DEC 2 0 2011

DOWN BY THE RIVER

THE GRACE VALLEY TRILOGY, BOOK 3

DOWN BY THE RIVER

ROBYN CARR

THORNDIKE
CHIVERS

This Large Print edition is published by Thorndike Press, Waterville, Maine, USA and by BBC Audiobooks Ltd, Bath, England.
Thorndike Press, a part of Gale, Cengage Learning.

The Grace Valley Trilogy #3.

The text of this Large Print edition is unabridged.
Other aspects of the book may vary from the original edition.
Set in 16 pt. Plantin.

LIBRARY OF CONGRESS CATALOGING-IN-PUBLICATION DATA

Carr, Robyn.
    Down by the river / by Robyn Carr.
      p. cm. — (In the Grace Valley trilogy ; #3) (Thorndike Press large print romance)
    ISBN-13: 978-1-4104-1623-0 (hardcover : alk. paper)
    ISBN-10: 1-4104-1623-2 (hardcover : alk. paper)
    1. Women physicians—Fiction. 2. City and town life—California—Fiction. 3. Country life—California—Fiction. 4. Large type books. I. Title.
PS3553.A76334D68 2009
813'.54—dc22   2009012241

BRITISH LIBRARY CATALOGUING-IN-PUBLICATION DATA AVAILABLE

Published in 2009 in the U.S. by arrangement with Harlequin Books S.A.
Published in 2010 in the U.K. by arrangement with Harlequin Enterprises II B.V.

U.K. Hardcover: 978 1 408 44230 2 (Chivers Large Print)
U.K. Softcover: 978 1 408 44231 9 (Camden Large Print)

Printed in Mexico
5 6 7 13 12 11

DOWN BY THE RIVER

ONE

Dr. June Hudson awoke to the ringing of the phone. It was still dark as pitch, but when she rolled over to look at the clock it read six-fifteen. She'd slept in, it seemed. She clicked on the cordless. "June Hudson."

"Who was that man?" her eighty-four-year-old aunt Myrna wanted to know.

June glanced over her shoulder at the man in question. Jim. He yawned largely and began to scratch his chest. Ah. So she hadn't dreamt it after all. He was here, beside her, in the flesh, after being away so long.

Aunt Myrna wasn't the only one who knew nothing at all about her secret lover. With just a couple of exceptions, the whole town had been kept in the dark. She was going to have a lot of explaining to do.

"His name is Jim and I'm going to bring him over to meet you the first chance I get, Aunt Myrna. Hopefully this very morning. You're going to approve, I promise."

7

"Where's he from? What's he do?"

I haven't figured that out yet, June thought. "Later, darling. There are too many details and I have to get ready for work. I'll see you soon."

She disconnected and returned the phone to the bedside table. This time when she looked at Jim, she shook her head and sighed, but she smiled. The phone rang again. "I'm not on call," she said. "We'll let the machine pick up."

He lifted one brow, amused. "Too many details?" he mimicked.

"Yes, and we'll probably have to make them all up." She jumped out of bed, naked as the day she was born. "I'm going to shower. Would you listen to the messages, please? If anyone calls for emergency assistance, bring me the phone. Okay?"

From the kitchen came the sound of June's father's voice, lifelike enough to make her flinch and grab for the sheet to cover up. Elmer Hudson was one of the exceptions who knew, but he didn't know everything. "Well, you've really stirred up a hornet's nest this time, haven't you?" Elmer asked, then laughed his wheezy laugh. "I think I'll take my coffee at the café this morning, just to be on hand if there's any excitement."

"He's a character, isn't he?" Jim asked.

"A laugh a minute." June made a face. "See if you can think up a good story while I shower."

While she waited for the hot water, she looked at her profile in the mirror. Her waist was fast disappearing.

A year ago she was the thirty-seven-year-old town doctor, single and without a prospect in sight. Six months ago, though she had a hot prospect, she was pretty sure she'd be childless. A few months ago, her prospect became even more serious and words of love were said along with desperate goodbyes. Two weeks ago her tummy was reasonably flat, but the moment she found out she was four months pregnant, her middle began to strain at her waistband. Then, approximately the second Jim returned home for good, home for her, she blossomed. Now she had a nice little round belly growing.

Last night, as the weekend Harvest Festival was breaking up and the last revelers were dancing, he appeared out of nowhere. It was as though the entire festival, the entire town had disappeared, and it was only the two of them, embracing, touching, kissing. And then, without making any proper introductions, they'd gotten out of

9

there as quickly as they could. But how naive. The town hadn't disappeared; the town had *watched*.

She heard the phone ring again and knew the whole town was going to call her this morning, asking for the facts. She should probably be grateful they hadn't started calling last night.

The actual truth — which they wouldn't be telling anyone — was that June had met Jim last spring when he brought a wounded man to her clinic, late at night, wearing a disguise, and held a gun on her while she removed a bullet from his comrade's shoulder. Call it intuition, but she had never quite believed this big handsome man with the beautiful sparkling blue eyes could be a criminal, though he certainly appeared the part. Shortly thereafter, right about the same time she fell helplessly in love with him, he admitted the truth — he was an undercover DEA agent, working inside a cannabis farm deep in the mountains, a farm they were getting ready to bust. After the raid, Jim was sent on one final assignment before retiring from a successful career in law enforcement. Neither June nor Jim realized they already had a baby started.

June, a small-town doctor raised by her father, the town doctor before her, was always busy thinking about the health and welfare of other people. Even though she'd been nauseous, sluggish and suffered through crying jags — something she'd never before experienced — she hadn't suspected a thing. By the time she described her symptoms to her business partner, John Stone, she was well along.

She got out of the shower and, while toweling dry, went into the bedroom. She wrapped the bath sheet around herself. Her wet hair hung in dripping curls to her shoulders. "Remember just before you left on that last assignment, I told you I thought I probably couldn't have children."

"I remember," he said, giving his head a nod. He was sitting up in the bed, sheet to his waist, and he held a cup of coffee. June's collie, Sadie, who was not allowed on the furniture, was curled up on the bed at his feet. When she lifted her head to regard June, she seemed to have taken on regal airs. "Shows what you know," he said.

"I was already pregnant. I just realized that."

"For a doctor, you don't pay such close attention to details."

"Well, about other people I do. You made coffee?"

"Uh-huh. And squeezed Sadie over the

11

grass and gave her breakfast."

"You just might come in handy. But before you get too comfortable, you're going to have to come into town with me. You need to meet a few people. We don't have a lot of time to waste."

"Why's that?"

She slowly opened the bath sheet. There it was, a protuberance that, much too soon, would be screaming for her supper. His eyes grew warm as they caressed her new shape. "It's time you met my family and friends," she said.

"Maybe you should take the day off," he suggested. "We could go to Reno or Lake Tahoe. Get married."

Suddenly, inexplicably, she felt her face grow hot. *Married?* Right away? What did she really know about him, besides that she loved him madly and he snored? So much was still a mystery. She wasn't about to marry him before she had a few more details.

But she wasn't about to start their relationship off on the wrong foot, by refusing his very chivalrous suggestion. She leaned across the bed and gave him a quick kiss. "It's too late to be coy, Jim. Tell me, how are we going to describe our . . . *courtship.* As it were."

12

He rubbed her cheek with the knuckle of his index finger. "I've found that the fewer the number of lies, the less complicated the cover. So, try this. I used to work in law enforcement back East and am retiring here, out West. I met you early last spring when I happened to be in the area and gave a friend a ride to the clinic for medical treatment for a minor injury."

"But he was a criminal! A drug farmer!"

Jim shrugged. "Yeah . . . but we were friends. Or so he thought."

"Ah, so that's how it works," she said. She sat on the bed, her legs curled under her, like a girl waiting for more of the story. The phone rang and they both paused and listened. Into the machine they could hear Dr. John Stone. "Hi, June. Just wondered if you're taking the day off. Or at least the morning. I can handle the clinic alone if you have . . . ah . . . other things to do. Heh-heh-heh."

"Smart-ass," she said to herself. Then, "So, Mr. Post, what kind of law enforcement?"

"In twenty years . . . a little of everything. In the last few years, more paperwork than anything else."

"Is that true?" she asked.

He nodded. "Unfortunately."

"And what have you been doing out here?"

"Scouting around for a place to settle. Grace Valley might have been a contender even if I hadn't fallen for the town's doctor."

"You know," she said, impressed, "you're very good at this."

He leaned toward her. "I'm a professional. Or was."

"How am I going to know when you're lying to me?"

He reached for her and, putting his large hand on the back of her neck under her wet hair, pulled her to him. He kissed her gently. "For some reason I can't explain, you have always known the truth about me. The only other person with whom that is true is my sister, Annie." He smiled. "I feel differently about you than I do about her."

"Well, that's a relief." She bounced off the bed. "You can have the shower. And hurry up. Let's get going before the town has any more fun with this."

June and Jim rode toward town in her little pickup truck. Sadie usually had the seat Jim was occupying, and June wouldn't even talk about putting her in the back, so Sadie was squished between them. June dialed up John on her cell phone.

14

"I just wanted to let you know I'm on my way into town and I'm bringing my . . . my . . . I'm bringing Jim with me so everyone can look him over and give him the stamp of approval."

"Why, June," John said, feigning hurt. "I'm sure the man of your choice is none of our business."

"I wish," she answered, and laughed in spite of herself.

June slowed as she came around a curve and encountered a disabled truck up on a jack by the side of the road, its left rear tire missing. The vehicle was old and overladen with bundles, boxes and a couple of child-size mattresses. Two little kids, either girls or boys who hadn't had haircuts in forever, stood behind the pickup. They were ratty-looking and dirty and wore forlorn expressions. They didn't wear jackets, though the early morning air was cold. If they were underdressed, there was a good chance they were also underfed.

There was no tarp to cover the family's goods and the sky was threatening. It was October and soon the rains of winter would begin and not ease up until late spring.

A family of modest means, all their worldly goods loaded in a truck, trying to find a place to start over, was not an unusual sight on the roads surrounding the valley. With the cold weather came the cessation of logging and a slowdown in construction. Farmers would let their temporary workers go and people would have to seek help from the state and county to get by.

"Damn," she muttered, slowing. "Give us a little extra time, John. We're going to stop a minute. There's a truck with a flat and a family that might need some help."

"Take your time, June. We don't have all the balloons blown up yet, anyway."

"Don't you even —"

"June, pull over quick," Jim said. "I think someone's sick."

June stopped her pickup right beside the old disabled one and jumped out, pocketing her phone in one swift movement. A split second later she recognized what was happening. Both the driver's door and the passenger's door stood open. A woman sitting in the passenger's seat was hanging on to her pregnant abdomen, leaning back as far as she could in the seat, her face twisted with pain, one foot braced against the dash. Standing over her was a young man, probably her husband.

June grabbed her medical bag from the bed of her truck. "Jim! A little help here, please," she yelled on her way around the dilapidated old truck to the passenger's side. "I'm a doctor," she said briefly, brushing the man aside. She took no note of him, nor did she expend any energy on manners. Fluids and blood ran from the floor of the truck onto the ground and June had only to lift the damp, flowered dress the woman wore to see that the baby was crowning.

"Get one of those mattresses from the back of your truck and lay it in my truck bed. And hurry," she told the man. "Jim, come here and lift this woman out of the truck and lay her down on the mattress in the back of mine. Let's go, go, go!" she yelled.

The man wore a look of confusion for only a second before he did as he was told, but amazingly, he didn't do it quickly. June had a reason for the instructions she'd given. Jim was by far the larger and stronger-looking of the two men. The husband was very thin and gaunt; his cheeks were sunken and his pants hung on him. Subconsciously she had assessed their condition as poor and hungry — perhaps the cause of his slow movements — but consciously she was getting ready for a delivery.

Jim lifted the woman out of her truck and waited behind June's. The man was slowly untying ropes that held the mattresses in

17

place, though it didn't look as though that was necessary. His movements were so lethargic that June dropped her bag, ran to where he stood and unceremoniously tugged the small, thin mattress out of his truck and tossed it into hers.

The instant the mattress was lying in the bed of her truck, Jim gently placed the mother on it. June plucked the phone out of her shirt pocket, handed it to Jim and said, "Press Redial and tell John what we're doing. Ask him to bring the ambulance." She pulled a pair of gloves from her bag.

"We ain't got no money for no ambulance," the man said. "I delivered the last one, I can take care of this one."

"No, you can't. It's posterior. I'm going to have to turn the baby's head. Now, find me some sheets or towels or even clothes. Something to wipe up with, to cover your wife and baby." She snapped on her gloves. "What's your name, dear?" she said, one hand on the baby's head, one hand gently palpating the uterus.

"Er . . . Erline. Davis."

"And is this your third?"

"Fourth," she said. "One's dead."

"Have you had problems with childbirth before?" June asked her.

"Just that once. He was a stillborn." And

then she screamed, a loud, harrowing scream that caused everyone but June to freeze.

"In a hospital?" June asked.

"Yes. Yes. The ones at home did fine."

"Childbirth is a strange and unpredictable thing. Can you take short, shallow breaths and keep from pushing while I attempt to turn the baby's head? It's going to hurt but it will be over quickly."

"I . . . I can try."

"That's all I ask, Erline." While June carefully manipulated the baby's head, the expectant mother groaned and panted. "We're there, Erline, that's it." June lifted her head like a doe sniffing the air for hunters and yelled, "Where's that sheet?"

She could vaguely hear Jim in the background trying to explain to John who he was and what he needed. The other background noise, behind the panting and groaning of Erline, was the sound of the father griping at his little kids and at least one of them whimpering.

June pulled off her jacket, then removed the white velour V-neck sweatshirt she wore over a thin shirt. She lay it beside the delivering mother, then said, "Okay, you're all set. When you're ready, I'm ready."

There was a brief silence and stillness, as

though the mother was gathering her physical and emotional strength. Then with a mighty growl she pushed and birthed the baby's head. June used a bulb suction she had in her bag to clear the baby's nose and mouth, but it was hardly necessary. Despite the challenges the wee one had faced in childbirth, it was already grinding out that shrill, hungry wail. With one experienced finger, June eased forth a shoulder and Erline delivered a baby boy into her hands.

"Ah, Erline, you did that like a pro. It's a boy. I'd say about seven pounds, maybe a tish less." She wrapped the baby in her sweatshirt, wrapped the long dangling arms around the little bundle and lay him on his mother's abdomen. She pulled off her gloves and dug around in her bag for some clamps. She applied them to the cord, but she didn't bother to cut it. It would be better for John and the emergency room personnel to see everything intact, provided he got here soon. She then spread her jacket over them both, covering as much of the shivering mother as she could.

"I couldn't find no sheet," the man said to June's back.

She turned. "You have a son, sir. He looks healthy, but he has to be checked over at the hospital."

"We ain't got extra money for no hospital," he said, but he didn't look her in the eye. He was digging in his baggy pants and pulled out a fold of bills. It wasn't particularly thick, but as he peeled off two twenties, the stench of green marijuana, an unmistakable skunklike smell that clung to the hands and clothes and *money* of people who cut the plants for drying, filled the air.

He tried to hand June forty dollars, and in so doing, looked her in the eye. His were dilated. Now she understood his lethargy, his poverty. Lots of different types grew dope in the backwoods. There were people who wanted the money involved and thought of marijuana as just another green plant. They might fill a spare room or section of garden with plants for extra cash. There were big-time growers and dealers who had camps as large as towns and fields as vast as a Midwest soy farmer, the kind of growers Jim had originally gone undercover to catch. And then there were deadheads like this one, an addict who grew pot for himself and what little cash he needed to get by on to grow a little more pot.

"I don't need your money," June said. "I'm sure you qualify for assistance. And I sure don't want any money that stinks of the plant. Put that away before you get into trouble. Has your wife been smoking?"

"Naw, she don't when she's pregnant," he said.

"I don't at all," Erline insisted.

"I seen her take a hit or two," he said.

"I'm only interested for medical reasons," June stressed.

Jim joined them. In his arms were the little girls, who were probably two and three years old. They both had blond stringy hair and were wearing cotton pants and T-shirts ill suited for the weather, and sandals on their bare feet. Jim had a fierce and unreadable expression on his face. The older of the little girls had a bright red spot on her cheek, as though she'd been slapped, and she struggled to keep back her tears.

The man put his money away and started to reach out for the little girl. "Wouldn't you like to see your son?" June urged, trying to distract him. She gently pulled on his arm, moving him to the back of the truck where his wife and child lay.

Fortunately for everyone, John arrived in the ambulance and they were able to quickly load Erline and her baby into the back. June put the little girls into the front seat and told Jim, "I'm going to have to drive them so that John can attend to this patient. I'll meet you in town a little later. Is that okay with you?"

"Do I have a choice?"

"Sure. You can park my truck and you and Sadie can come with us."

"What about him?" he asked, tilting his head toward the man with the stinky twenties.

"I'm not too concerned about him. I'm concerned about them," she said, tilting her head toward the ambulance.

"Go on," he said. "I'll see you at the café. I'll go take some of my medicine while you work."

She smiled, knowing her father and some of the locals would be waiting for him. "You're a brave man."

He took off his jacket, the sleeves of which were soiled, and wrapped it around her shoulders. "Is this what life with you is going to be like?"

"Well, not really. I don't do this on my way to work every day."

"But it's going to be bizarre, isn't it?" he asked gravely.

She stood on her toes and kissed him. "For a flexible guy like you, it should be a piece of cake." Then she jogged to the driver's side of the ambulance and jumped in. She pulled away with lights flashing.

Jim looked at the father, who stood and

stared, dumbly, at his jacked-up truck. "What do you say we throw your tire in the back here and I'll give you a lift into town. Maybe you can get it fixed, get your truck running and go to the hospital."

He shrugged. "I should just get the tire fixed and head out on my own. I never did think it was a good idea to have all them kids."

"You think anyone would come looking for you?" Jim asked, one brow lifted.

The man scowled and slowly, without much enthusiasm, rolled the heavy tire toward the pickup. Jim, impatient, picked up the tire and pitched it into the bed of the truck. When the man got to the passenger door he stopped, looked at Sadie and said, "I'll ride in the back. I'm not much for dogs."

Just as well, Jim thought. Sadie's not much for idiots. But all he said was "Suit yourself."

Two

Even though Grace Valley had grown from a population of around nine hundred to more than fifteen hundred in the past ten years, things were actually very slow to change. In fact, Valley Drive, the street that ran down the middle of town, had only seen a few minor improvements. There were just a half dozen businesses, including the police department, the church and the clinic.

Sam Cussler's garage sat at the far west end. He'd owned it for forty-five years. It was weatherworn the day he signed the deed and he'd never seen the need to prettify it. Sam, twice widowed, worked harder at fishing than at pumping gas. And in Grace Valley, typical of small rural towns, most people kept their own vehicles running, so Sam wasn't called upon to do much mechanical work. In fact, he'd usually leave the pumps on and townsfolk would write him their IOU and slip it in his mail slot. He'd go around town and collect when the fish weren't biting.

Down the block was the police department, set up in a three-bedroom house and run by Tom Toopeek and his young deputies, Lee Stafford and Ricky Rios, all lifetime residents. Tom had been brought to Grace Valley by his parents when he was a mere tot and had spent his childhood as one of June's best friends. Tom's six siblings had left Grace Valley to make their marks on the world. Tom not only stayed, but he built his house onto his parent's original cabin and added five of his own children to the mix. Lee and Ricky were handpicked by Tom as soon as the town could afford deputies. They were sent to a police academy, after which Tom personally trained them to adopt his philosophies in how best to serve a small town.

Also on Valley Drive was a flower shop, closed for the time being because its owner, Justine, Sam's late wife, had recently passed on. There was George Fuller's café, open for service every day of the year including Christmas, a bakery run by Burt Crandall and his wife, Syl, the clinic and the Presbyterian Church, which boasted a new pastor, Harry Shipton, who was considered to be a breath of fresh air. Behind the café and church a riverbank as wide as a football field sloped gently toward the Windle River. Most town gatherings were held there — such as the Fourth of July picnic or the Harvest Festival. George Fuller had built a couple of brick barbecues and people would bring blankets and lawn chairs.

There was a post office out on Highway 482 and a seasonal farmer's market set up to the south. The schools — elementary, middle and high school — were located between Grace Valley, Westport and Rockport because students from other small towns were bussed in, according to need.

Grace Valley was just one of dozens, perhaps hundreds of small towns that speckled northern California from San Francisco to the border of Oregon. And while they had many similarities, they also each had a special and unique personality. The major industry was the land — farming, fishing, logging, vineyards, ranching — and the beauty that brought both tourists and transplants from the urban sprawl. Along with tourists and transplants came inns and bed-and-breakfasts, specialty shops, the occasional restaurant or tasting room, but these were commonly near the highways and not in the heart of town.

Industry didn't bring the new folks to

town, but rather entrepreneurship supported by those new folks and new tourism. Once someone realized several artists and crafts artisans had relocated to the peace and beauty of the valley, a gallery would suddenly appear. After a rash of tourists were noticed poking around the little towns, a few bed-and-breakfasts sprang out of refurbished old houses like spring tulips. As vineyards expanded their crops, tasting rooms would emerge. And as traffic along the highway increased, so did the number of quaint restaurants.

There were those whose income did not come from the town or the land. Myrna Hudson Claypool was a very successful novelist and Sarah Kelleher was just one of several well-known artists. And then there were rich folk who built between the shadow of the mountains and the vast beauty of the Pacific Ocean just because they could.

But there were others who came to the valley not so well fixed. With growth came opportunities in construction, logging and farming, and with opportunity came people in search of work. Or people passing through on their way to the cities in search of a paycheck because their seasonal work had dried up in some other town. It was an unfortunate fact that plenty of people sought work of an illegal sort, poaching fish or wildlife, or growing marijuana. The draw to such professions would be the promise of easy money.

The young man in the back of June's truck, huddled against his flat tire, was just such a case. His name was Conrad Davis, and by the looks of him, it would appear the money hadn't come as easily as he had hoped. Jim was in a hurry to get this young man's tire fixed and send him on his way. After working undercover for the DEA all these years, his nose was good and his instincts better. This guy had a thin, hapless, no-account look about him, but Jim sensed there was something more going on. Conrad was slow moving, which could be accounted for if he was high, but he had an angry grimace on his face that belied pot smoking. Potheads were usually lackadaisical, not ill-humored. Jim suspected there was more at work than just marijuana. Maybe he was going up and down . . . a little pot, a little crystal meth.

Jim pulled into the gas station. He hadn't spent enough time in and around Grace Valley to know that there were more than the usual number of cars present on Valley Drive, mostly around the café. The garage door was open and Jim spied a tall, tanned and formidable man inside. Though his hair was completely white, his shoulders were broad and his face had a youthful appearance. He held a broom in one hand and a fishing pole in the other, as if trying to decide which to employ. As Jim got out of the car and walked toward him, the man retired both against the wall.

"I figured this for a busy day," Sam said. "Busier than usual."

Jim stuck out his hand. "I'm Jim Post. I'm . . . ah . . ."

"Sam Cussler," he said, taking the hand. "I know who you are, son. More or less."

The pieces fell into place immediately. June had related many stories about the town and its people. "It's a pleasure, Mr. Cussler."

"If you're going to stand on ceremony, it's going to take us a long time to get around to fishing. You do fish, don't you, son?"

"Whenever possible, Mr. . . . . Sam."

"Good. There's a need for that around here." Sam peered past Jim to spy Conrad struggling to get the heavy tire out of the back of the truck. "He's a tad puny for that big old thing, ain't he?"

Jim had almost forgotten about Conrad. He moved quickly to get the tire from him and rolled it toward Sam. "I was coming into town with June this morning when we happened past this young man and his family and their disabled truck. The missus was having a baby. June delivered the baby, took the young woman, baby and two little kids to the hospital and left me with him . . . and the flat." Jim glanced over his shoulder at Conrad, who stayed close to the truck. He leaned back against it, his hands plunged into the pockets of his baggy pants. "The tire isn't all that's flat," Jim said, transferring the tire into Sam's hands.

Sam intercepted it with a low whistle. "Looks like he drove on it a spell."

"He need a new one?"

"Very likely. I can try to fix it, but I wouldn't guarantee anything."

"Any chance you can just sell me a new one? I'll cover the cost," Jim said. He didn't want the kid flashing any of his drug money around town. He just wanted him taken care of and out of there. "I'll get him back to his truck."

"Now, don't worry about that, son. I can take him. I imagine you have people to meet at the café. And this is my living, even if I don't do it often enough to pay taxes."

Jim peered down the street. "Are there usually that many people there for breakfast?" he asked.

Sam grinned broadly. "Not hardly."

The dawning came slowly. Jim was going to get a looking over. "Hmm," he said. "Well, much as I'm excited to meet everyone, I promised June that I'd take care of this young man personally, and if I start breaking promises now, I suppose she'll have second thoughts about me."

Sam's brows drew together in question. He'd known June all her life and he seriously doubted there was any truth to what Jim said. Sam figured there was something more to it. Probably something more to this young man. "You don't want to keep 'em waiting long," Sam advised.

"I'll make it a quick trip and get right back to town," Jim promised.

"Whatever you say, son," Sam said, taking possession of the tire and rolling it into the garage.

A half hour later Jim was tightening the last lug nut on the tire at Conrad's truck. The tire he'd just put on for the kid was the best one on the truck; Sam had sold him a retread at a good price. He straightened and stretched his back. Without a jacket in this cold, damp morning, it hadn't taken long for Jim to stiffen up.

Sam would have done this, and likely he could have held his own. But Jim was watching the kid the way a cop watched a suspect. He might be puny, but if he had a handgun stashed in the back of his truck, size would be irrelevant. He didn't want Sam to be robbed or hurt — or both.

"Thanks, man," Conrad said. "I owe you one."

"You don't owe me anything, kid. You know the way to Valley Hospital in Rockport?"

"I haven't decided if I'm going there yet," he said. Then he smiled a crooked, insincere smile. His teeth were nasty.

Jim took a breath for patience. "Wherever you go, make sure you don't end up back here. Got that?"

"Oh, man, I sort of *like* it here. People are real friendly."

"That could change in a heartbeat, *man*."

Jim got in June's truck before he said or did anything more, leaving the kid standing beside his pickup. He made a U-turn, heading back to town, and thought that maybe retirement wasn't going to be as dull as he feared. Especially around here.

John admitted mother and baby to the maternity ward and nursery. June made sure the little ones were settled in a safe play area in the social services department at the hospital while they waited for their father. The staff was on alert. If the father didn't show up or appeared impaired in any way, the social worker was prepared to put the children in emergency foster care.

That settled, June and John began the drive back to Grace Valley.

"Is he here to stay? Is he going to make an honest woman out of you?"

"You don't waste any time, do you? Yes, it appears he's here for good."

"That's a relief. Is he going to make an honest woman out of you?"

"Did you know I'd been thinking about having a baby, anyway? On my own? Because not only was my clock ticking, but my calendar pages were flipping like mad. Though I admit I'm a hopeless romantic. I like it far better this way, which as you know was totally unplanned."

"Okay, I'm going to go ahead and pretend I didn't notice that you didn't answer the M question. But don't think I'm going to be the last one to ask."

"Believe me, I don't kid myself about anything anymore."

"How is it you never mentioned him?" John asked.

"Hmm. That's a little complicated."

"I'm sure it is, but you might want to

come up with an answer for that one. It might take peoples' minds off the other question. Go ahead. Practice on me." He looked over at her, a curl from his usually perfectly coiffed blond hair dangling onto his forehead.

"Well, we didn't spend as much time together as my condition would suggest."

He whistled. "Good job, June. You couldn't get any more vague than that."

"Okay, look. I met him last . . . I don't know . . . early in the year. It might've been around the same time you moved to town. He came into the clinic after hours with a friend who had a minor injury. They were in the area for something or other. Camping or hunting, whatever. I patched up his friend and just a few days later he showed up at my house on a Sunday afternoon to thank me. We sat on the porch, drank iced tea and fell in love."

"Aw," he said, stringing it out musically. "That's sweet."

She did her best to ignore him, discovering she did indeed need a rehearsal. "When he was in the area, which wasn't all that often, his stay was really brief. And you know, we don't have any hotels or inns in town. Once he had a room over in Westport at that place by the steakhouse. . . ." Lying but not lying, she found, could be a little fun. Like playing chess, you have to remember where all the pieces are.

"Now comes the tough one, missy," he said. "How'd he take the news? That you're pregnant?"

She didn't have to make anything up. "That's easy. He appears to be thrilled."

"That's wonderful, June," he said, and for once he didn't tease. He'd been the one to examine her just last week and surprise her with the news that the pregnancy was advanced. Doctors weren't infallible. "You really didn't have any idea, did you?"

"It was the farthest thing from my mind."

"I can't imagine," he said. "Susan and I knew Sydney was on the way when she was about three weeks gestation."

"You're an OB first and family practitioner second. You're supposed to be obsessive about that. Plus, for whatever reason, I kind of figured I wasn't going to ever have a baby. At least not as easily as this."

John laughed loudly. "I bet you were pretty lazy about birth control."

Stunned by his accuracy, she asked, "Now, why would you say that?"

"That's what women who haven't gotten caught always think."

■ ■ ■ ■

June almost had a heart attack when they drove into town. There were so many cars parked on Valley Drive and in the church and clinic parking lots, it resembled a town meeting. The last time she'd seen congestion like this, word had just hit town that a deathly handsome new doctor had come to the clinic to practice with June. Women came from miles around to catch a glimpse of John Stone.

"What the heck is going on?" she asked.

"Oh, as if you don't know," John said.

And then it became obvious. Everyone was inside the café; it was virtually bursting at the seams. Her truck was parked across the street at the clinic where Jim must have left it, right next to her father's truck.

There being no readily available parking spaces, John stopped the ambulance in the street, blocking a couple of pickups. "I'll take it over to the clinic to clean and restock in a little while. I'm not going to miss a second of this," he said, opening his door and jumping out.

"John," she protested. "The owners of these trucks might want to get out."

"Not until after they've heard your story,"

he shot back, heading into the café.

The last thing she wanted to do was go in there, but worry about what might be happening to Jim propelled her out of the vehicle and into the café. A roar of "hellos" and "heys" and a general cheer went up at the sight of her. The crowd parted, and as she passed through the throng, men patted her on the back and women gave her shoulders brief squeezes. At the front of the café stood the guest of honor, leaning back against the counter and holding a coffee cup. The preacher and police chief flanked him on one side, her father and Sam Cussler on the other. They all held coffee cups as if they were tankards.

Jim did not appear to have been harmed in any way.

"Well, there's our girl," Elmer boasted excitedly. "Give her a cup, George, but don't put any liquor in it. She's pregnant!"

"Dad!" she gasped, appalled. She immediately began to color and glared at Jim. But he simply shrugged his shoulders helplessly. More than a few chuckles rose from the crowd.

George passed a cup over the counter to Elmer, who passed it to June. She looked into the cup, which appeared to have milk in it. She made a face. She *hated* milk.

"Sorry, June," Elmer said. "I tried to sit on it, but I got a little excited. I thought I was going to the grave without a grandchild. Have you had an ultrasound? Do we know the sex yet?"

"None of your business!"

"When's the wedding?" someone from the crowd asked in a shout.

"When's the baby due?" came another shout.

"Where'd you find this guy? He ain't from around here," asked yet another.

June twisted her head around, trying unsuccessfully to find the people responsible for the questions. But her glance took in a great deal — John's wife, Susan, the clinic nurse; Birdie Forrest, her late mother's best friend and June's godmother; Burt and Syl Crandall from the bakery; Charlotte Burnham, her retired nurse; Jessie Wiley, her secretary and receptionist. A great many friends and patients. The clinic must be closed.

Elmer was busily circulating with a bottle of Jack Daniel's, pouring a dollop into a few coffee cups, including Jim's. Passing the bottle off to someone in the crowd, he leaned toward June and gave her a kiss on the cheek. He gave a nod in Jim's direction and a wink. "He held up pretty well, June, facing everyone solo."

"Dad," she said pleadingly. "The poor guy!"

"Poor guy, hell. Look at him! When have you ever seen anyone more puffed up?"

Jim smiled and a chuckle shook his shoulders, but he was not in any way puffed up. He was being a damned good sport, and she was going to owe him big time. But what if he bolted? She wasn't sure what bothered her more, that he could take all of this pressure so unflinchingly or the possibility that he'd tear out of here.

An arm stretched over June's shoulder with an empty cup. "Hey, Doc," John begged.

"Get John here a little something," Elmer commanded. "He's going to need it if his partner's getting married and taking maternity leave!"

Again, cheers rose with a laughing roar. June's cheeks flamed.

"Now, everyone taken care of?" Elmer asked. "Because I'd like to toast the young couple and . . ."

"They're not *that* young," someone yelled.

Elmer raised his cup. "To my daughter, her intended and my grandchild!"

"Here, here!" The crowd heartily intoned. Many a drink was tossed back.

June unhappily sampled her milk, then said to Elmer, "Isn't it a little early for that?"

"I'd say we're all a little late," he returned, his eyes pointedly fixed on her middle.

There was a part of her quite grateful for the fun and games; she'd anticipated scorn. She was pretty far along in years to be an unmarried woman, with a secret lover to boot. She mentally acknowledged that, then pushed it to the back of her mind because the teasing was likely to go on for a while, and it was already annoying. Plus, this teasing could easily turn to badgering if she didn't appear before them reciting vows. But every time she thought about making that kind of commitment, her face lit up like a firecracker and her insides twisted into a knot.

"When's the wedding?" Harry asked them.

June stammered so Jim answered, keeping an eye turned to June, who squirmed in discomfort. "We haven't had time to even discuss the when and where. You'll have to give us time on that."

"Doesn't look like you have a whole lot of time," someone said.

"You'd better step up to the plate, young man," someone else roared.

"Now," Jim said, holding up a hand.

"You're going to have to leave that to June, and it should be clear just from looking at her that she's still a little stunned by this whole thing."

"You're not hedging, are you?" Elmer asked pointedly.

"Absolutely not," Jim assured him. "Patience isn't really a virtue around here, is it?"

"Was I mistaken, or did I hear she's well along?" Elmer asked.

Jim lifted his cup. "She's not going to get any less pregnant while we discuss the particulars," he said, drawing laughter from the crowd. "We'll take care of it when the time is perfect."

She couldn't help but feel warmed by his rescue, when it must be puzzling to him that she wasn't rushing him off to the altar.

"What?" a familiar voice demanded. June's godmother separated herself from the crowd and stood before June. "Did I hear right?" Birdie asked. "You don't have a wedding date?"

"Birdie, we've barely had time to talk about it," June repeated. "We'll come up with something and let you know."

"Over my dead body," Birdie said. "You're the closest thing to a daughter I have. And there's going to be a *wedding!*"

June reached for Birdie's hand. "You know, you really need to leave this up to us," she said pleadingly.

"You just leave this to me," Birdie said, giving her hand a reassuring pat.

But June was not reassured. She cast a worried glance at Jim, but he only shook his head as if to say, "This is your town . . . and your hesitation."

Then June felt the baby fluttering inside of her. A smile found its way to her lips. A smile that Birdie completely misinterpreted.

"See?" Birdie said. "Everything is going to be wonderful."

About a half hour later, after many hugs and congratulatory kisses, June left the café with Jim. "You held up very well in there," she said.

"You didn't do so well," he said. "It hasn't escaped my notice that there's something you seem to be avoiding."

She took his hand. "I'm so sorry. It's not because it's you. It's the very idea."

"What are you saying?"

"Only that I'd appreciate your patience. And that we should talk about it before we do it."

"Unlike the way we went about getting pregnant . . ."

"I don't mean to put you in a bad position," she said. "I've always wanted to be married, to have a family. But I've been on my own a long time. I'm set in my ways. That's probably why the first time you mentioned marriage, something in me just froze up." She reached for his hand. "I need to get comfortable with the idea. I do love you." He didn't look at her and didn't respond. "Hey. Did you hear what I said?"

But he was staring down the street toward Cussler's garage. Sitting out front, tilted a bit to one side, was the dilapidated old truck, weighted down with all the Davis family's possessions.

"Son of a bitch," he said.

Inside the café the partying died down to a quiet roar, an occasional burst of laughter, the clatter of glassware in the background. Elmer, Sam and Harry sat in a booth, finishing their libations, which by now were down to coffee. People were drifting off, having checked out and toasted June and Jim.

"I suppose I ought to get over to the clinic and see if John needs me. I don't imagine June's going to be much good to him today."

"I heard her say she had to take Jim out to Myrna's for a looking over," Sam said.

"I'd like to see how that goes, but I wasn't invited," Elmer said, hefting himself out of the booth. "We having poker at the parsonage on Thursday, Harry?"

"You bet. Is everyone in? Even Myrna?"

"I'm sure wild horses wouldn't keep her away."

Harry made a face and shook his head. "Nobody loves Myrna more than me, but if she doesn't miss a poker night one of these weeks, I'm going to have to file for bankruptcy."

"You're preaching to the choir, Reverend," Elmer said, making his departure. It was a well known fact that Myrna had been cleaning up at poker for many a year. She rarely had a downslide.

"Is the mail dependable around here, Sam?"

"I wouldn't know, Harry. No one ever writes me."

"I can't tell if it's the post office or my friend. I made a loan to someone a few months ago and, well, I know he's good for it. . . . Or maybe he's not and I was foolish. Anyway, he said he sent it, but —"

"Don't say another word, Harry," Sam said, pulling a thick wad of bills out of his pocket and folding out some twenties. "I can give you a little something to tide you over."

"That's awful nice of you, Sam. I hate to

take advantage. . . ."

"Think nothing of it, Harry. Since Justine passed away, I have no one and nothing to spend it on." He counted off a hundred dollars and put it on the table in front of Harry. "Anytime I can be of help."

"Much appreciated, my friend. I'll get it back to you the second my check arrives."

THREE

Perhaps the most beloved resident in Grace
Valley was Myrna Hudson Claypool. June's
aunt Myrna had lived in the valley longer
than any other resident, having been
brought by her parents at the age of four.
Her father, Charles Hudson, had been a
successful Bay Area banker who had built a
mansion for his much younger wife, where
they could live in comfort, raise a large family and entertain lavishly. In so doing,
Charles had founded a town, though he
didn't get to live in it long. Eight years after
moving into Hudson House, Myrna's
mother died giving birth to her second
child, Elmer, and two years after that, when
Myrna was barely fourteen and Elmer but
two, Charles joined his wife in eternity.

For the next seventy years Myrna lived an
eccentric and fascinating life. Rather than
playing with other little girls or being
courted by young men, she raised her

younger brother from infancy and saw him through a college education and medical school on the generous funds left to them by their father. All through this period of single parenting, she devoured books; reading saved her from loneliness. When Elmer was gone from the house to further his education, she began writing novels — first Gothic, then mysteries and finally suspense stories. By the age of eighty-four she had published more than sixty books and was still hard at it.

Though no one knew the measure of Myrna's wealth, she had extended her generosity to the town as though it was a part of her family. She gave a piece of land for a town cemetery, carried a million-dollar note to fund the building of the clinic, and just last summer at the Fourth of July picnic, surprised June with a brand new ambulance. She employed the sixty-five-year-old bickersome Barstow twins, Endeara and Amelia, simply because no one else would and without work they would be destitute. And she did this despite the fact that they weren't much help around the house and couldn't cook any better than Myrna, whose cooking was legendary for its inedible quality, a fact that had never prevented her from having large dinner parties.

One of the quirkiest and most entertaining stories about Myrna was her marital history. She didn't indulge until she was in her forties and then married a stranger to the town. Morton Claypool was a traveling salesman who loved to read, thus their attraction to each other. He spent little enough time in Grace Valley, which appealed to Myrna as well, she being an older matron and quite set in her ways. Then after twenty years, Morton went off and didn't return.

That she was quite piqued by this disappearance Myrna kept mostly to herself for a couple of reasons. First, to her wifely chagrin, months had passed before she'd even noticed he hadn't returned home. And second, she suspected another woman, a rather embarrassing fact. Rather than let it upset her unduly, she lifted her chin and wrote her way out of the funk of a disappeared husband. Literally. In many of the books that followed Morton's departure, a murderous wife gets even with a philandering husband by killing him. Book after book, the murders varied in style but somehow get more gruesome with each telling. The first one she wrote for personal vengeance at being jilted, but the subsequent ones were for pure entertainment. The town thrived on both the books and the conjecture.

Then bones were found in her garden, an event that threatened to topple Myrna and her writing career. Speculation grew into an accusation and the assistant district attorney looked at pressing charges.

The bones turned out to be from more than one skeleton, eliminating the possibility that they were Morton's. But during that scare, June, Elmer, Myrna and her attorney, John Cutler, all began investigating Morton's disappearance in earnest. Their efforts were not rewarded; Morton seemed to become "more missing" all the time.

June explained this to Jim as they drove to Myrna's house. "We learned that six months after departing from Grace Valley, he retired and drew a pension, but it was mailed to a post office box. He continued to have a portion of his pension withheld to pay social security while the pension lasted, but the company he'd worked for went bust and the pension dried up. Then there was no record of his death or of his collecting social security. Poof."

"Your aunt must have been very upset," Jim said.

"Well . . . um . . . You'll understand this

better when you get to know her a little, but no, Myrna didn't seem to be very upset. She was a little miffed that the sheriff's department dug up her yard looking for a body and said, 'They're all going to feel so stupid when this is over.' I was upset, almost unconsolable, bursting into tears at the mere thought of my precious little old aunt going to jail, but as we learned later, all that crying probably had more to do with being pregnant than being distraught. My father was fit to be tied. Tom Toopeek was in a nasty mood about the whole thing. But Myrna held up well, never doubting for a second that she'd be vindicated. In fact, last time we talked she hadn't even given up writing the 'missing husband capers.' " June sighed. "You'd think she'd have learned by now."

Though June said that, truthfully she wouldn't have Myrna any other way. She could be so wonderfully oblivious, so un-shakable. Doubtless the murdered spouse tales would go on indefinitely, getting only more shocking.

Endeara answered the door, but behind her, peering out of the kitchen, was Amelia. Endeara stared up at Jim — he was more than six feet tall and very broad shouldered — and June could have sworn the woman

51

swooned slightly. Amelia's sigh was audible all the way from the kitchen. It was an extremely rare occurrence to find them both at the house at the same time. They quarreled so much that Myrna insisted they job share, coming to the house one at a time.

There they all stood, June and Jim on the front porch, Endeara and Amelia staring soulfully at the handsome man beside June. "Are you going to invite us in?" June asked, but neither of them moved an inch.

June heard the click-click-clicking of her aunt's shoes on the hardwood floors. Myrna pulled off her glasses and let them dangle around her neck as she came around Endeara. "For goodness sake," she complained, gently pushing her maid out of the doorway. "Come in, darling, come in. This must be your man." Myrna, perhaps five foot one, stood aside so they might enter. Her white hair was a little springier than usual. She'd fixed a large bun on the top of her head with her pencil stuck through it, but it rebelled and little curls escaped around her face and ears.

June and Myrna pecked cheeks, then Myrna stepped back and said to Jim, "Now, let me look at you." She gave him a study that was almost roguish for a little old lady. "My yes, you're certainly attractive enough for my niece. But are you rich enough?"

"Auntie!"

"I have barely two nickels to rub together, but I plan to earn my keep."

"Ah, I see. So you've already struck a bargain, have you?"

"I promised her that I would do anything she asked."

June lifted a single brow and regarded him dubiously. When had he promised that?

"Then I hope she's begun a list to keep you busy a long, long time. Now, come into the sitting room and I'll have the girls bring us some refreshments. Endeara, snap out of it," Myrna demanded. "Amelia, get a grip!"

The twins disappeared huffily, both taking refuge in the kitchen.

"And if I hear one bicker out of either of you, you'll never get another favor out of me. Do you hear?" There was subdued grumbling, clearly from both of them.

Myrna hooked her arms into June's and Jim's and led them to the sitting room. "I thought this might be a bad idea, but I was in a fix, you see. When Endeara came to work this morning I told her that you'd be bringing your gentleman over to meet me. Well, she took on this superior air. She thought she was going to have one over on her sister." Myrna looked up at Jim and explained, "All the two of them have done all their lives is argue and spit at each other, which is why I'll only have one of them at a time, unless there's an urgent need for both. And don't I pay the price when that happens!"

When they reached the sitting room, she pointed them to their chairs and took the settee across from them in the middle. "But there I was, with Endeara thinking she had the advantage. So I was forced to call Amelia and tell her that if she could behave herself, she might come and have a look at you, too." She smiled like the rascal she was. "I do believe they approved.

"Now!" she said, clapping her hands together. "Tell me all about yourself!"

So came the story — in brief.

"And your people?" Myrna asked.

"I have a married sister in the Midwest. She has a couple of teenagers and she has been bossing me around all my life."

"Ah, you're close."

He shrugged. "I suppose, though we don't see too much of each other."

"And how many times have you been married?"

"Never," he said.

"Engaged?"

"Not even engaged."

"Then what makes you think you can marry my June and be a sufficient husband to her? You're rather old, after all."

June rolled her eyes. She had known it was going to be at least this bad.

Jim leaned toward Myrna, resting his elbows on his knees. "And if I'd said I'd been married once and was divorced?"

"I'd ask what makes you think you've got it right now?"

"If I'd been married and divorced three times?"

"A mighty bad track record, don't you agree?"

He leaned back, laughing. "You're impossible to please, aren't you, Mrs. Claypool?"

"Probably," she said good-naturedly. "Lucky for you, then, that you don't have to worry about pleasing me. Isn't it?"

"Indeed," he agreed.

She let her eyes gently close with the nod of her head. "Do you play poker, Mr. Post?"

"I never have," he lied, "but I'd be willing to let you teach me."

She laughed a little too gleefully and glanced at June. "He's a live one. Good job, June."

At that moment Endeara came into the room bearing a tray of champagne glasses and a small bowl of strawberries. Behind her trailed Amelia, holding a large bottle of chilled champagne.

"You'd better bring me tea, Endeara. On top of everything else, I'm pregnant." Endeara nearly dropped the tray of crystal and managed to set it down on the tea table in front of Myrna just in the nick of time. Amelia hung on to the champagne bottle by its neck and covered her open mouth with the other hand.

"Gracious," Myrna said. "I didn't ask the right questions after all. Jim, would you be so kind as to open the bottle for Amelia? And Endeara, tea for my niece?"

When they left the room again, Myrna said to June, "I hope you don't intend for them to keep it secret? It's impossible, I assure you."

"Don't worry, Auntie. Thanks to my father, the whole town knows. And I only told him last week." The cork made a loud pop as it came out. "I was just getting around to telling you when Jim appeared. I hadn't expected him to arrive so soon."

"It seems a good thing he has appeared. Tell me something, dearest. How have you kept him secret so well?"

"Well, Auntie, I haven't seen as much of him as I would have liked, as he's been working out of state. I knew he'd be retiring in a few months and then I planned to spring him on the family and the town. In the meantime, though, I guess I just didn't want to share."

Jim poured champagne into two of the glasses. "And I didn't want to be shared," he said.

"I don't know how you did it," Myrna said, lifting one of the glasses. "Not with the hours you keep and the way people keep letting themselves into your house when they want to see a doctor. Well, here's to you, June. The master of deceit." She took a little sip. "And a baby, too?"

"We had so little time together, I can't imagine how that happened," June said, genuinely perplexed. "But I'll make a confession. Had I known this was going to happen, I'd have introduced Jim around a while ago. It must look to everyone like I jumped into bed with him the second we met. It wasn't quite that way," she said. But it was close.

"I have something for you," Myrna said. "Just the thing. Sit still."

She dashed out of the room excitedly, as quickly as an eighty-four-year-old woman can dash, leaving Jim and June to stare at each other. June whispered, "How are you holding up?"

"I think I'll survive. Your aunt is a kick. Hell, your town is a kick. It doesn't look like I'm going to be bored."

"You have anything to keep you busy, like knitting?" She was answered with a frown. "There's a lot I need to learn about you." Endeara brought her tea on a tray with a basket of tiny crackers.

Jim patted her knee. "Fortunately there's plenty of time," he said. June sipped her tea. "And I'm not holding anything back," he whispered.

The tea wasn't hot and it had a funny taste. The twins didn't usually screw up tea, which made her very suspect of the ingredients. She didn't hear exactly what Jim said, but the combination of his warm breath in her ear and tea that tasted strangely like dishwater made her stomach turn over. She set the cup down on the cocktail table and grew pale.

"Are you all right?" Jim asked.

"I'm not sure. A wave of . . . The worst . . . Funny, you'd think I'd get used to this."

"What?"

Her hand went to her stomach. "The totally unpredictable lurching of my stomach." She grimaced. "Out of the blue, for no reason at all, I'll be just overcome with . . ." She made a face and swallowed convulsively.

"The fact that I've been whispering in your ear that you can get to know as much of me as you like hasn't made you sick to your stomach, has it?" he asked, half joking.

"Of course not," she said, but she spoke with difficulty. This had happened to her a number of times, this queer and sudden sickness, but if she waited it out it would pass. She hadn't yet thrown up during this pregnancy. "I just need to be still and quiet. For a second or two."

"Amazing," he said. "You can deliver a baby without flinching, but a cup of tea in your aunt's sitting room has you green at the gills."

"Shh," she said, patting her tummy gently and closing her eyes. *Pass,* she commanded the feeling. *Pass.*

"Just so long as you swear it isn't the thought of marrying me that's making you nauseous," he gibed.

"You're looking for trouble," she said through gritted teeth.

"Okay," he chuckled. He sipped his champagne and tapped his fingers on his knee. He looked around the ornate, overcrowded antique room while June took deep, slow breaths in through her nose, out through her mouth. He smiled at her, though she couldn't see. Even as she struggled with pregnancy-induced stomach upset, he found her compellingly beautiful.

The sound of Myrna's heels on the floor announced her return. "Here it is!" she said cheerfully. Myrna stood before them, holding a dress hanger high above her head. Flowing down to the floor, sheathed in thick, clear plastic, was a wedding gown. "I've saved this for you all these years, dear," she said. "Now you can get married in your mother's dress!"

An odd, strangled sound came from June. She turned away from her aunt and Jim and promptly threw up on the rug.

Over the years June had had patients tell her that with morning sickness, unlike food poisoning, the flu or any other nausea-producing condition, the second it was over, it was completely over. Just a few moments before she had struggled with a biting, churning illness that caused her to pinch her eyes closed, grit her teeth and pray. But once released, she took a couple of deep breaths and voilà, she felt like jogging. Jogging to the kitchen to make something to eat, in fact. It was nothing short of miraculous. Under no other circumstances but pregnancy did stomach upset resolve itself so efficiently.

Except for the humiliation of it. "Oh, God! Auntie, I'm so-o sorry!"

"Well, I'm sure you didn't do it on purpose," Myrna said weakly.

Endeara first peeked, then rushed from the kitchen with a cool, damp cloth. June rejected it. "Seriously, I feel absolutely fine now. As if I never felt ill. Except, of course, I'm mortified. That's *never* happened to me before."

Amelia came running with a pail and rags. "Pregnancy is the strangest thing," she was saying.

"Oh, please, Amelia, you must let me!" June insisted.

"Never mind," Myrna said, draping the wedding gown over the back of a chair. "I think we'll find the scenery in the sunroom more to our liking." Myrna tsked and said quietly, "I do hope your mother wasn't watching."

June bit her lip. It was all a coincidence. Jim's mention of marriage and the appearance of the wedding gown had not made her throw up.

"I should help clean up," June said, but the twins would have none of it.

"You've tended enough sick people in your time," Endeara said.

"You've earned some tending," said Amelia.

The sunroom was next to Myrna's office, across the hall from the kitchen. It was here that she retired from her writing every day at five to have her martini — a celebration of a good day's work. The room was bright and airy and overlooked the Hudson House grounds which, under normal circumstances, boasted gardens, trees, vines and lawn, not to mention a view of the valley all the way to the coast. But at the moment it was a mess of compromised landscaping, holes and torn-up shrubs. Myrna sighed audibly as she entered the sunroom, then chose a seat that put her back to the yard.

"We'll discuss the wedding another time," Myrna said, more softly than was typical for her. "I'm very fond of this particular rug."

"Aunt Myrna, the two things had *nothing* —"

"Of course, my darling. You just relax and take your time. You won't be rushed by me. Why, I raised a child on my own, not a man in sight, if you'll recall." She looked rather wistfully at Jim. "However, had I one like . . ." Her voice trailed away.

Jim, however, was focused on the rubble outside the sun room. He frowned. "June told me the police did some digging out there," he said.

"Some digging?" Myrna repeated. "They were looking for a body. The body of my late husband, Morton. That is, if he is late." Then she smiled. "Don't tell anyone I said so, but it wasn't a completely ridiculous notion on the district attorney's part. I've been writing such scenarios in my fiction for years, so they thought they were on to something. They don't know how hard it is to be a writer, nor how difficult it is to be abandoned by your husband."

June's expression registered surprise at the remark. She'd never before heard her aunt express that particular sentiment, but she should have known that, even though Myrna never showed it, it certainly must have hurt.

"But that's behind us now," Myrna said.

"I'd be happy to help you put the yard right again," Jim said.

"That's very thoughtful, young man, but I plan to make the D.A. pay the freight on that. Though I don't really blame them for the suspicion, one has to be accountable for one's actions. And on that score, I've been seriously considering making a major change in my future themes."

"Really?" June asked. "No more knocking off philandering husbands?"

"The whole idea has gotten a little stale, even if it has made me rich. I have Edward to thank for that, when it comes right down to it."

"Edward?"

Myrna gave a veiled smile. "You aren't the only woman in this family who's had a secret man, although mine is considerably farther removed. Despite many attempts, we've never managed to meet in person."

June scooted to the edge of her chair. "Who is this, Auntie?"

"A gentleman writer, an historian, to whom I've corresponded for nearly twenty years. I've written to a large number of writers over the years. It's very common among our breed, since we work in solitude. But Edward has been quite constant. He began as a fan who was working on his very first book — an account of the Lewis and Clark expedition."

Myrna rose and, without bothering to explain herself, went to her office and retrieved a book. She handed it to June. *The Promised Trail* by Edward Mortimer. June flipped to the back of the dust jacket. "No photo," she said.

"Edward's a tish older than me and very shy. He said he found himself faced with a choice between resurrecting his old army photo or demurring altogether."

June closed the book and smiled at her aunt. "How is it you've never mentioned this . . . Edward?"

Myrna shrugged. "No particular reason. Or maybe there was. Maybe I didn't want anyone to think me a silly old fool, because, as it happens, I've grown very fond of him over time."

"I think that's lovely," June said.

"I ran the killer-wife idea by Edward and he went for it. Or maybe he ran it by me and I went for it, I can't quite remember. He thought it was my best work, perhaps because I was so . . . so . . . furious when I wrote it. And it took off like a sky rocket. So he said, in his letter, 'Don't be silly, Myrna, do it again with a different twist. You've stumbled onto something your readers love.' And, of course, I gave him advice as well. Writers tend to rely on each other for that kind of support." She cleared her throat. "Edward is the only person I've ever confided in to that depth. I'm typically very private."

"Is there any chance you'll meet him in person?"

"I doubt it. Some years ago I drove all the way to Fresno where he was to appear at a library talk and book signing, and wouldn't you know it, he was taken with an attack of gout and couldn't get out of bed. I don't mind travel a bit, but I can't light out in that old Caddy for a five-hour drive at my age. It would be reckless!"

"Well, if you ever see the opportunity present itself again, you just let me know," June said. "I'll take you wherever it is." She stood up. "I think we should go, Auntie. I've left John stranded for too long at the clinic."

"But you'll be back soon?"

June kissed her aunt's crepey cheek. "And often."

On the way back to town, Jim said, "You do want to get married, don't you, June?"

"I think so," she said.

"You *think* so?"

Her hand immediately protected her tummy. "Don't snap at me. I've been single a long time!"

His eyes bored into her for a moment, though he should have been watching the road. Finally he spoke. "You've been pregnant a long time, too."

FOUR

The people of Grace Valley were usually guilty of spreading gossip so fast that people would hear rumors about themselves before they had a chance to tell their own best friends. Like word of June having a secret man in her life, a baby on the way and no wedding date set — that news was all over town before she even had a chance to introduce Jim to her only aunt.

But there were times that word didn't travel fast enough. News perhaps important enough to sound the alarm could sometimes sit like sludge and not move. Just such news was the presence of Conrad Davis in town when Jim had pointedly told him to scat. Jim was the only person who had been close enough to have gathered a sense — a professionally trained sense — that Conrad was bad news.

When Sam went to the gas station after breakfast at the café, he found Conrad and his laden truck. "Well, you didn't get all that far, did you, son?" Sam asked in a friendly manner. "Problems with the truck?"

"No, sir," Conrad said sweetly. He looked down and shuffled his feet. "I was taking the wife and kids down to Fresno where my cousin said he thought there was work, when she popped like a cork by the side of the road." He raised his eyes and allowed a shy smile. "A boy. Thank God for that woman doctor."

"Yep. She's a peach."

"So now I got the wife in the hospital and I need to get there, but . . ." He paused, thinking. He looked down again. "I don't reckon it'd be safe to leave this truck full of stuff in the parking lot over there. I'd come out and find it all gone."

Sam looked at the tied-down, sorry mess of household goods and personal belongings. Frankly, nothing in there looked worth burning, much less stealing — especially not that stained and bloodied mattress sticking out the back end. He lifted a white eyebrow.

Conrad followed his eyes. "Erline gave birth on that. I'd of thrown it, but I ain't got no others. The kids gotta have something between them and the ground." The young man's eyes grew moist. "It ain't much, that

68

load, but I need a place to store it so I can go over to the hospital and get my little girls. Can't risk losing all that. Kids' clothes and all."

Sam had always lived simply, but that was by choice, not because he'd been down on his luck. The fact was, Sam made money without hardly trying.

"What kind of work you do, boy?"

"Construction. Janitor. A little mechanical, but not much." He cleared his throat. "I'd do just about anything to keep a roof over my family's head, sir."

Sam didn't need an employee. Heck, Sam didn't even need to be around for the gas station to run itself. He'd had his share of hard times, having buried two wives, but he'd never been poor and he'd never had the worry of how to feed a family. There hadn't been any children for him.

This young man could be a grandson.

"When did you last eat, son?"

Conrad rolled his eyes skyward, as if the answer lay in the clouds. "Not yesterday," he said finally. "I think it was Saturday. We were camped for the night and I caught some fish."

A smile broke over Sam's face. "A man who can fish never needs be hungry. Tell you what, let's go on down to the café, get a bite to eat and talk about some possibilities. This is no Fresno, but if we could find you something to do, do you think you could be persuaded to stay on awhile?"

Conrad's face lit up. "Here? Hell, this here town's way better than Fresno. Fresno's an armpit. You ever been there?"

"Can't say as I have." Sam laughed.

"This town's a whole lot better than Fresno. Way prettier. And the people are nicer, too."

"People tend to be real nice in Grace Valley," Sam confirmed. He dropped an arm around the kid's shoulders and began to pull him down the street toward the café. "Come on, let's get a bite. George rarely messes up breakfast, and he has the best coffee in a hundred miles."

Conrad seemed to pull back. "Sir, my load, sir. Can I just park her in the garage?"

"Don't you worry about that load. Not in Grace Valley. I personally guarantee it's safe."

Conrad's expression became wistful. "Sure would like to raise my kids in a place safe as that," he said quietly.

"You never know," Sam said. "Maybe that'll work out."

Harry Shipton sat at his desk in the parsonage, awash in a sea of papers with his checkbook register and calculator in the middle. He kept figuring, futilely. The answer was always the same. He was overdrawn. Again.

His hand reached for the phone out of habit and he snatched it away before he placed the call to his ex-wife, Brianna. It was humiliating for her to always be right — he was a dunce with money. His priorities were elsewhere. He was great with people, with spiritual encouragement, even with counseling. It had always made Brianna laugh, that he could so successfully counsel couples in trouble while his own marriage disintegrated before his very eyes, almost without him seeing it.

Well, at least they didn't have children.

At least? He had wanted children. Brianna had wanted children. But the children hadn't come.

His phone rang. "Pastor Shipton," he answered. The woman on the other end of the line told him that her elderly father had been taken to the hospital early in the morning. It was very likely a stroke. The old man was only semiconscious. "Oh, my goodness, I'm so sorry to hear that. Is he in Valley Hospital? I'll go there this afternoon and sit with him for a while. But meanwhile, is

71

there anything I can do for you?" Prayers, the woman requested. Other than that, she couldn't think of a thing. "I'll activate our prayer tree immediately. Now, don't you worry, your father is a good man and the Lord will take good care of him. And you."

"What would we do without you, Harry," the woman said.

"What would I do without *you?*" he replied. "If anything changes, call me at once."

They said their goodbyes and Harry got right on the phone. He first called Leah Craven, then Betty Lou Granger, explaining that he needed the prayer tree activated for their fellow parishioner. Next he called George at the café and asked if he had a frozen meal he'd be willing to donate to the family, as their time was consumed with hospital sitting and they probably couldn't take the time to prepare a decent meal. Next he called Philana Toopeek, Tom's mother, and asked if she might wish to throw some of her wonderful baked bread into the mix. She promised to have her husband take it over to the family in need before the dinner hour. And then Harry took a moment, clasped his hands together atop a disastrous pile of bills and beseeched the Lord to care for their friend and brother in the hospital. The warmth of community love spread through him like a glow and he opened his eyes from prayer feeling stronger. As always.

But it only lasted for as long as it took him to remember that he was overdrawn at the bank and owed for cash advances on three credit cards.

This inability to manage his meager salary as a preacher had cost him his marriage. He and Brianna had started out in good shape. She drew a respectable salary as a school-teacher and it balanced against his modest income quite well. They even managed a little savings toward their future together. But their biggest mistake was falling into that conservative old habit of letting the man manage the money. Harry was simply miserable at it. He always paid the higher interest as he juggled the bills, ended up wasting money on nonsense, invested in losers, passed by winners. Ultimately they were in a deep hole.

"We'll just have to take the money out of our savings, Harry, and from now on, I'll be paying the bills."

He would never forget the look on her face when he told her there was no longer any savings. His investments were supposed to be sure things; they had been sure flops.

She was devastated. So they sold their house, paid off the debts, restocked the savings account and started over.

Harry had meant to surprise her by recouping the money. He found a couple of investments that should have paid off in less than six months. To hedge against failure, he spread the money around, a diversified and balanced portfolio. To his delight, a couple of his long shots came in high, doubling his investments, so he set up some margin calls. Then he had to liquidate a little to pay a debt. A couple of investments cratered and he liquidated other stocks to buy at a low, sold some stocks short and, wouldn't you know, they came in high, causing him a loss. He had some markers called in, exercised a couple of margin calls, had some options come due . . .

"What?" she had screamed at him. "You *lost* the savings? Again?"

"It wasn't supposed to go like that," he'd said lamely.

So she left him. He could hardly blame her. It wasn't a question of love, they loved each other still. And if they'd had children together, she would have set up a college fund and he would have blown it on some bet or investment or long shot that was supposed to pay off big. Every once in a while he thought his luck was changing, then wham! Down he'd tumble again.

If it weren't for money, Harry would have a perfect life. He loved God, loved his church, loved the people, loved the work. He was never happier or more at peace than when he was kneeling, or in a pulpit delivering a meaningful and uplifting message to the flock, or when helping someone with a problem or need. But too soon that part of his life would pass and he would grapple with paying the bills again.

He had a hundred bucks, an overdrawn checking account and credit card bills due. Grace Valley was a chance for a fresh start, if only he could turn things around. If he could just pay his bills, he'd never take another chance on anything. He'd hire one of those money-manager types who would collect his paycheck and dole out an allowance, and he'd never stray off his budget. Never.

He opened his top desk drawer and took out a racing form. It had worked before, it could work again. He had a really good tip on a horse. If he came in, he swore to *God* he wouldn't place another bet. He punched the numbers on the phone.

Tom was alone in the police department, sitting at his desk in his office, which was the largest bedroom in the converted three-bedroom house. One deputy was on patrol and the other was resting so he could work that night. Tom, whose day had started even earlier than usual, was just thinking about lunch when he heard the tinkling of the bell on the front door. "Back here," he yelled, pen poised over paper.

A loud snort that fell into a snore issued from one of the two other bedrooms that had been converted into a cell. The bed was being used by Rob Gilmore. He'd had a little too much to drink the night before and his wife, Jennie, had locked him out of the house and called the police chief.

Tom looked up and waited. Whoever had come by was sure taking his time. Tom didn't hear any footfalls, but he could hear the hallway floorboards squeak. He put his hand on his sidearm just in case, though being ambushed in his office was the last thing he expected.

At last Jim Post stood in the frame of the door. He gestured with a thumb over his shoulder. "What's his story?" he asked.

"His wife put him out," Tom answered.

"I can see why. Listen to that. Sounds horrible. Sure am glad I don't sleep that loud." The noise came again. "Jesus, how long has he been doing that?"

"Since I brought him in here at 4:30 a.m."

Jim shook his head. "You must have nerves of steel."

"I don't get nearly the credit I deserve," Tom pointed out with some humor.

Jim took another step into the office. "Got a minute?"

Tom threw down his pen and indicated one of the two chairs that faced his desk. Tom had only just met Jim, but in many ways he felt that he was an old friend. This was June's man, for one thing, and June was the closest thing to a best friend Tom had, excepting his wife, Ursula. Being the town cop, he did a lot of business with the town doctor. Additionally, they had grown up together. In fact, if Tom recalled correctly, they were blood brothers. That would have been before June realized she was a girl. The memory caused him to smile to himself.

"Something funny?" Jim asked.

"I was just remembering that once, when we were kids, June Hudson was my blood brother. We cut our hands and everything. And now she's your . . . What is she? Your fiancée?"

"At the least," Jim said.

Tom considered it a stroke of luck that he took to the guy June had chosen. Add to that, Jim Post had spent his career in law enforcement. Once they knew each other better, there would be stories to trade. Tom looked forward to that.

"There are a couple of things I want to talk to you about. Are we alone? Except for what's-his-name in there?"

Tom nodded. "As long as you can hear him, he's not listening to you."

"Gotcha. Okay, number one. Confidentially, if you don't mind. I'm retired DEA."

"I know."

The surprise registered on Jim's face. "No, you don't. You just guessed."

He shrugged. "Have it your way. You were part of the raid last summer."

More surprise. "Did June tell you that?"

Tom rested his elbows on his desk and leaned forward. "What do you think?"

He rubbed his chin and pursed his lips. "She told you about the gunshot wound. The late night visit to the clinic. And from there you made assumptions."

"Actually, I have one or two reliable sources."

"That makes me uncomfortable," Jim admitted.

"Well, relax. We're on the same side, after all."

"I was mixing it up with some real badasses," Jim admitted.

78

"Mostly behind bars now, thanks to you and a few others. The DEA brought in the army, for God's sake. And those that slipped away aren't going to hang around here."

"Yeah, well, this is what we hope," Jim said.

"I keep a pretty close watch on things," Tom said, trying to reassure him. "See if you can relax. You have other matters to —"

"One more thing," Jim said. "Did you happen to notice a pickup loaded with household goods parked at Sam Cussler's gas station?"

"When?" Tom asked, which made it obvious he hadn't seen it.

"When I was leaving the café with June to drive out to her aunt's house, the truck was parked outside the garage. When I brought her back to the clinic just now, I noticed the truck *in* the garage. June and I happened upon that truck out on the road. It was disabled. The man's wife was in labor and June delivered her in the back of her own pickup. There are also two little girls. John Stone brought the ambulance and took everyone but the husband to the hospital while I bought him a new tire from Sam."

"You had a busy morning," Tom observed.

"I changed the kid's tire and told him not to hang around. He tried to give June a couple of twenties for delivering the baby. He had a pocketful of drug money."

Tom leaned back. He picked up a pen and tapped it a few times. Finally he asked, "Why do you suppose he's hanging around here?"

"I have a lot of theories. His pupils were as big as ink blots this morning when the baby was coming. He was high. Sluggish and inattentive. I don't think he's looking for a fresh start. Though I've never seen him before, I'm pretty sure he came out of the mountains where he either worked for a grower or had a small operation of his own."

"If it was an outdoor farm," Tom said, "it might've shut down. Pot growers aren't the only farmers who fall on hard times when the weather turns. We see some layoffs around here in winter. Social services gets real busy. Maybe he's just one more hard-luck story."

"When you see his eyes . . . when you talk to him . . . you're going to know what I know. He's not what he pretends to be. He's not just another hard-luck story."

"You expect me to arrest him for the look in his eye? Or run him out of town because we don't like the smell of his cash around here?"

"I expect you to keep a real close eye on

him. Because he's up to no good. I'm sure of it."

Tom smiled lazily. "You aren't all that retired, are you?"

Jim returned the smile. "Old habits die hard."

"I can imagine," said Tom, who had barely had a day off in twenty years.

"Plus, old Sam seems like a good guy and I'd hate to see him burned by the kid. It's gotta be Sam helping him out."

"Sam's pretty savvy, but just to be safe, I'll put a word of caution in his ear." Tom stood and stretched. "You had lunch?"

"I'll have to take a rain check," Jim said. "I have errands to run. And I think I've had all the café exposure I can take for one day."

The afternoon sped by for June, for she had more than the usual number of patients with decidedly minor complaints, mostly curious about her new status as expectant mother and, it was assumed, prospective wife.

She found herself frequently thinking, you gotta love a small town. The questions were not couched in any phony politeness. "Well, how *long* have you known him then?" And "When is this baby due, exactly?" She was an expert at evasion. She would answer

"Long enough" and "Babies tend to come when they're good and ready." But by far the most common question was "When is the wedding?"

And her answer? "When we have a date, you'll be the first to know." By the end of the day at least forty people were deemed to be first.

By the time the dinner hour approached, June had had a full day. She was clearly sinking. She knew that exhaustion was par for the pregnancy course, but she hadn't been so plagued before. "I'm absolutely wilting," she told Susan Stone.

"Yeah, I think that's the worst part, the total and consuming fatigue. Worse even than the nausea."

"I don't know about that," June said, a hand going to her stomach. "Did I tell you about my visit with Aunt Myrna today? She dragged my mother's old wedding gown out of the attic and I threw up on her Oriental rug." She made a face. "I think it was the smell of mothballs. And the tea Endeara made me, which tasted like dishwater."

Susan erupted in laughter. "No! Really?"

"Would I make that up? I was mortified!"

Jessie, upon hearing the laughter, came down the hall from her secretary's cubicle. "What's so funny?"

"June threw up on her aunt's rug," Susan reported.

"No way!" Jessie said.

"Way," confirmed June.

John came out of an examining room to join the discussion. "What did the daddy do?" he asked.

June had to think a minute. "I think he looked the other way," she said.

"But he didn't run for his life, did he?" Susan asked.

"No, he hung in there. It was truly horrible." June sank wearily to a stool in the hallway. "You know, he's almost forty and never expected this —"

"Hell, June, *you're* almost forty and never expected this," John reminded her.

"I'm almost thirty-eight. Don't rush me. But you're right about the expecting part. . . ."

"You never expected to be expecting?" Jessie asked.

June lifted an eyebrow and peered at her young, pretty twenty-year-old office manager. "Let this be a lesson to you. Anyone can find themselves in the family way, without warning. So be careful."

"Well, since you brought it up," Jessie said haltingly, "that's exactly what I've been wondering. How someone like you . . ."

"Excuse me" a voice called from the waiting room.

"Thank God," June said, dragging herself up and heading toward the voice. Over her shoulder she said to Jessie, "I can't talk about that yet."

John whispered into Jessie's ear. "I can talk about it. She wasn't prepared. At all." He leaned back, lifted his brows and looked down at the young woman. "Do we understand each other, Jessica?"

Her cheeks grew rosy. "Um, yes, John."

Susan whacked him in the arm. "Don't embarrass her, you lout." To Jessie she said, "Jess, you and I will have lunch tomorrow and talk turkey. 'Prepared' is my middle name. You're in good hands."

June found that the owner of the voice was Harry Shipton. He had just slipped into the clinic and didn't look very well. "Oh my, Harry. What's the matter? You look awful."

"Thanks," he said sheepishly. "I'm not feeling too well, actually. Had a rather long afternoon. Do you have time for a last-minute customer?"

"Of course, Harry. Come on back. We'll get a history and make up a chart for you and —"

"Maybe we could save all that for next

time," he said. "Could I just talk to you for a minute? In private?"

June frowned, confused. "Sure. Would you like to go into my office, or an examining room, just in case . . . ?"

"Your office will do."

Harry was quite tall and lanky, with the biggest feet, but he seemed to slump slightly as he followed June to her office. He acted as though he just didn't feel well, that a bug had gotten the best of him. "Hi, Harry," Jessie, Susan and John all said as he passed them in the hall. "Hi, all," he said weakly.

Harry took the seat in front of June's desk while June went around to her chair. Sadie perked up as the two entered and had to pay a little welcome to the pastor before she could lie down and nap some more. A few silent seconds passed.

"Well, Harry?" June prodded.

"June, bear with me. This is very embarrassing for me," he added morosely.

"You've come to the right place, Harry. I know a lot about being embarrassed today."

He gave her a tremulous smile. "I suppose you've been teased all day about your, you know, condition."

"That's the half of it. What's wrong, Harry?"

"Can I invoke doctor-patient privilege

even though I'm not really physically ill?" he asked.

"Sure. I'll keep your confidence."

"June, I'm a screwup."

"Aw, Harry."

"I am. I'm good with people, but I've never been good with a budget, and I've bungled my checkbook. I wasn't paying attention and now I'm overdrawn and it's over a week till payday."

"Oh, dear," she said. "Do you have a credit card?"

"Maxed," he said helplessly. "Truth is, June, I came over here hoping that John, Susan and Jessie would already be gone. I came to ask you for a loan. If I can't borrow two hundred dollars before tomorrow morning, I'll have to pay a huge overdraft penalty. This is so embarrassing."

She reached across her desk toward him, taking his hands in both of hers for a reassuring squeeze. "Why are we always so hard on ourselves, huh, Harry? Who among us hasn't made a mistake or two, huh? Look at me. I did it in front of the whole town. Well, I didn't *do it* in front of the whole town, but I might as well have."

That made him chuckle. "By the way, your young man is very nice, June."

"He's not young and neither am I," she

said, pulling her hands back and opening her top desk drawer. She retrieved her checkbook and flipped it open. "We've both always been single and neither of us has had children and we were completely surprised by this blessed event. I imagine we look like fools." She scribbled onto a check, tore it out and handed it to him. "Why don't you sign up for one of those debt-consolidation loans, Harry. Get the credit cards wiped out so you don't get stuck with all that high interest."

He took the check, his expression brightening considerably. "That's a very good idea, June. And thank you for this. I'll pay you back as soon as I can. With interest."

"I'm not worried, Harry. I know where to find you."

He looked so tremendously relieved that June had to remind herself that to some people a two hundred dollar mistake in the checkbook was a disaster. Harry had probably worked himself into a real lather of worry over it. June's life was simple and she didn't have a lot of money, but she didn't need a lot of money. Her patients paid her in goods and services as often as insurance claims and she was usually somehow ahead. Even so, she remembered a time or two when Elmer had covered her. And yes, it had been embarrassing. But then doctors had a much more marketable product than preachers. Not a more valuable product, just one more easily translated into money.

"You'll never know how much it means to me, June, that you trust me for it."

"Not at all," she assured him.

Jim Post had almost no experience in the wooing of a woman; he had been married to his work. The only thing he knew how to do with absolute certainty was play a role for the sake of undercover police operations, so he decided he would adopt a persona of suitor and seduce June into a comfort zone from whence she would melt into his life and they would, together, have a baby.

Well, the baby would come no matter what. But it would be better for all of them if they forged a union into which they would bring this child, this baby girl. And in order for that to happen they would have to get beyond June's overwhelming sickness at the mere thought of marriage.

He'd been busy. He'd been to Rockport to buy fresh salmon and vegetables, then to Standard Roberts's fields of fresh flowers, then home to June's little house, where he had rummaged around in search of table linens and good dishes. He had purchased sparkling cider for their toast, but also a single malt Scotch for himself. After all, he wasn't pregnant.

Jim wasn't a bad cook for a bachelor. He didn't lean toward the gourmet or cook as a hobby or anything as precious as that, but he certainly knew how to put a decent meal together. June might have had her fill of salmon long ago, living this close to good fishing all her life, but there was nothing quite as safe and delicious in his mind, not to mention a huge treat for someone who had been back East for the last several months. A little lemon and dill butter, some capers, garlic mashed potatoes, broccoli . . . He lit the candles on the dining room table, remembering a night not so long ago when he'd bought her a little black dress as a surprise and danced with her in this small room. Size six, as he recalled. He didn't think it would be altogether wise to dig through the closet and find it right now.

He heard a vehicle; June said she would get a lift home from either John or Susan. He dimmed the lights in the dining room just as the door was opening.

"My" was all she could say. Sadie pushed past June and ran to Jim for a pet.

"I hope you like salmon."

"It would be against the law for me to dislike salmon, given where I live. You've gone to an awful lot of trouble."

He pulled her into the living room, removed her jacket and sat her down on the sofa in front of the blazing hearth. "You relax while I get you something to drink and put on the finishing touches." He knelt on the floor and gently pulled off her boots, resting her feet, one at a time, on the coffee table.

"What if I get used to this treatment?" she asked him.

"That's my intention. To spoil you into submission."

Her hand went to her slightly swollen middle. "I already submitted, remember?"

He was about to say "Not all the way," but held his tongue. "I'll be right back," he said instead.

She stifled a yawn as he went to the kitchen. "Feed Sadie while you're in there, will you?" Then she yawned largely and let herself relax into the cushions of the sofa. The fire was so warm and welcoming. The smells, so savory and alluring. The day, so long and tiring. She yawned again, thinking home had never felt quite so delicious.

When Jim returned with a stemmed glass of sparkling cider, he found her sound asleep, her head slumped onto her shoulder.

FIVE

The phone at the Toopeek household rang, sending Tom and Ursula both bolting upright. Four-thirty in the morning. Tom grabbed it first. "Toopeek," he answered.

The gravelly unidentified male voice rasped, "Man with a gun out at Rocky's."

"Great. What's he going to do with the —"

Click.

"Hello? Hello?"

Rocky's was an isolated roadhouse frequented by the lowlife clientele of three counties because it sat on the edge of all three. Unfortunately, it sat a little bit more on the Grace Valley side of upper Mendocino County. Tom's jurisdiction. Tom dialed the number from memory. It began to ring.

Ursula fell back against the pillows. "What is it?" she asked sleepily.

"Man with a gun at Rocky's." The phone just rang and rang.

"What else is new?" she asked. "Everyone out here has a gun or twelve."

It rang and rang and rang.

Tom hung up and swung his long legs out of the bed. His bare toes curled against the insult of the cold wood floor. "Someone must be threatening or even shooting."

"How do you figure?"

"No answer at Rocky's. The man with the gun is either not letting them answer or someone tore the phone out of the wall. Again."

He picked up the phone and dialed another number. This time there was an immediate answer. "Rios."

"Ricky, I just got a call from —"

"I know. Rocky's. It's a couple of the MacAlvie boys. Cousins. They got laid off from the mill up at Mad River and they were either having a celebration or a commiseration that turned into one of their usual fights. I'm on my way."

"Good. I'll back you up."

"Hey," Ricky said, "I got it, Tom. Plus, I radioed Humboldt County and got Bill Sanderson. The MacAlvies are theirs. Humboldt can join the party. Go back to bed."

"It's okay. I'm up."

"We're all up," Ursula muttered, sticking

her legs out in search of slippers.

Ricky was on duty till 7:00 a.m. He had fielded the call through the police station and arranged his own backup from the county sheriff's department. But someone had made a point to call Tom's house, which upped the seriousness of the trouble by a notch. Because of that, Tom decided he'd put in an appearance. Maybe it was a worse-than-usual fight. He could only hope they'd kill each other by the time he got there. The MacAlvies were no good.

Rocky Conner was a leathery woman in her forties who looked like she was in her sixties. Her life had taken its toll. She was the fourth generation to run that ramshackle watering hole and was named for her great-grandfather. She claimed her people had served up drinks to tired and thirsty men all the way back to the Gold Rush.

Rocky's was off the beaten track and known only to locals. Though it wasn't exactly a place to buy a drink by invitation only, it came close. Tourists were not welcome. Strangers were usually met with unfriendliness unless they arrived on Harleys and had plenty of money to buy rounds. Rocky ran the place alone, but she had her regulars looking out for her. She'd only been robbed once in all her years at the roadhouse and that poor fool had gotten shot in the back as he made his getaway. Every last patron in the bar gave evidence that he'd fired a weapon, but Tom never did find the gun that killed the man. "Thicker than thieves" had real meaning in the backwoods.

There'd only been that one robbery, one death, but Rocky's place had been busted up by fights more times than anyone could count.

A situation at Rocky's might be the only case in which law enforcement personnel from three counties were willing to cross town and county lines to help out, because the counties of Humboldt, Trinity and Mendocino met in the bar itself. It sat in the shadow of Legend Mountain, down the Windle River from Grace Valley several miles and well out of the way. At least there was always someone to back up Tom and his deputies. Just the same, Tom had told Rocky a hundred times that if a good wind came up and blew that damned old shack ten feet to the northeast, his life would be measurably improved. To which she would always say, "I'd miss the hell out of you if that happened."

He didn't run the siren, but he flashed the lights atop his Range Rover and made some serious tracks to Rocky's. The flashing lights of three patrols greeted him; the place was all lit up. He saw a Humboldt County car, a state police vehicle and Ricky's squad car. There were a few ratty-looking men hanging out by the front door and Rocky was leaning against the county squad car with a cup of something in her hands. The culprits had their palms against the building and their legs spread.

Tom drove his Range Rover up close and jumped out.

"Hey, Toopeek, what's your hurry?" Stan Kubbicks asked.

"How's it going, Stan?" he replied.

"We're just mopping up here," he said. "You coulda stayed in bed."

"I like an early start," Tom said, approaching the building.

Ricky was patting down one of the MacAlvies while Bill Sanderson handled the other. Ricky pulled a knife out of his suspect's sock and tossed it onto a small pile of contraband that had been removed from the two of them. Tom saw three knives, one of them a switchblade, brass knuckles, a shank — the type made by prisoners in jail — and some unlabeled pills in a small vial. Both MacAlvies were dripping blood from their faces. Both law enforcement officers wore rubber gloves and took great care with their searches.

"Nice little armory," Tom said.

"Yeah, and they left half their artillery in the bar," Bill answered. "I already told Ricky, you're going to have to take 'em, Tom. We got a full house tonight."

"Must be a full moon," Ricky said. "I was busy all night."

Once the cuffs were on them, Tom shone the flashlight in both their faces. There were some cuts and swelling and bruises, but nothing that looked too serious. "These two ought to be all right with some ice and tape. We can let the lady doctor sleep. Put them in the back of your squad and I'll follow you in," he told Ricky.

"Figures. I spend half my life washing out the back of that car. Now they're gonna bleed all over it."

"Mine's clean," Tom said. And smiled as he added, "And I'm the chief."

"Yeah, Chief, you're the chief." He yanked his suspect around. "Come on, asshole. Let's get you to jail."

Ricky's man, Ben MacAlvie, moaned and complained, but the other one took one step and went down. Bill crouched down, rolled him over and looked for a carotid pulse. By the time the pulse began to beat under his fingertips, Vern MacAlvie was snoring. Bill looked up at Tom. "He's passed out," he said, incredulous.

Rocky sauntered over on her short, thick legs and poked him in the ribs once with her toe. He snorted a couple of short ones, but didn't rouse. She looked up at Tom. "If he'd passed out an hour ago, either he'd be dead or the fight woulda petered out. Either way, there'd'a been less damage." She emptied the contents of her cup on his face and he sputtered madly, establishing he was not in a coma. "Damned trashy MacAlvies," Rocky grumbled.

That last caused Tom to lift a curious brow in her direction as she sauntered away. It was definitely the pot speaking of the kettle.

Then his eye caught a familiar face and he nearly gasped out loud. One of the four or five men who lingered outside the bar at dawn was his old high school chum, Chris Forrest. He couldn't believe his eyes. He'd never known Chris to be a drinker, and for sure not the kind of drinker who'd be at a dive like Rocky's at four in the morning. And not only did he appear in his cups, he was a trifle scuffed up, as though he'd been caught in the fray. Then he realized *Chris* had called him, disguising his voice very poorly.

Tom helped Bill lift up Vern MacAlvie, and once he was on foot, left him to get the detainee in Ricky's car. When he approached Chris, the other man looked down, his hands in his pockets. All he could think of to say was "Chris?"

Chris raised his eyes. "I'm looking for a ride," he said.

Chris was the only son of Judge and Birdie Forrest and had been Tom and June's best friend all through childhood, right up to high school graduation. He was the homecoming king to June's homecoming queen. Then, as many Grace Valley kids were known to do, Chris went away to make his mark. He'd landed in San Diego where he and wife, Nancy, also of Grace Valley, had twin boys.

Just a few months ago Chris had returned to the valley with his boys, now age fourteen, in search of a place to raise the little delinquents. Their mother had had enough of their petty crimes and disrespect. All that had been resolved, but not in the way anyone would have planned. Brad and Brent had stolen their grandmother Birdie's car and plunged it down a ravine. The boys were nearly killed; their injuries were going to take a long time to heal.

"I bought myself a fixer-upper," Chris told Tom on the ride home. "The place is a wreck, but now it's a wreck with two hospital beds in the living room. My boys are in traction and there's no time to work on making the house livable. The physical therapist comes every day and tortures them till they scream in pain. Nancy left a good job, and not only does she miss her work and friends, money is so tight we have to watch every cent. She cries herself to sleep at night, and even then, it's not for long . . . the boys wake up several times, needing pans and pills." He sniffed back self-pity. "Sometimes it's all just too much."

"I can imagine."

"I just needed to get out of the house."

"I can understand," Tom said. "But, Chris, why go to Rocky's? You know that place is like a hockey game in progress."

Chris gave a huff of laughter. "Yeah. But it was three in the morning. Nothing else was open."

"Still . . ."

"I didn't get much to drink, anyway. I'm just so damned tired it went straight to my head," Chris said. Then he looked at his knuckles. "I got a piece of Vern MacAlvie, though." He laughed.

"You're lucky they didn't get a piece of you."

Chris was quiet for a minute, and Tom gradually became aware that the soft sounds next to him were from Chris crying. He looked out the window, hiding his face from Tom. "At first I thought Nancy coming back here would help us work on our, you know, issues," he finally said. "But I've got her living on a shoestring in that dump of a house and I don't know how we're going to get through it."

Tom knew they must be exhausted from the sheer demands of critical-care patients, not to mention the financial burden. Birdie had told Ursula in the quilting circle that their insurance would only afford hospitalization for so long. That's why the boys were now getting home care long before the house was ready to be a home. Even with Birdie and Judge stopping in to help, even with the therapists and visiting nurses, Chris and Nancy were beat. And Chris couldn't work as much as he needed to if he helped with the boys.

"You might have to ask for help," Tom said.

"Ask who?" Chris bitterly replied.

"Your friends. That's who."

"My friends? My boys got into so much

trouble with my friends, you think anyone would want to help them now? They stole from Burt Crandall's bakery and egged the whole town. They vandalized George's café, tipped over trash cans, beat up your kid, for God's sake. No one's going to feel sorry for them now. And this," he said, looking over at Tom, tears wet on his cheeks, "is mostly because I wasn't there as a father."

Tom gave him a light sock in the arm, but really he wanted to stop the car and shake him good. "Stop feeling sorry for yourself. Remember what you know about your people. Your town."

Chris got the handkerchief out of his pocket and gave his nose a good blow. "I know they can be pushed too far sometimes, that's what I know."

Tom's radio squawked. "Rios to Toopeek, where you at, Chief?"

"Right at Paradise and 162, Ricky."

"We got truck versus deer at 162 and 86, you copy?"

"I can take that."

"Thanks, Chief."

Tom turned on the lights and siren; the morning was foggy, particularly dense in the low areas between hills. "Slight detour, Chris. I'm afraid it can't be helped."

"No problem. I'm the tagalong."

"We can talk about this later, though."

"Hey, it's a tough patch, but we'll work it out." He wiped his face, sniffed back the remnants of tears.

In just moments they could see the headlights of a truck down the road through the early morning fog, which could be hell on both wildlife and drivers. Hal Wassich, a farmer, stood beside his truck with a shotgun. On the ground at the side of the road was the carcass of a large stag.

Tom and Chris both got out. "Hey, Hal," Tom said.

"I had to put him down, Chief. Got him square on the hip, crippled him bad." Hal shook his head and a stream of blood ran onto his shirt from a wound he didn't appear to know he had sustained. "Ever hear a stag that size scream? It's godawful, that's what."

Instead of putting the flashlight to the animal's carcass, Tom shone it square on Hal's head. "Chris, get an ice pack and some bandages out of the truck, would you? Hal, what'd you smack your head on?"

He reached up and touched his gushing forehead. "Damn. I must a bounced my head off the steering wheel. That sucker hit me like a tank. He's big as one, too, ain't he?"

"You got a big one, that's for sure," Tom said, squinting at the injury. "Hal, you cracked your head wide open."

The grisly farmer grinned, showing a couple of missing teeth on the bottom. "Lucky for me I got nothin' in there to fall out, ain't it?"

"Damn truth," Tom agreed, smiling with him.

Chris had bandages, tape and ice from Tom's first aid kit and took over the cleaning of Hal's head while Tom checked out the truck and the carcass. The stag was crushed on one side. If he'd managed to limp or drag himself into the woods, he'd have died a slow and miserable death. As for the truck, the bumper was bent, the hood was concave and the windshield was shattered. There wouldn't be any driving it away from this spot.

Chris had Hal sitting on the tailgate while he cleaned off his head wound. "You doing some kind of ride-along with the police?" Tom heard Hal ask Chris.

"Naw. Tom was giving me a lift home from the bar. I had a couple too many to drive."

Hal laughed outright. "You sober enough to deal with my head?" He pronounced it "haid."

"Yeah. Fortunately it's a huge cut and I

can see it plain as day."

That made the old farmer laugh harder. "You still sellin' insurance, boy?"

"Yeah, that's what pays the bills these days."

"I never figured you for paperwork, you know? I always figured you for doing something with your hands."

Now it was Chris's turn to laugh. "Is that because I could barely get passing grades in school?"

"Well now, I can't say I ever knew the state of your grades. But you was in shop with Hank, weren't you? Hank . . . he's a couple years older than you. But I remember you made your mother this fancy coffee table with a planter in it. Nice piece of work."

"I've done a little woodworking here and there . . . shelves, repairs, simple things," he said.

"As well, we had you in 4-H and I remember you had a nice hand with the animals."

"We haven't even had a dog in years," Chris said.

"If you want one, just say the word. That old bitch of ours whelps every spring. She should've dried up four years ago, but she keeps 'em coming. Border collie, sometimes mixed. Good dogs."

"I might take you up on that," Chris said.

"We got a couple of pups now. Six months, not housebroke. They're herders. Keep to the barn. Hey, Chief!" he yelled. "You gonna let me keep the deer?"

"Sorry, Hal. I have to call Forestry."

"Jesus, Chief! Think you'd at least let me have the son of a bitch who tore up my truck."

"Maybe Forestry'll let you have him."

"Those sons of bitches never give up a thing. Remember that bear what scared the bejesus out of the whole town? You think anyone got her?"

"A bear's a different thing."

"Hal," Chris said. "You're gonna have to get some stitches. There's no way this thing is gonna heal with just tape. It's huge."

"You want me to call a tow truck?" Tom asked him.

"Naw, just loan me that phone to call Hank. I'll get him out here with his flatbed and chains. Damnation. I think my day's ruined."

"Your insurance should take care of the truck at least," Chris said.

"Would if I hadn't let it lapse. Isn't it the damnedest thing? Just when you think things are going pretty good, something jumps out at you."

"I hear you," Chris said.

The ringing phone woke June.

"Do you ever get up to the alarm clock?" Jim asked from beside her.

"June Hudson," she answered.

Behind her Jim muttered, "Or, God forbid, just let the sun wake you up?"

"Shh," she hushed him.

"I'm really sorry to do this to you," John Stone was saying. "But I'm all the way in Rockport with a patient with a hot appendix and if the surgeon doesn't show, I'm going to . . . Well, I'm calling because Tom's running a special on facial stitches and head wounds. He's got two MacAlvies at the police department. They got in a fight out at . . . I can't remember."

"Rocky's," she said. And she thought, I hate stitching up the MacAlvies. Someone almost always gets sick.

"Yeah, Rocky's. Must be some little night-club."

"Oh, you know it. Are they badly cut up?"

"Not too bad, Tom said. But he thinks you should look at them. And he's taking Hal Wassich to the clinic. He hit a deer with his pickup and cut his head open on the steering wheel. Do you know him?"

"Uh-huh. Farmer. He's been here forever. How bad?"

"Tom said it's a deep occipital gusher, but he's conscious. Must have a hard head."

"The hardest. Okay. I'll take care of them. See you at the clinic later."

She hung up and leaned over to kiss Jim on the head. "Go back to sleep. I'm going to go put in some stitches and come home for a shower. Then you can have the truck if you want it."

He rubbed her arm. "You feel okay?"

"Yeah, fine. I slept like a baby."

She pulled on a sweatsuit and tennis shoes, put a ball cap on her head and snuck out of the bedroom without turning on the lights. She didn't notice the dining room as she passed through, but saw the roasting pan soaking in the sink. She backtracked and looked in the dining room. One place setting — hers — and burned-down candles still sat on the table. A bottle of what looked like champagne sat in a bucket of water. It all came back to her.

She went to the bedroom and knelt beside his side of the bed. "I fell asleep on you last night," she whispered. She twisted some of his thick chest hair around her finger. "Are you mad?"

"Not at all. You must have been exhausted.

You barely woke up to go to bed."

"I'm so sorry. You went to a lot of trouble."

"Hmm. I had a big night planned for you."

"Can I get a rain check?"

"Sure. But as far as I can remember, it's Tuesday. Meat loaf night."

Every Tuesday for years, unless there was some sort of emergency, she made her deceased mother's meat loaf recipe for her father. It was important to Elmer; she couldn't discontinue that, as Jim obviously knew.

"I'll see you in a little while," she promised.

June went first to the clinic to take care of Hal Wassich, and then, before cleaning up the treatment room she'd used, she went down to the police department to check on the MacAlvie boys. They both snored as she cleaned their facial cuts and applied a couple of bandages over antiseptic. As long as they slept, working on them was easy. They both smelled like breweries, but there was no arguing or fighting.

She went back to the clinic to clean up and when she came out, it was almost dawn. She saw that the light over the grill was on in the café and decided to walk over there for a cup of cocoa. When she got to the back door, she could see the silhouettes of three men down by the river — one tall with silver hair, one medium height with a big stomach, one short and bald. Sam, George and Elmer.

She walked on down. As she got closer, she could hear the sound of rushing water. The Windle River was usually calm and docile. In summer, when it was dry and hot, it was little more than a creek in most places. Sam dropped an occasional line there.

This was the first real sign that winter had arrived. The old men in town were watching the river to be sure it wasn't flooding. And they would watch it right through spring as the last of the mountain snow melted.

"Hi, Dad," she said. "Sam. George."

"Hi, honey," Doc answered. "Awful early for you, isn't it?"

"I had to tend a couple of cuts. I put some bandages on passed-out MacAlvies and stitched up Hal Wassich, who hit a stag and cut his head open on the steering wheel."

"Good thing he didn't hurt anything that matters."

"Dad!" she scolded. "So what's going on here? Thinking about some fishing?"

"River's up," Sam said.

"Higher than usual," George said.

"Weather's too damn warm, that's what."

"Warm?" She shivered. "I'm freezing!"

"Not cold enough. It's warm for this time of year and we're getting too much rain, too little snow in the mountains."

"It always rains a lot through winter," June pointed out.

"It always stays wet all winter. Drizzle and fog are our friends — heavy rainfall and warm temperatures that melt mountain snow can do us in."

"We gotta keep a close eye on this here," Sam said. "It's been twenty years since she came out of her banks, but when she does, she does it fast. One minute she looks like a nice little stream, the next minute she's a raging river."

"It'll be okay, guys," June said, stifling a yawn. "I'm going to go home, shower and start the day over." She turned to head back to the clinic for her truck and saw that a car had parked in front. "Maybe I'll see who this is first," she said.

"Want me to get that, honey?" Elmer asked.

"No, thanks, anyway."

In a way typical for June, she wasn't able to get back to her house. In fact, it was noon before she even had time to call Jim. And then there was no answer.

SIX

Jim Post didn't have a vehicle when he came to Grace Valley because, up to that point, the truck he drove had belonged to the government. A company car, if you will. Part of separating, retiring, was turning in the keys. It didn't take him very long to see that it would be impossible to share the little truck with June. She would go off on a call to put in a few stitches, promising to return in an hour or less, and he wouldn't see her until that night.

The very first time she was more than an hour late, Jim called Tom and said, "I know this isn't something you call the police for, but I need a truck."

"Oh?" Tom had replied.

"Let me explain. I need to get to a car lot somewhere so I can buy or lease a truck. I can't share a truck with June and I can't sit out here at her house without wheels. You with me?"

He was. "And how can the Grace Valley Police Department help you with this . . . ah . . . problem?"

"I need a ride. I only have about three new acquaintances and nobody's phone number. How do I go about calling a cab around here?"

Tom couldn't help but laugh. He didn't even bother to tell Jim there was no cab. Well, at least not in Grace Valley. "Sit tight. I'll hook you up."

About forty minutes later the pastor showed up in his twenty-two-year-old station wagon. Harry drove him to Rockport, waited around for him to find a Ford truck with an extended cab that he liked, borrowed fifty bucks from him and followed him back to the valley.

"I like this," Jim had said, shaking Harry's hand. "A full-service church. This could turn me to religion."

"We aim to please. Anytime you need anything, give me a call. Oh, and I'll pay you back as soon as I get my check."

"Don't worry about it, Harry. A cab would've cost me at least that."

The rest of the month passed somewhat slowly for Jim, as he was just settling in and hadn't quite figured out what he was going to do in his retirement. He made the family meat loaf for June and her dad, something he enjoyed far more than he expected to. He checked out various hardware stores in the larger towns near the coast, just in case he decided to build something, like a room addition or baby furniture. He called his sister, Annie, in Madison and told her about June and the baby . . . and was put on the spot about his plans, or the lack thereof. He did the chivalrous thing and let Annie assume *he* couldn't be pinned down to a date. But maybe it wasn't chivalry. Maybe he was just embarrassed.

And while Jim pretty much fought boredom, for June and Tom Toopeek it was just the opposite. They were coming into a rough season, which would peak just after Christmas and wouldn't ease up till spring.

There were layoffs, which led to ennui, drinking and domestic strife, and economic crises, which led to depression, more drinking, more fighting . . . The circle widened. The skies stayed cloudy, the weather damp and cold, which didn't do much for creating work or easing depression. Flu came on and assaulted even the hardiest, but picked on those out of work, out of money, out of heating oil, and those who suffered from bad nutrition.

Tom's nights were late, his mornings

started too early. And the clinic was always full. If Jim wanted to spend any quality time with June, he learned it was best to show up at the café around break time, or maybe catch lunch with her, which meant her and the regulars. If he waited around at home until quitting time, he might or might not see her for dinner. And the combination of hard work and pregnancy made her a teensy bit testy and very tired. She was edgy sometimes, snappish. And sleep came easily. The second her head hit the pillow she was gone.

But Jim was patient. He liked watching her sleep, so all was not lost.

In fact, he would often think, nothing is lost and all is gained. After twenty years of having only one commitment, to the struggle to maintain law and order, there was a kind of peace in this lifestyle that required nothing more from him. He wasn't an idiot; he knew it was a temporary idyll soon to be shattered by either boredom or some problem — hopefully not relationship-oriented — or even by the squalling of a hungry or colicky infant. But for now, while June got used to the idea that he was here to stay and their family was growing, he would enjoy the quiet. He would watch her sleep.

He had never considered what his notion of true love might be. He had even begun to think that in this life he wasn't going to get the perfect partner, the woman he'd live and die for. But he had. No matter the complications, he had never felt so secure. So sure.

In the midst of a busy clinic day, Jessie summoned June to say, "Birdie Forrest is on the phone. She says she can't stop her heart from racing."

June didn't even check to see if there was a patient waiting to see her. She grabbed her bag and fled to her godmother's side. She found Birdie in the glassed-in front porch of her house, rocking nervously. The room was icy cold because they didn't heat it in winter; Birdie must have been flushed and tried to cool down. Judging by the look on Birdie's face, she was trying to stay calm. There was perspiration on her upper lip, despite the chill.

"All right," June said, kneeling beside her and taking her pulse. "I'm here, you're going to be fine." Her pulse was one-twenty and thready. June gave her one aspirin, the universal precaution against heart attack, though she wasn't terribly concerned about that. She suspected something else altogether. "What were you doing when your heart started to race?"

"Just folding some of Judge's under-shorts," she said weakly. "Am I all right? Because if I die, he'll run out of clean shorts in a week."

"It looks pretty good for Judge's clean shorts. Does your chest hurt?"

"No, not so much. But I'm so light-headed and feel all . . . vague. I feel vague."

June tried to keep the chuckle from her voice. "Well, you're not vague at all. Your pulse is slowing . . . can you feel it?"

Birdie concentrated for a moment. "Yes," she finally said. "Oh, June, you're so gifted."

"I haven't done anything, Birdie. Tell me, what were you going to do after folding the clothes? What's on the agenda for the after-noon?"

"Oh. Let's see. I put a casserole and cake in the oven that I'll take out to Chris, Nancy and the boys later. A little trip to the grocery if there's time. I have a couple more loads of wash — I've brought some of theirs home to do. They can't keep up, you know. And that house . . . They just don't have the . . . ah . . . *facilities.*"

"I can imagine," June said sympathetically. "Taking care of two bedridden teenage boys must be a nightmare. You must be very worried about them."

"I wish I'd locked my car," she said.

"Birdie, they took the keys off the kitchen hook. You couldn't have prevented them from stealing your car."

"I wish I'd locked the door, then."

"Your pulse is almost normal, darling. Do you know what happened? I think you've had an anxiety attack."

"Piffle," she said. "Impossible."

"Why is it impossible?"

"Because if Judge couldn't throw me into an anxiety attack in all the years I've put up with him, nothing could!" She stood up and smoothed her wool plaid skirt. She had worn skirts with white blouses, cardigan sweaters and clompy oxford shoes since June was a tot. When she was younger, Birdie had wound her hair into tight little brown pin curls that were now white, but nothing else in her style had changed. Change disturbed Birdie. And though Judge was a cranky old handful, he was static. Her life had been turned upside down by the sudden appearance of her son and grandsons. And now this additional stress — a near-fatal car accident with her car!

"I want you to have some routine blood work done tomorrow morning," June said, reaching into her bag for a lab order slip.

"I'm not expecting to find anything, but better to be safe than sorry. And after work today I'm going to run over to Chris and Nancy's and look in on the boys."

"Oh! Would you? Oh, thank you, June!"

There was no pretending — Birdie had had about all she could take of this stress. She would have to be settled down somehow. "In fact," June said, "when I'm done at the clinic I'll come by here and get that casserole and cake. I'd like you to take a night off."

"Oh, but June, much as I'd like to, I just can't leave them —"

"Doctor's orders, Birdie. I said I'll go out there and check on them."

"That's very sweet of you, dear. And then, when can we talk about your wedding?"

She swallowed. "Well, not today. I just don't have the time."

Jurea Mull and her two teenage children lived in a tiny house in a poor section of town, but every day was a wonderful day for them because it was the best they'd ever had. Up till a few months ago Jurea's whole life had been spent in the mountains, first as a child in a large family that lived very meagerly off the land, then as the wife of Clarence Mull, a Vietnam vet. Their home, the place where they'd raised their two kids, was little more than a shack in the back-woods, an isolated existence that they had once seen as protective.

Clarence had suffered since the war from post-traumatic stress disorder and bipolar disease. He could cope only if he felt he was hidden from the general population. This medical condition had nothing to do with his intelligence, which was high. He had been what they called a dropout vet, living in the forest near Grace Valley when he came upon Jurea's family and found that they had been hiding their daughter from view because of the morbid scarring of her face. The claw end of her father's hammer had ravaged the entire left side of her face, and the lack of medical attention had resulted in Jurea's disfigurement. Clarence, in his sickness, immediately recognized in her a soul mate, a fellow prisoner from the world at large.

They'd made their life in the woods, where Clarence first taught her to read and write and cipher, then taught their children. That is, until they were discovered by June Hudson and Tom Toopeek. They helped the Mulls move into town so that Jurea could begin a series of plastic surgeries, the children could attend public school and

Clarence could get both veteran's benefits and some medication. He'd been doing very well on psychotropics until, as is fairly common, he stopped taking his drugs and fell back into his delusional world. While he was in the hospital getting straightened out, Jurea, sixteen-year-old Clinton and fourteen-year-old Wanda were on their own.

The house just a half block down from the Mulls had stood vacant and vandalized for a long time, long before the Mulls came into town. Jurea had no idea who owned the place, or if anyone did. But to her surprise she saw Sam Cussler pull up to that house. He had a young man with him and they went inside.

Jurea was by nature very shy, but she'd been pushing herself to interact with people more, especially now that she'd had the first surgery on her face and it was so dramatically improved. If she was to be a citizen of the town, a parent to students and a member of the church, it was imperative that she learn to mingle. So she put on her jacket and bravely walked down the street to say hello to Mr. Cussler. She waited until he came out of the house with his friend.

"Well, Jurea, you saved me a trip down to your house," Sam said. "This here's Conrad Davis."

"How do you do," she said slowly, carefully.

Conrad sunk his hands deeply into his pockets, looked at the ground and gave a brief nod. He's as shy as me, Jurea thought.

"Conrad here has a young family," Sam said. "Three children, one just born. He's a little down on his luck at the moment and —"

Conrad's head came up suddenly and he interrupted Sam. "Got laid off," he said.

"That's right," Sam went on. "This old place hasn't had an owner in I don't know how long. It stands here just a miserable sight in need of attention while there're people like Conrad and his young wife in need of a roof. So I think we'll just slip him in here and for the price of a little fixing up, he'll have a place to live."

"Isn't that fine," Jurea said. "And where is Mrs. Davis?"

When Conrad didn't answer at once, Sam did for him. "Social Services has her and the little ones in a Rockport hostel while Conrad here's been looking for work. I have something he can do, but the family really can't come here till the house is habitable. And heatable."

"If you'd like, Clinton, Wanda and myself would be obliged to help you clean it up a little, once the kids are home from school."

"That'd be very neighborly of you, Jurea. Isn't that neighborly, Conrad?"

"What happened to your face?" the young man asked.

Stricken, Jurea's hand rose automatically. It had been ten times worse than it was now — her cheekbone had been caved in and her eye scarred shut — yet in all her life no one over the age of seven had ever come out with the question as bluntly as that. Fortunately Jurea was always hungry to learn, and always an optimist, so she took it as an opportunity to practice the handling of a difficult situation. "When I was a small child, I walked right into the path of my daddy's claw hammer. My scars were so much more terrible than they are now. I've had some plastic surgery."

Jurea didn't notice Sam frowning at Conrad. In fact, Conrad didn't notice. "Well, bless your heart," Conrad said, but there was something in his tone that was just slightly mean.

"We'd better get going, Jurea. I'm determined to get some plywood hammered over those broken windows today," Sam said. "We'll be back a little bit later."

"I look forward to meeting your wife and children," Jurea said. "And once Clinton and Wanda get home, we'll wander down and see if we can lend a hand."

"You're a kind soul," Sam said.

He walked ahead of Conrad to his truck and got inside. He just sat there for a while after his passenger was in and settled. He was thinking.

Life hadn't been too pleasant for Sam lately. He'd just buried his second wife, a woman younger than him by more than forty years who'd died a slow and painful death from cancer. He was feeling low and lonely when this poor boy with his truck full of pitiful belongings had pulled into the garage and recited his sob story of hard times. It had long been Sam's custom that when he was feeling a little less than good, the best way to perk up his spirits was to help someone less fortunate. It had also long been his experience that whenever he needed perking up, the Lord would slip a less-fortunate individual into his life at the perfect moment. Conrad had just returned to the valley to collect his household goods after his weeks-long unsuccessful search for a job. In his seventy years, Sam had never regretted a good deed.

He looked over at Conrad, who slumped in the seat next to him. "I went out on a limb to help you, boy, and you were just rude to a friend of mine."

Conrad looked at him square in the eye. "Was I? That was a mistake."

Sam thought about this a second. "Maybe it was," he said. "Or maybe the mistake is mine. We'll see."

There were very good reasons why June had not, until now, gone out to Chris and Nancy Forrest's house to see how the bedridden twins were doing. First of all, she'd been almost insanely busy, so busy professionally that she was having trouble finding time for the complex new chapter in her personal life. Plus, she was not their family doctor, though she had attended the emergency of their car accident. Too many doctors in the mix could confuse things, so now her visit would be in the role of a friend.

But there was even more to it, like her complicated history with Nancy and Chris Forrest. June and Chris had been steadies in high school, with Nancy her constant rival. When June went away to college, Chris and Nancy ran off and got married, an event that, when she thought about it, could *still* take her completely by surprise. He had been writing her love notes at college while screwing around with Nancy in Grace Valley! Even in love with another man and

125

pregnant with his child, it could piss her off all over again if she thought about it much. But she didn't *act* angry. At least she didn't think she did.

In the almost twenty years since they'd run away together, Chris and Nancy had lived in southern California. It was only a few months ago that Chris and the boys had returned to Grace Valley, and it was only two months ago that June had learned that Chris was not divorced, as he had claimed, but only separated from Nancy. And the separation had been Nancy's idea. Brad and Brent were such a handful of trouble and Chris such an oblivious parent, that Nancy thought maybe he should be the one to take over. So Chris had come home. Like any red-blooded American man, he thought his mother would probably help.

Obviously, it hadn't gone well. The kids had been in constant trouble around town, culminating in their theft of Grandma Birdie's car, which they plunged off the road into a ravine.

What had started as a domestic problem, marital and familial, had escalated into a crisis. They were in the fixer-upper Chris had bought before the accident. No doubt it had been a good idea at the time. Before the accident there had been time to make

126

slow but steady improvements on the house even with his job, but there certainly couldn't be much time now. Nancy had left her San Diego job to rush to her boys' sides; their income was probably at an all-time low, while stress was at an all-time high.

As promised, June retrieved the casserole and cake from Birdie and drove out to Chris's house in the country. It was situated on a nice piece of land on the rise of a knoll with a long driveway up from the road. Prime property. The house, however, had been falling apart long before Chris bought it. Only the most basic improvements had been made — plumbing and electrical, thank God — when Brad and Brent had been hospitalized.

As June raised her hand to knock on the front door, she heard one of the twins hollering, "I want my pain pill!" while another yelled, "Ma-a-a-a!" Though she wanted to flee from the chaos inside, she knocked. Nancy yanked open the door, an impatient frown on her face. She blew an errant lock of hair off her face.

June could see a lot from the doorway. The floors were bare, there were rooms without doors, the bathroom at the end of the hall had only a curtain to offer for privacy, some windows were boarded, the kitchen cupboards had been torn from the walls and were in the midst of being refinished, ancient appliances were in use, probably until the new kitchen could be finished, and electric bulbs dangled from the ceilings in place of fixtures. In the middle of the living room stood two overpowering hospital beds, complete with traction rigging and tray tables.

"Good Lord," June said as she looked past Nancy into the house.

"If your children are going to have a car accident and be laid up for a while, it isn't practical to have just bought a fixer-upper," Nancy said. "Not exactly *Better Homes and Gardens*."

"My house was a lot like this," June said. "It took me forever to get it in shape." June noted the dark circles under Nancy's eyes. "One thing at a time," she advised, giving her the casserole dish as she balanced the cake in her left hand.

"June. How lovely of you."

"I wish it had been lovely of me, but Birdie made these. And I am totally ashamed. I should have been out here a couple of weeks ago. Not to mention giving you a hand with meals and chores."

"I hear you have quite a lot on your mind, too."

June's hand went immediately to her middle. "But you should have sent up the alarm, Nancy. You need help around here."

"June, don't be naive," Nancy said sullenly.

"What do you mean?"

Nancy ignored her question and said, "Come in, June. If you're patient, I'll put the coffeepot on right after I finish Brent's range of motion exercises. I can't really stop in the middle — it's so painful for him we have to get it over with. Then maybe I can visit for a minute or two."

"Forget about it, I'm watching the caffeine for the time being. And I'm miserable about it, too. Go ahead with Brent. I'll put this casserole on the stove for you."

When she got to the kitchen she could see that it was even worse up close. The sink wasn't attached to the wall, there were no shelves in the pantry, and what few kitchen items there were had been stacked on orange crates on the floor. Groceries were either in the ancient refrigerator or still in bags. "Nancy, what do you do without a working kitchen sink?" June asked.

"Ma! It's time for my pain pill!" Brad yelled while Brent, whose leg was being stretched and pulled by his mother, gritted his teeth and moaned loudly. He gripped the bed rails and struggled to keep back tears.

"Bathtub," Nancy yelled back. "I know, honey, I know. First Brent, then I'll get it. Just give me a couple of minutes."

June went to Brad's bedside. "What do you get, Brad?"

"Percocet," he answered. "It's right back there on the card table."

June looked at the prescription bottle, shook out a pill, poured him a glass of water from the pitcher and dosed him. Then she helped herself to some lotion from the card table laden with everything from medication to linens. "Roll on your side," she told Brad. "I'll work on your shoulders a little bit."

His leg was in traction and maneuvering was a problem, but he managed enough so that June could pull up his T-shirt and massage his shoulders. Now his moans of pleasure mingled uncomfortably with Brent's cries of pain. "Hang in there, Brent. When you're through with the hard part, I'll give you a little rubdown."

"Can I have another pain pill?" he asked, his voice tremulous.

"You had one before we started," his mother said.

"But *she's* here! She's a doctor!"

While June massaged Brad's back, she took note of some pressure spots on his skin from bedrest, spots that could turn into dangerous bedsores overnight. She answered Brent, "It isn't a good idea to have more than one doctor writing you prescriptions. Just hang in there, the pain medication will kick in soon. I know orthopedic pain is the worst. Nancy? Is your visiting nurse massaging these boys? Looking them over for pressure spots and bedsores?"

"She only comes three times a week. We all look them over and massage them. She mentioned the other day that we could use some sheepskin, but there hasn't been time to —"

The front door opened and Chris came in, the look on his face one of terror. "June? Is everything all right?"

"Fine," she said. "I'm just visiting."

He grabbed his chest. "Thank God. I had my cell phone and Nancy didn't call, but when I saw your truck . . ."

"I seem to have that effect on a lot of people," June said. "I dropped off a casserole and cake your mom made for your dinner . . . and I thought I'd make myself useful."

"Thanks," he said. "Where's Mom?"

"I told her she had to take the night off,

131

Chris. She had a spell this afternoon. Nothing too serious, I hope, but her heart was racing and she was flushed. I think it's the stress."

"There's plenty of that to go around."

"You should know she wanted to come out here, anyway, but I insisted —"

"Well, if she's okay, we need her," he said.

"She needs a night off," June said firmly. "Doctor's orders. Until I look at some blood work and we can be sure she's fine."

"Chris, are you going to get that sink hooked up and running tonight?" Nancy asked.

"Did I not just get home?" he countered unpleasantly.

"I'm only asking!"

"I said I'd try!"

"Look, folks, I know you're tired —" June attempted to say, but Chris just walked past her toward the back of the house. He did pause to give Nancy a peck on the cheek, a very short one, but she didn't look especially grateful. You could cut the tension with a knife. For once the boys were quiet.

"He's home early again," Nancy said.

"You must need his help," June ventured.

"Not as much as we need his paycheck."

June thought for a moment about the cozy little house that awaited her and wondered what it might be like to be Chris, or worse still, to be Nancy, locked in this bedlam, working like a farmhand to take care of these kids. No wonder they sniped at each other.

When Chris came back into the living room — the hospital room — wearing jeans and a sweatshirt, Nancy finished with Brent's exercises and rolled him onto his side so she could rub his back. He was worn out from the pain and lay listless under her probing hands. Chris paused by his bed and ruffled his hair. He moved to put an arm around Nancy and she sidled away slightly to avoid him.

"Okay," Chris said. "I deserve that. I'm sorry, everyone."

No one said anything for a long, uncomfortable moment.

"Well," June said briskly. "I've got to get going. Nancy, I promise not to be so long in getting back here."

"Thanks, June. It was good seeing you." Though her words were polite, she sounded very tired, near tears.

"You, too. Hang in there."

"Let me walk you out, June," Chris said.

"Don't worry about it, you're busy," she said, but he opened the door and saw her to her car, anyway.

"I'm sorry you had to see that, June," he said. "Sometimes Nancy and I just get on each other's nerves from the pressure and everything."

"Perfectly understandable. But, Chris, when I told Nancy she should have put out an alarm that she needed help, she told me not to be naive. What does she mean?"

"You know," he said with a shrug. When she answered with only a nonplussed expression, he elaborated. "We have so many amends to make around here. Not just for the trouble the boys caused right up to the accident, though I suppose people are going to be a long time in letting that go, but also Nancy and me. I mean, we ran off and ditched our town. We hardly ever came back, as if we thought we were too good. Plus, we hurt you, the town's favorite daughter." He took a breath. "People aren't going to be real anxious to help us out right now. We're strangers to them. And it's our own fault."

She was stunned speechless. "Chris, that isn't true! I don't think anyone realizes just how tough a time you're having!"

He smiled and gave her cheek a pat. "Nancy's right. You're naive."

"But . . . I . . ."

"I'm going to see if I can get that kitchen

sink attached, redeem myself a little. See you around, kiddo." And he disappeared back into the house.

As she drove up to her own house, she saw that the porch light was on, as well as the light in the garage, a free-standing, one-car building. Curiosity drove her to check it out. She pulled open the double doors and found Jim measuring a length of wood balanced on two sawhorses.

"Oh, my," she said, her face lighting up. "You have a tool belt! You look like one of the Village People!"

He frowned slightly. "Was that a compliment?"

"It sure was. What are you doing?"

"You have a whole section of porch rail that's rickety. I don't want you to lean on it and fall through."

"You're a carpenter?"

"Naw. Mostly I'm a repairer."

"I've been wondering . . . We haven't had a second to talk about this, but what do you plan to do now? Really retire? Get a job? Take up fishing with Sam or poker with my dad?"

"Haven't decided," he said with a shrug. "Until I do, I thought I'd tinker. Unless there's something —"

"Oh, I couldn't!" she said, putting her

arms around his neck. "You've already done so many sweet things for me. Errands, cooking, cleaning, taking care of Sadie . . ." Then she had an idea and the effect of it lit up her eyes. "But, if you find you're bored, I think I know where you might ply some of your talents."

Seven

Jim wasn't real sure that it was his place to organize what amounted to a barn raising, but he *was* sure that he'd carry any burden June asked of him to the ends of the earth.

When Jim thought about how he might spend his retirement, it had never looked like this. He had seen himself on a sailboat or tropical island, basking in the sun. Or up to his thighs in a mountain stream, fly-fishing. Then there was that mountain-cabin fantasy, hunting his own food. It had never been a little house in a small town filled with eccentric people who minded everyone's business but their own.

But he loved it. It would have been enough that he loved June; he could have made anything work for her. Yet he hadn't met a resident of the town he didn't like, and he was completely astonished at how willing they'd been to accept him. A lot of that was love for June, but he knew very well that if they hadn't liked him, if they hadn't thought he was good to her or good for her, they'd be giving him a lot of trouble. They'd try to run him off. They were a friendly group, a trusting group, a willful group.

He went first to Elmer to talk about June's idea. He found the older man at the café having a late breakfast, so he sat up at the counter beside him and ordered coffee. June was already at the clinic seeing patients and it appeared most of the early morning regulars had gone. They passed a little chitchat on the weather, which was dismal, before Jim got around to the subject at hand.

"June has asked if I would go to the Forrest house and see how I can help with their renovations. Even though I'm not the best hand in carpentry."

"Well, isn't that a kick in the butt," Elmer said, startling a grin out of Jim. "That's her old boyfriend, you know."

"So I've been told." Over and over and over, he thought.

"Never was good enough for her, not even when he played quarterback in high school."

"That's good to hear."

"Now I guess he's got himself in a real mess," Elmer said.

"That's how June described it. A fixer-upper that hasn't had much fixing up done to it. And they're at the end of their respective ropes because of the twins."

"A mess of their own making, I might add," Elmer couldn't resist saying.

"She didn't elaborate on that," Jim said. "But she did say there's no hope of them having a livable house by Christmas. And they're at each other's throats."

"Why are you telling me this?" Elmer asked.

"I told her I'd offer some help out there. I wondered if you wanted to come along."

Elmer made a face. "Damn it all," he cursed. "I'm close with Birdie and Judge, and I don't wish that aimless kid of theirs any harm, but I've always regarded Chris Forrest as a no-account pain in the ass."

This brought Jim more pleasure than he could possibly have imagined, even though at no time had Elmer mentioned caring any more than that for him. And what they never talked about, when or even whether Jim and June would marry and legitimize his first and perhaps only grandchild, hung heavily between them. Rather than push June about that matter, he strove only to please her. And if working on her old boyfriend's house pleased her . . .

"How'd she talk you into it?" Elmer asked.

"She didn't have to talk me into it."

"Oh, brother."

Jim sighed. He didn't wish to look less than manly in the eyes of the man he hoped would soon be his father-in-law. "She caught me making some repairs to her porch rail and got the idea I'm a carpenter, though not much of one. I don't have a lot of daily appointments. And I find that, after a twenty-year career of working long hours, it doesn't suit me to sit around the house and wait for the doctor mommy to show up."

Elmer's fact lit up. "Well, there you go! I was afraid you were some kind of panty-waist." He lowered his voice and leaned close. "But June thinks . . . ?"

"That I'm doing this because I adore her."

He slapped his knee and laughed loudly. When he stopped, he frowned slightly. "You sure you've never been married?"

"Positive."

"Hmm. You've got it figured out pretty good for a novice. You know, there's something else on my mind."

Oh-oh, Jim thought.

"June's no kid. She's got good judgment and all, and I know she's been wanting a family for a long time, even if she did seem to be short a husband. So whatever she wants is no business of mine, as long as she's healthy and happy." He lifted a gray brow and peered at Jim over his glasses. "Although she still appears to be short a husband."

Jim, who had fearlessly stared down the barrels of criminals' guns, felt his neck grow slightly damp as he faced this little, bald-headed old man. "Have you talked to June about this?"

"She doesn't like when I meddle," Elmer said.

"Has it ever stopped you before?" Jim asked boldly, needing to know.

"That's impertinent. You *do* want me to like you, don't you?"

Now, this was a spot his sister Annie had put him in, wanting to know why they hadn't set a wedding date. The real buried question was, *Who's* standing in the way of you setting a wedding date? There was no winning in any answer. If he said he was reluctant, he looked like a cad. If he said June was, he was worse than a cad for selling her out. If he said both of them, well, wouldn't everyone want to know what the problem was? Which harkened back to questions one and two.

So all he said to Elmer was "More than you can possibly imagine."

"That so? Well, I just wanted you to know that I was troubled by that detail."

In the worst possible way he wanted to say "Me, too!" But he knew better. So instead he said, "I hate seeing you troubled." Jim had been interrogated by armed criminals while working undercover and felt more confident than he did now.

A slow smile spread on Elmer's face. "Well, what are we going to do about that?"

Jim thought a moment. "I think we should find Sam Cussler and maybe Harry Shipton, drive out to the Forrest house and see how bad it is. Then we'll have time to go over to Westport or even Fort Bragg to get what we need."

"Harry? I don't know that Harry can even pound a nail."

"Maybe he can pray for the rest of us, then."

Elmer shifted off the bar stool and got to his feet. He pulled a few bills out of his pocket and slapped them on the counter. "All right, let's go have a look. Sheesh, you're a slippery devil."

Lunchtime at the clinic brought a lull in the action. John had gone over to Valley Hospital on his rounds and Jessie was using her lunch hour to study at her desk, so Susan had gotten some hot tomato soup and grilled cheese sandwiches from the café for herself and June. They were having a picnic on June's desk.

"It's been pretty nonstop around here the past couple of weeks," Susan said.

"Hmm," June agreed, sipping soup from her spoon. Not just nonstop in the clinic, but in her life, racing from work to Jim to work to emergency calls to Jim to family commitments. No matter what she was doing, she was always late. Always. She had even missed a couple of dinners entirely. And where did the time go? Jim had been here since the first week in October and it was already November!

"George sure knows how to mix up a good bowl of soup," Susan said.

"Hmm," June answered, nodding. And in weather like this — the constant drizzle of early winter — soup and a blazing hearth really appealed. It was hard to leave that warm bed in the dark of early morning, especially now that there was a warm body beside her. And torture to drive to work through the chill mist and fog when it would be hours yet before sunrise. And even then, sunrise didn't bring much light or warmth. June often wondered how she went from feeling invigorated by the crisp colorful fall to drenched in the darkness of winter without even noticing the transition.

"It must be strange, going from a single career woman to half of a couple, fat with child."

"Mmm-hmm," June offered.

"Oh, for Pete's sake!"

June jumped. "What?" she asked, startled.

"Do you have any idea how quiet you're being?" Susan asked.

"Huh?"

"Well, here we are, alone for the first time in who knows when, with no patients waiting in line, John at the hospital, Jessie absorbed, and all you have to say is 'hmm'?"

"Did you ask me something?"

"Not really. I was patiently waiting. For you to talk. To say something. What's it like? What's *he* like?"

June took a second. "Well, he's pretty much too good to be true. When I told him we were pregnant, he came as soon as he could. And for keeps. He's retired from the . . . police."

Susan rolled her eyes.

"Why'd you do that?" June asked.

"Never mind. Go on. Tell me more."

"Well, he's been completely patient about everything. He hasn't complained one tiny bit about all the demands that are made on me, especially right now. This is a terrible time of year for illnesses. He tidies the house, runs errands, cooks dinner. And even if I'm called out and miss the dinner he cooked, he just saves a plate . . . that I may or may not get to eat." She took a spoonful of soup. "I don't think I could be that good if our roles were reversed. I think it would piss me off."

"So, are you planning a wedding? Or are you going to elope?"

"Hmm," June hummed.

"Stop that!"

"Well, Susan, I have a problem," she said frankly. "And I have absolutely no one to talk to about it. Can it be you, or are you going to blab?"

"Of course it can be me! Am I not the soul of discretion?"

June made a face. Susan might indeed have sound judgment about when to speak and when to hold her tongue. Certainly no clinic confidences had leaked out since she'd been the nurse in charge. But girl talk was another matter. June could pretty much count on Susan's best friend Julianna Dickson being cut in on the gossip at some point.

But who else could she talk to? Not Elmer, not about this. Birdie had more than enough on her mind as it was. Aunt Myrna, the darling, could be a flake. Ursula Too-peek would be a good choice, but she was busy with five kids, a full-time teaching job, a police chief for a husband and her in-laws living under her roof.

"Oh, what the hell," June said. "There is this thing that Jim and I are not talking about, and it is as heavy as a four-thousand-pound boulder hanging in the air just above our heads. Getting married."

"Why haven't you talked about it?"

Simple question. Not so simple an answer. "Because . . . Because . . . Jeez, I don't know why. Because I've been single all my life and it's a really big step."

Susan leaned farther over the desk, frowning, and said, "Isn't having a baby a big step?"

"Having a baby is a very big step, but that's done. It's here. No matter how nervous I am at the prospect, I don't have any choice. I still have a choice about making the great big marriage commitment. And I'm not sure I'm ready."

"Oh, boy, is this going to stir things up," she said.

"Yeah, I'm pretty sure you're right about that."

"You said you're not talking about it. Does that mean he hasn't asked you?"

"Oh, he's asked me. Sort of."

"How did he 'sort of' ask you?"

"He said, 'Why don't you take the day off and let's go to Reno or Tahoe and get married.' "

"Oh," Susan said, nodding. "That qualifies. You said no?"

"I said I couldn't take the day off."

"Oh, for Pete's sake!" she said.

"I guess I'm going to have to talk to Jim about this," June said sheepishly.

Susan picked up her soup bowl and drank from it. It was such an unexpected maneuver for this dainty little blonde. When she lowered the bowl she smiled at June, showing her a tomato soup mustache and making her laugh. She licked off her upper lip and patted her mouth with a napkin. "I don't know what's wrong with me. I could eat a horse. I must have a tapeworm or something."

"Where do you put it?"

"Listen, I have to be careful. When you're five foot three, one extra bran flake shows. So, you'd better talk to him. Maybe he's not ready for marriage, too, and was just trying to do the right thing. If you're both not ready, you can work on getting ready. It doesn't really matter, as long as you're on the same page. And as long as your child is the priority."

"I've gone from never having anyone around, to having someone around all the time."

Susan bit her lip. "Are you starting to feel a little . . . crowded?"

"Not really, strangely enough. I kind of like it." She smiled and then her smile faded as a recurring thought popped into her mind. "It seems fine, but I keep wondering if I'm going to suddenly, and without warning, *hate* sharing my space with another person. Does that happen to people?"

"Happens to us every morning. We should have a bathroom with at least two sinks."

"You're saying some of this is just normal?"

"Uh-huh. You going to eat the rest of that sandwich? I'm famished."

"Help yourself. Before, when I said something about Jim being retired, you rolled your eyes. What was that about?"

"Oh. I figured if he was in law enforcement before, you might have met him about the time of that raid on the marijuana camp."

"Why would you think that?"

"Well, logically, in order for the feds to have a big raid on a huge cannabis plantation where they arrested dozens, there must have been agents in the area for months beforehand. The timing is right."

June was quiet and serious for a moment. "He was camping. With a friend. Last spring."

"That's what all the undercover cops say to their girlfriends," she said, winking. She stood up and collected their dishes onto the tray to take back to the café. "Take my advice, June. Don't put anything that needs talking about on the back burner. Things that sit there too long tend to get burned beyond recognition."

Jim and Elmer took a look in Elmer's garage at what tools he'd collected over the years, then in June's. Elmer had spent what free time he had fishing and playing poker, so aside from the most rudimentary tools necessary for basic repairs, he was a little short. Likewise Jim's modest collection in the back of his truck and in June's garage. Sam, they figured, might be better fixed, having a gas station and all. Once they knew what they had, they'd pay a visit to the Forrest household and assess their needs.

When they pulled up to the gas station, they pulled up to trouble. Syl Crandall's bakery truck was sitting at the pump and Syl was having a very loud argument with

Conrad Davis.

"Oh, Lord, what was Sam thinking," Elmer said to Jim.

The men got out of Jim's truck in time to hear Syl say, "If Sam wanted to change his policy, then Sam should've told his friends!"

"If you don't have the cash, I can come around the bakery and get it —"

"It's not that I don't have it, young man, it's that I usually pay Sam by check once or twice a month. I use a lot of gas to make deliveries."

"We're working on cash now," Conrad said.

"Is that so?" Elmer asked, approaching them. Jim shored him up from behind and glared at Conrad. It seemed to take Conrad a second to remember him.

"Just collecting for the gas, man," he said.

"Where's Sam?"

"He's over at this old house he found for me and the family. It's been left empty and he said we could use it."

"Elmer, this young man says he's running the station now and we're not to leave IOUs anymore. You hear anything about that?"

"Nope. Better take Mrs. Crandall's IOU, son. That's how she's used to doing business with Sam."

"Things've changed now that I'm running

the station. He said it doesn't make any difference to him how I run it, long as I take good care of it. I swept it out and everything."

"And Sam is . . . ?"

"I *told* you! He's over working on that house!"

Elmer took a step toward him. "Where's the house, son?"

"The street's Marigold or something like that. It's just a few blocks over, behind that big church a ways. Right by this woman with a chopped-up face."

Syl gasped. "That's Mrs. Mull," she said unhappily. She stuffed the IOU in Conrad's pocket and stomped to the truck. "I never," she muttered.

"I think it's against the law to leave without paying, *ma'am.*"

"Call the police!" she shouted. She got in her truck and drove one block to her bakery.

"I've known Syl Crandall for a hundred years," Elmer said. "I can't imagine what you said to her to get her that riled, but I'm guessing it was pretty bad."

"Look, you buy gas, you pay for the gas. How hard is this?"

Jim put a hand on Elmer's shoulder from behind. "Let's go talk to Sam."

"Yeah! You go talk to Sam! He'll tell you!

I'm running the station now and when I pump gas I get paid for the gas!"

"You'll sell a lot more gas with honey than vinegar," Elmer said.

"Huh?"

"Never mind. Never mind." Shaking his head, Elmer got back in the truck. "What in the blazes was Sam thinking?"

It became evident very quickly when Elmer and Jim found the house down the block from the Mull's. There were only a couple of glass windows in front; the rest had been covered with boards. There was a curl of smoke coming from the chimney. It was a poor little place, but something about that swirl of smoke warmed it up considerably.

Just as the men would have knocked on the door, it opened. Jurea let out a small gasp of surprise, which immediately grew into a smile when she recognized Elmer. "Oh, Doc Hudson, you gave me a start." In her arms she held a wicker basket full of clothes that appeared to need laundering.

"Morning, Jurea. I don't guess you know June's . . . June's . . ." He turned slightly and looked up at Jim, frowning. Then, without any solution in sight, he smiled back at Jurea. "Jurea Mull, meet Jim Post, the newest newcomer to the valley."

Her smile was shy and sweet. Of course. Jim knew instantly who she was. June had been telling him stories of the Mulls and their exodus from the hills since the first week they met. He'd been more than a little curious about her face and the transformation. He had no idea how charming he was when he reached for her hand, though it still grasped the basket. He actually had to pry it loose just a little so he could squeeze it. "Jurea, it's so nice to meet you. June has told me all about you and your family."

Elmer snorted. "Humph. Well, at least you and my daughter seemed to take some time for talking. Sam here?"

"Sure, he is. Come in, but mind that door. This old house is so full of holes we can't hardly keep the wind out, and there's little ones in here."

There, in the corner of the living room by the wood stove, sat a young woman in a wooden rocker holding a bundle that was surely a newborn. There was a rug on the floor, and while bare in spots, it at least served to keep a bit of warmth between two little girls and their game of blocks. And not far away, kneeling to repair a floorboard with a warped and ragged edge, was Sam. The scene had such a look of domesticity, it appeared almost the natural order of things.

"Hey, there. The calvary," Sam tossed over his shoulder.

Elmer walked over to him, put a hand on his shoulder and said in a near whisper, "Sam, what have you gotten yourself into?"

Sam sat back on his heels. Just a few feet away Erline Davis sat with the baby, her little girls playing contentedly at her feet. In this setting, as opposed to the front seat of a truck in the throes of labor, she had a pretty and peaceful look. And she looked far too young to be the mother to this many children.

"Winter's on us," Sam said. "Up to now, Erline and the little ones were in a shelter and before that they camped."

Elmer sighed, thinking of what Conrad was pulling down at the gas station. Sam would have to get him out of there or be robbed blind. "Well, Sam, I guess it's true what they say. No good turn shall go unpunished."

Jim hadn't intended to head up a town project, but he could sense that this was some kind of beginning. With the Davis children so young and vulnerable, the place they were staying had to be shored up and safe, even if it was only one room. Central heat was out of the question, but the fire-place and wood stove made the small living room warm. There weren't any appliances, but the electrical work was serviceable, and in the old pickup were some cooking pans, dishes and a hot plate.

Jurea wasted no time in taking Erline under her wing and showing her how to make do in a house that offered little in the way of luxury. Elmer left a message for Corsica Rios, a social worker from Family and Children Services, who would see that the Davis's got a little help with food and clothing.

While getting them taken care of, the men couldn't help but see that Jurea and her family could use a little fixing up, too — what with Clarence in the hospital. Afterwards, while having lunch at the café and talking about these chores, George interrupted them. "I'd be glad to do my part to help out at the Forrests' if you'd lend a hand this weekend out at the Cravens'. Leah's my waitress and her sixteen-year-old son Frank washes dishes. It's just her and the five kids. They keep up pretty good, but with the cold weather on us, it wouldn't hurt to make sure they're all set for the winter."

Harry said, "I'm not much of a carpenter,

but I can tote and carry with the best of them."

"Before we can do anything at all, we have to take a look at what we're taking on. We're going to have to go out by the Forrest house and take inventory."

Hal Wassich was having a hot cup of coffee with his son Hank and a couple of the locals when he heard the name come up in conversation the first time, so he paid better attention to what was being said. Then he wandered over to the counter where the men sat. "Did I hear you say you're going over to the Forrest house to lend a hand?" he asked.

They turned and looked at the grisly old farmer. Elmer jumped in surprise when he saw the bright pink scar running down his forehead. "Lord, man, you really whacked your noggin."

"Hit a six-point buck, that's what. Chris Forrest was getting a ride with the chief that morning and he taped me up as best he could. He never said anything about needing a hand. He should've known he could count on my family."

"Seems he's gotten shy about his needs," Sam said. "Since his boys gave the town such a lot of trouble before that accident."

"He's got two banged-up teenagers in

hospital beds in his living room, and that house he bought was a fixer-upper. I don't think he's even got the kitchen sink working yet, not to mention carpets on the floor. And June said they've strung curtains across bedroom and bathroom doors."

"Rumor is the best help they have these days is Judge — and you know what a pleasant sort he must be to work with."

Hal whistled. "We better get on out there and see what's what. Hank?"

"Yeah, Pa?" he answered from across the café.

"Finish your coffee, son. We got something come up."

About an hour later, Nancy Forrest answered knocking at her door. There, on her rickety porch, stood an impressive gathering of men who'd come in a half-dozen trucks. There was Jim and Elmer, Harry and Sam, Hal and Hank Wassich, George Fuller and his son. A few others had joined them before they left the café — Standard Roberts, whose flower fields would be too wet right now to keep him real busy; Lincoln Toopeek, who was semiretired, anyway; Ray Gilmore, who was found at the bakery and joined in; then, at the fork in the road, they happened upon Bud Burnham, who'd do anything for a little time away from his wife,

Charlotte.

"Hi, I'm Jim Post. I'm June's . . . June's . . . Well, no one's really been able to figure that one out yet." There were a few chuckles among the men, but not Elmer. "Someone said you and Chris might need a hand out here. Some fixing up? Some carpentry? Some plumbing? And we have specialists in trash hauling, polishing, waxing, washing and whatever it is you need done."

Nancy put both her hands over her startled mouth and began to cry.

EIGHT

Even if the wintery temperatures were not cold enough to give the river watchers peace of mind, it was at least cold enough to make June's layers of clothing seem natural. Only Jim knew that she could no longer zip her slacks closed. She covered the evidence with a long T-shirt, and over that a baggy sweater that reached below her hips.

Susan gave her a sidelong appraisal. "Are you ever going to graduate into actual maternity clothes?" she asked.

Every morning when she rose and dressed for the day, when all of her clothes, from bra to boots, felt more snug, she would realize how fast time was fleeing. While Jim was busy helping all over town, while cold and flu season was in full swing, while the bleakness of winter deepened toward Thanksgiving, June grew.

"Are you concerned?" June asked her nurse.

"Actually, yes. See, there comes a point at which your unzipped pants won't stay up, and at the worst possible moment, you find them around your ankles. I've been there."

Okay, so maybe it wasn't only Jim who knew.

"Even if I had the time, I wouldn't know where to look," June admitted.

"Never fear," Susan said. "I'll get catalogs. And your aunt Myrna called. She wondered if you might have time to run by Hudson House. She'd be happy to give you lunch."

June wasn't taking any more chances. "Call her back and tell her I'll *bring* lunch. At about twelve-thirty."

Not only did June grow, she grew ever more hungry. The nausea of early pregnancy was replaced by ravenous hunger. She called George at the café and asked him to make a foot-long submarine sandwich with everything. Aunt Myrna might eat a fourth of it, if she were starving. She stopped at Crandall's bakery and picked up four double-chocolate-fudge brownies — the large size. One for her, one for Myrna and one for each of the twins. Unless someone didn't want theirs . . .

It was just a tish past twelve-thirty when she arrived to find Myrna waiting impatiently for her. "Thank goodness you're here. I thought I might have to drive in to the clinic to have a word with you. I can't remember when I've asked anyone for advice, but June — he's coming."

"He's what?"

"Coming! Edward Mortimer! He's traveling to Grace Valley to see me. After all these years of letters, without so much as a phone call between us, he's coming! What in the world am I going to do with him?"

June still stood in the foyer. "My goodness. When?"

"Thanksgiving." She said it in a panicked whisper. "Thanksgiving," she repeated.

"Myrna, we have at least a couple of weeks. Do you suppose we could have lunch?"

"Oh, I couldn't eat a thing," she said, whirling away from June. "Come to the kitchen then, you can eat."

When they were settled in the breakfast nook, June spread her picnic out on the table. She fetched a knife and two plates, cut a piece of the sandwich off and put it before Myrna despite the fact that the older woman waved her away impatiently. Secretly, June hoped Myrna wouldn't eat it. She was famished. But before digging into her much larger portion, she asked, "Just why are you so frazzled? I thought you wanted to meet him in person."

"I have always wished for him to visit. I even attempted to meet him in Fresno years and years ago. You must understand, dear, we've been writing each other letters for many years. On one hand, we're the best of friends. But on the other, were complete strangers. . . ." Her voice drifted off wistfully.

"How did all this start, Myrna?"

"Edward was a true aficionado of my work," Myrna went on. "I think he knew more about some of my plots than I did."

"How sweet," June said, between chews.

"Yes, isn't it? Back then, before we all worked on computers, a lot of us would write letters. I used it as a means of warming up for the day. It was every bit as creative an art as our novel writing or poetry. And I spared no talent in my gift of entertaining. I ranted and raved and carried on about Morton once and Edward wrote me back that my letter set him ablaze, it read with such passion and rage. He asked me if I'd ever considered killing him off in a book."

"So it was Edward's idea," June said.

"Oh, I guess it was," Myrna said. "But I was this close to thinking of it myself."

While June ate her generous lunch, Myrna

unfolded a story of friendship that went back almost twenty years. Edward encouraged the idea of her notorious husband-killing books, and on occasion read and critiqued her manuscripts, as well. He was the only one to do that, according to Myrna. No other friend or fellow writer saw her work before her editor. Not only was this pen pal lurking behind Myrna's career, always supportive and at times actually helping, but Myrna was also acting as mentor to Edward who, after retirement, was finally getting an opportunity to write.

He'd worked in a ho-hum job, he said, bringing in just enough money to get by. He hadn't been necessarily unhappy, thanks to books and friends and travel, but he hadn't been fulfilled. Then finally, in his senior years, came his opportunity to write some of the history he'd studied as a hobby all his life. An avowed bachelor in his sixties, he came late to the profession, but published his first nonfiction book a few years after his first contact with Myrna.

"He's a very talented writer, but I still like to think my assistance had something to do with him finishing that first book and getting it published. I read the manuscript several times, giving him editorial advice and correcting errors. I even championed him to my editor! He didn't buy Edward's book, but still . . . When you think about it, I suppose I was only doing for him what he'd done for me. I think we relied on each other for about twenty-five or maybe thirty books, between us."

"Who knew you had this mystery man in your life, keeping your prose tight and your plots grisly!"

"As I said, I've been in touch with lots of writers over the years. This one, though, this one emerged as special. He's been with me a long, long time."

"Then why are you so nervous? Meeting him should be a wonderful experience. And what better time than Thanksgiving?" June covered her mouth as a small burp escaped. "We'll cook, however. Dad and I and Jim." It was just then that she looked around the kitchen and realized that neither Barstow twin had made an appearance. "Where are the twins?"

"I couldn't have them around to eavesdrop on this long, drawn-out story. I sent Amelia home when I received Edward's letter."

June's eyes lit up at the mere thought that no Barstows would be sharing the brownies. She opened the white bakery package slowly, almost reverently. "What is it you think I can do to help, Auntie?"

Myrna leaned toward June. "First, don't even mention this to your father. I'll tell him when I have it figured out. Second, what am I going to do with him, June? I can't have him *here!*"

"Why ever not?"

"Besides the Barstows getting underfoot, what if I don't like him so much in person? What if he doesn't like *me?*"

"That's not probable, now, is it?"

"Well, June, we come across quite differently in letters than we do in the flesh. Wouldn't you agree?"

"Possibly true, but we also get to know each other much better by revealing our personalities in letter after letter. I imagine that's why all these people fall in love in chat rooms on the Internet."

"Exactly!" she said. "Then they meet and find out they've been misled!"

"Myrna," June began suspiciously. "Have you misled Edward somehow?" She half expected her aunt to say she'd lied about her age or something. But Myrna was vigorously shaking her head. Her aunt was notoriously honest.

"What if he finds me . . . eccentric?"

June's laugh was so sudden and loud, there was no hope of concealing it as a cough or sneeze. Myrna frowned. "Now,

Auntie," she said. "You can't expect miracles."

"Cheek."

"If you've written him for almost twenty years, I'm sure he already knows you're just a tad colorful."

"You were never punished enough as a child," she grumbled.

"Oh, Auntie . . ." She laughed.

"And look at you eat! You're going to be as big as old Charlotte Burnham before long!"

June daintily placed what was left of her second brownie on the white paper in which it had been wrapped. "Now you're just being vengeful."

"Oh, I'm sorry, dear. You set me off with that utter nonsense about me being an odd old duck —"

"I never . . . !"

"Whatever you said, it sounded to me like I'm an odd old duck, which I am, but I don't like people thinking so." Myrna got to her feet and left the nook, talking all the while. "There's something I want you to hear. You'll see what I mean." She was back in a flash with a letter in her hand. "Now, listen to this, June.

'Myrna, my dear, there are times you

annoy me so that if I were a day younger, I'd be on the next bus out to Grace Valley to have it out with you. Other times you come off so warm, so tender, I can't believe it's really you. Then there's your humor, and of course your deadly seriousness. Whether you argue with me or tease me, no one has ever made me happier. And, I'll go ahead and say it since you won't, I just wouldn't be the same without you. I've come to depend on you. I think you might be my closest friend. Ever. And that is only because we exist in these letters and not in the flesh, in which case we might actually be sweethearts. Ah, such a picture!' "

"Oh! Aunt Myrna, how lovely he is!"

"Yes, isn't he? And what if he gets here and can't stand me? Or I can't stand him? Either way, the letters, which I've so enjoyed and depended on, would be over."

June thought about that for a moment. "I see what you mean. Given all the options, you'd prefer not to change anything about this."

"Exactly! But . . . Well . . . He's coming and I won't be rude and tell him he can't. I just can't imagine what —"

"Have you allowed for the possibility that

you might fall head over heels for each other?" June asked.

"Now you're being silly," Myrna said, but there were two round red stains on her cheekbones.

June gathered up her brownie, the paper and bags she'd brought lunch in, and stood. She leaned over and gave her tiny aunt a kiss on the forehead. "Everything is going to be fine. Wonderful, in fact. You'll have Dad, Jim and I all to help, and we'll treat Edward to a wonderful Thanksgiving. If you really don't want him to stay here, make arrangements for him at the B and B down 482, but I don't think I'd trust Agatha Worth with your man!"

"He's not exactly mine," Myrna said.

"As good as! I have to get back to the clinic. Are you going to be all right, or should I give you a little something to settle you down?"

"I wish you would, dear. I'm a trifle excited."

"Fine, I'll give you this advice. Have a cup of hot tea, put your feet up for a while and, instead of fretting, make positive pictures in your mind of all this working out wonderfully. Affirmations, Auntie."

Myrna made a face. "I could have sworn I'd be getting a Valium soon."

"Ha! You wish! I'll call you later and see how you're holding up!"

Sam felt somewhat at a disadvantage, having never raised children. Aside from the occasional lawn boy or part-time helper to sweep up around the station, he hadn't had employees, either. It was therefore very hard for him to understand why young Conrad Davis would give up a chance to earn honest pay for honest work, work that was so easy and pressure free. Sam certainly didn't need help at the station; it ran itself. The only possible way he could make this any easier for Conrad would be to invite the boy to stay in bed and deliver him a paycheck every week.

Sam had told Conrad twice that he was not to insist on cash payment for the gasoline. IOUs from his regular customers would be fine. And he was to wash the windows and check the oil unless he was specifically asked not to. So Sam spent a morning across the street from his station, lurking behind tall lilac bushes, watching his station, feeling guilty to be sneaking around. He saw exactly what he expected to see. Conrad wasn't going to much trouble to help the customers. He washed a couple of windshields, checked the oil a couple of times, but no single car or truck got the full treatment. He argued for cash, which he put in his pocket, and only one customer refused and insisted on leaving his IOU.

After a couple of hours, Sam walked out from behind the bushes and crossed the street to his station. Conrad hadn't even noticed where he came from.

"Hey, old man," he said. "What brings you to town?"

"Just been sitting over there, across the street, kind of watching how you do business, son. I guess none of what I asked you took hold, did it, now?"

"What're you talking about? You been spying on me?"

"Well now, let's see. I was watching you, my employee, conduct business here, at my station. Would that be spying? Or would that be quality control?"

"You old codger, you —"

Sam put his hand out. "Let's have it, Conrad. What you collected this morning."

Conrad hesitated. Anger twisted his features and he squirmed, but eventually he pulled a wad of bills and one IOU out of his pocket. He slammed it into Sam's hand. Sam's hand, much the larger, grasped both the money and Conrad's fist and he squeezed, holding on. Sam's eyes bored into

170

the younger man's. After he thought he might have made his point, he let go. Then he slowly counted the money, which was not organized by bills.

Conrad couldn't watch. Had he known Sam was right across the street, he'd have gone inside the station and transferred some bills to his other pocket.

". . . Fifty, fifty-five, sixty, one, two, three . . . Not a bad business for a morning, huh? And twice what the station took in the last two full days."

"What are you saying?" Conrad asked defensively.

"I guess what I'm saying, son, is that I don't need you anymore. This isn't working out. Customers I've had for more than twenty years are letting me know they don't like the way you handle things around here."

"What do you want from me, old man?"

"Not a single other thing, son. Except maybe you stop calling me old man. You and the missus go ahead and squat in that house for the time being. Maybe you'll find more work around here . . . or maybe you'll decide there's a better place for your family. But if I let you pump gas in Grace Valley one more day, my closest friends are going to drive all the way to Rockport to gas up."

Conrad was quiet for a minute, staring at

that wad of bills in Sam's hand. Then he said, "One more chance, old — Just tell me how you want it done and that's just how I'll do it. One more chance."

Sam felt himself almost break into a sardonic smile. The young man wasn't *asking* for another chance, he was *telling*. "Sorry, Conrad."

"What? What? Just like that?"

"Just like that, after a few warnings. And I'm going to go ahead and let you keep what you skimmed the last week or two, hoping you use it to take care of that young family rather than do some selfish thing." He shook his head sadly. "This isn't your fault, son. I shouldn't have stuck my nose in your business, trying out my brand of help on you. All those expectations and we weren't, neither one of us, up to it."

"Yeah, you got that right, old man," he said, plunging his hands into his pockets and moving sulkily away. After taking about ten steps he stopped, crouched to pick up a rock and threw it point-blank at the station doors. A window shattered under the assault. Sam didn't flinch; Conrad brushed his hands together in satisfaction, then continued his walk down the street.

Boy, did I pick that one wrong, Sam thought.

■ ■ ■ ■

The shorter days hadn't changed Tom's schedule much. In fact, he was rousted from bed earlier in the winter than in summer and spring. Plentiful work and long workdays tended to wear people out, help them feel they'd been successful regardless of how much they'd earned, and there was far less trouble in the valley.

This early morning Deputy Lee Stafford had answered a domestic disturbance at the Craven household. That got Tom's attention. It was usually a good idea to get backup for domestic calls, given the volatile and unpredictable nature of them. But the Craven family had a long and tragic history with domestic problems. The late Gus Craven had been jailed numerous times for beating his wife and five children, and then one horrible night, when he'd been drunk and out of control, Leah gave him a whack on the back of the head with a shovel, ending his battering days forever. A jury of her peers had determined that it was the whack Gus had long been begging for.

But family violence is a hard thing to nip in the bud. It's generational. Ironically, the one thing a child most abhors about a physically abusive parent is the very thing he or she might inherit — a tendency to hit.

Sadly, Tom was not too surprised to find that the physical altercation had been between sixteen-year-old Frank and his mother, Leah.

Tom and Frank had way too much history for a boy his age and a police chief, and way too personal to boot. Frank had, for a time, romanced Tom's eldest daughter Tanya. And in some unreasoned fit of rage, Frank had struck her, just as Frank's father had struck his mother.

But all that was before; Tom was concerned with now. By the time Lee and Tom arrived at the scene, Leah was rocking in the chair on her porch, an ice pack on her eye, and Frank was sitting on the porch steps, crying. There were lights on inside, but all was quiet. All but the creaking of the rocking chair and the subdued sniffing.

"Everyone inside doing all right?" Tom asked Leah.

"Yes, Tom. Frank and I — We had an argument is all. Kids never even got out of bed."

"One of them called the police, Leah." Briefly, surprise registered on her face. "Lee, go in and check on the kids. Make sure no one's hurt or needing anything."

Lee went into the house. He was a good man for this duty; he had a couple of his own little ones. Lee and Ricky were both about thirty years old, Ricky being the bachelor.

"Let me have a look, Leah," Tom said. She slowly lowered the ice pack and revealed a bruised cheekbone. He touched it softly; she winced just slightly. "It doesn't look real bad, but I suggest you drop into the clinic later, have June or John take a look."

"It'll be okay," she said. "I've had worse."

"That's fine talk," Tom said. "Sounds like this family is right back where it was when Gus was alive." Leah looked into her lap and Frank muttered something. "What's that, Frank?"

"I said, it was an accident!"

"I'm sure it was. At least, you never intended it. Why don't you go get yourself a jacket, Frank."

"Naw, I'm okay. I'm not cold."

"We're going for a ride," Tom told him.

Leah rose out of her chair. "Oh, Tom, no! Don't take him in. It wasn't as bad as it seems. He got in late, we argued, I pushed him too —"

"We're just going for a ride, Leah," Tom said, though he could take Frank to jail and charge him with battery if he wanted to. But Tom wanted to accomplish two things. First, he wanted to separate the combatants. No matter how contrite and sorry Frank might be at the moment, tempers could soar quickly when just the right comment was made and the whole dispute could arise anew. And second, he wanted a little time with the young man to talk about counseling, anger management and the like.

"It's okay, Mama," the boy said.

A couple of minutes later Frank returned to the porch with a jacket on and gave his mother a kiss on the top of the head. He then descended the steps and went to the Range Rover, his hand on the back door. "Get in front, Frank," Tom called. Perplexed for a moment, Frank finally let himself into the front.

Seeing that Leah and the other children were all right, Tom and Lee got ready to take their leave.

"I'm getting tired of coming out to this house," Lee said. "I thought this sorry business was over, with Gus gone."

"Shows what you know," Tom said. "I'll see you back in town."

Once in the car, driving, Tom turned to Frank and asked, "You want to end up like your dad?"

"Dead, you mean?" he asked with sarcasm.

"We're all going to end up dead, son. I mean with a temper you can't control. I mean hurting people you care about and then feeling like a big loser because of it. That's what I mean."

Frank didn't answer right away. "No one wants that," he finally said.

"There are things we can do to try to head it off at the pass, you know."

"We?"

"Son, I'm the one who got pulled out of bed before dawn to drive out to your house and see who's beating up who. I've been doing that a long time now, first with your daddy and now, it seems, with you. I figure we're in this together. At least partly."

Frank slid down in the seat. "That's a comfort," he grumbled.

Tom let it go. "I didn't know if I was going to have to start handling domestic calls that involved you, but I'll be honest with you, the statistics said I would. Now we're faced with a couple of choices. I can start locking you up each time, or we can get you in a program. You should already have been in one. . . ."

"I was."

"Is that so? You quit or something?"

Tom asked.

"No. I went the three months."

"You *graduated?*"

Frank looked over at him. *"Yes,"* he returned with the same incredulous inflection in his voice as Tom. "Guess that shows you how good a program it was."

Tom whistled. "Point taken. Well, we have to do something. We can't just act like it didn't happen, Frank."

"Maybe you should lock me up awhile," he offered.

Tom drove right past the police department and on down Valley Drive. "I know that isn't going to do any good. I wish it would — that'd make life simple, wouldn't it? Just grit your teeth, hang out in County for a while and be miraculously free of that compulsion to strike out every time things don't go your way."

"It wasn't exactly like —"

"Okay, how about every time someone is just so damned annoying and provoking that there seems to be only one way to get them to back off? How about that? That how it was?"

"Yeah! That's how it was!" he said.

Tom pulled the Range Rover up to the café, which was still dark. He put it in Park and looked at Frank. "Okay, try this on for size, big shot. Not everyone gets that annoyed and provoked. It's in the DNA, handed down from generation to generation. It's like a medical condition. And there *is* treatment."

"What are we doing here? I don't work till after school."

"I've got a key. We'll put on the coffee for George, get ourselves some orange juice and come up with a plan for you."

"Aww," he whined.

"It's me or Judge Forrest," Tom said.

"No contest there," Frank allowed.

"Good choice."

Tom pulled out an impressive key ring with keys to most of the businesses and storage sheds in town, but when he got to the back door, it was ajar about three inches. His arm came out across Frank's chest, stopping him in his tracks. He put a finger over his lips and steered the boy back to the Rover. He put Frank in, pulled the shotgun out.

He'd like to think George just forgot to lock the door, but George never had before. Although it was a town where theft was rare, there were two businesses on the main street that were careful with locks — the café and the clinic. In the café George had to worry about stores of expensive food and supplies, and the clinic kept supplies of a different nature on hand, plus some drugs. Not only were those doors kept locked, whoever was on night patrol checked them. "Lie down on the front seat," he whispered to Frank. "Lock yourself in."

He raised the shotgun, cocked it, filled the chamber and prepared to clear the building. He pushed open the door, sidled in, flipped on the light. He moved stealthily through the café, checked closets, bathrooms, booths. There was no one in there. Whoever had been there had left a long time ago. And had left the cash drawer gaping and empty.

"Well, I'll be a damned dog" came the voice of George from the doorway.

NINE

Grace Valley was by no means crime free. With the biggest drug farmers in California, possibly the United States, hiding in the vast mountain ranges east of the town, you could hardly say that.

That was different. That criminal activity had little to do with Grace Valley. And with the close watch Tom kept over the town, those outsiders kept to themselves and generally waged their battles with the feds.

Of course, there was crime in Grace Valley. Plenty. There were feuds and fights, way too many domestic disturbances, and being so closely situated to the infamous pot growers, Tom and his deputies had more than their share of controlled-substance abusers. There were drunk and disorderlies, runaways, theft of property and accidents. Like everywhere else there were people in trouble and people who made trouble.

But no one had ever pried open the door

to George's café and emptied his cash drawer. There was something so personal and invasive about that.

George only kept a couple hundred dollars in the drawer, just the right amount so that he'd never have to go to the bank for change. He made a bank run about once a week and took money home with him at night, that was kept in a safe in his bedroom closet. In all the years he'd been open, everyone knew his routine. He locked his cash drawer, locked his doors and took the excess money with him. The café, being on the main street along with the clinic and police department, was patrolled during the night if there was a deputy on duty, which was most of the time. It was kept well lit. But mostly, it was a friend of the town. To rob George, to rob the café, was like robbing the church, or your mom and dad.

"Never expected nothing like this," George told his cronies as he poured coffee all around.

"Was there anyone else broken into around town?" Elmer asked.

"No sir, Doc. Tom checked the clinic, church, flower shop and bakery first thing. He had Lee dust the door and the cash drawer for prints to send out to some high falutin crime lab, but there were surely too many smeary prints to get the burglar's. Sam? You checked the station, didn't you?"

"There's no money there, George. And if someone stole some of the tools, he'd be doing me a favor. Don't use 'em much, they're as old as God and I still have insurance because I've always been too lazy to cancel."

Elmer turned on his stool and regarded Sam slyly. "You're the only man I've ever known who could make poverty and lack of industry sound like a virtue."

"Lack of industry?" he argued. "I'm busy every second!"

"Poverty?" George seconded. "The man's probably the richest in the county, save Myrna."

"I ain't that rich," Sam said. "I put aside a dollar or two is all."

There was a round of amused laughter.

"You keep a wallet so fat, I'm surprised you don't have scoliosis from sitting lop-sided."

Sam, like a lot of men his age, liked to deal in cash and wasn't too enamored with things like check writing and mutual funds. He kept a savings account and had recently allowed the Rockport banker to talk him into a certificate of deposit, but it took some doing. He owned the house he lived in, and the station, and wasn't impressed by things like deductible mortgage interest. He was most comfortable with things that just added up.

And one thing that didn't add up just right was the fact that George was robbed a little less than a week after Sam had told that useless Conrad Davis to take a hike.

Sam finished his coffee and took his leave just as June was coming into the café. They said their good mornings at the door.

"Morning, everyone," June said. "George, I heard you were robbed! How in the world did that happen?"

"Looks like it probably happened with a crowbar," he informed her. "I know you're off coffee right now, but you're not off bear claws for breakfast, are you, June?"

"Certainly not! I think I could eat ten, but I'll just take two." She kissed her father's cheek.

Rather than looking up at her face from the stool on which he sat, he looked at her middle. "You're growing by the second," he muttered.

"Yes," she said, rubbing her tummy idly. "It's about ten per cent baby and ninety percent bear claws, I think."

"That baby's gonna be born with sticky fingers," George said.

"Fine by me," said Elmer, then muttered, "long as June's got something on her finger besides sugar glaze."

Sam noticed that the old truck was not parked in front of the house Conrad and Erline shared. Though it was early, a homey curl of smoke rose above the house. She must be up and had stoked the fire to warm the little ones. Still, he knocked softly. It was a long wait before her quiet voice inquired, "Who is it?"

"It's Sam Cussler, Erline. I know it's early, but —"

The lock moved and the door opened. Clearly she'd been crying. Her eyes were red, and that look that reshapes a woman's face from cheerful to mournful had transformed her. It was too early in the day to have already had an insurmountable problem. She'd been crying through the night.

She sniffed and tried to smile, but it was lopsided. "You know you're welcome here anytime, Mr. Cussler."

"Thank you, Erline. I was hoping to find young Conrad at home."

"No, sir, he ain't."

Sam's eyebrows lifted. "Could it be he's found some honest work?"

Her chin dropped and she resumed crying, softly. Sam just let himself all the way inside and closed the door behind him. He could see where they'd made camp on the living room floor in front of the wood stove. The two children and baby still slept atop that single, thin mattress, covered by what looked to be their mother's sweaters.

"Now, what is it has you crying, Erline?" he asked her.

"It's Conrad. I haven't seen him in days. He took the truck and left."

"Why haven't you told anyone?"

"I've already been so much trouble to everyone. Starting with Conrad, I suppose. If I hadn't gotten pregnant . . ." She wiped her nose on her sleeve. The redness of her nose wasn't just from crying; she was cold.

"Erline, the café got robbed last night. The back door was pried open and the cash drawer was emptied. I have a notion it might've been Conrad."

"If it was, he didn't come by here. I laid awake all night, listening for that old truck, hoping he'd come back and help us." She sniffed loudly. "Can't be he's left us for good, can it?"

"Erline, just how old are you?"

"I'm nineteen now."

"And that oldest of yours?"

"Three. There's been one a year. One died."

"And Conrad? How old's he?"

"He says twenty-four, but I don't know."

So, Conrad had had himself a youngster. A fourteen-year-old girl. And now look at what he'd left behind.

"He's done this before. He'll probably be back after he lets off some steam."

"What's your name, Erline?"

She looked confused. "You know my name. . . ."

"You and Conrad . . . you're not really man and wife. Where you from?"

She turned away from him then, went back to the children. She knelt and tucked the clothing around them tighter, then reached over to the stove to stir the embers around and make room for another piece of wood.

In many ways Sam was innocent. Unlike Tom and June, he wasn't continually forced to look at the seedier side of life. Yet, he could tell that if Erline wasn't forthcoming with the answer to his questions, there was something painful and shameful enough to hide.

She turned and looked up at him. "Conrad took me away from a much worse condition. If you can believe that."

He didn't even question it. Nor did he comment. "How's the food holding out?" he asked, and she looked away again. Certainly that, more than Conrad's absence, was what had her crying. "You all out now?" he pressed, and she nodded weakly. "Any money, Erline?" he tried, but he knew the answer even before she shook her head. Conrad had left the station with some money, plus what he'd skimmed from money he'd collected from customers against Sam's orders. You'd think the scoundrel could've left the mother of his children with enough money to feed them for a little while. "He use it mostly for drugs?" he asked her. And of course she nodded again, but she couldn't look at him.

The room was quiet for a long spell except for the miserable, soft weeping.

"Look here, Erline," Sam finally said. "If you can make up your mind to be finished with that losing piece of crap, I can get you some legitimate help. But no way am I going to help Conrad. If you plan to take him back, just tell me now, and I'll fix you and the little ones up with some sort of bus ticket to somewhere. But this is a decision you have to make. You're overdue, I'm thinking."

She stood up from the mattress. "I never

wanted it to be like this. I just never had any choice. He was all there was. That or starve."

"Well, looks like you're about to starve now for want of him. Your choice. I can get you some county help. Some money and food and maybe a little more improvement on this beat-up old shack. It happens Corsica Rios, a caseworker for the county's Child Protective Services, is a good friend around here. Her boy Ricky is a deputy."

"What do I have to do?" she asked him.

"You'll have to fill out some forms, I reckon," he said. "I'll go over to the café, put in a call to Corsica and bring you back a little milk and cereal for the children. Next I'm going to get some sturdy locks for what pass as doors on this sorry old house. But you have to promise, Erline, that you're not going to give whatever help you get over to that drug abuser."

She smiled slightly. Weakly. "That's an easy promise to make, Mr. Cussler. Life with Conrad ain't exactly easy."

Later that same day, Ricky Rios pulled up to the little house in his squad car. He carried four generous bags of groceries to the front door and knocked by tapping his foot against the portal. Erline peeked out nervously. Behind her came the sound of crying children.

"Can I come in?" Ricky asked. "I have some food for you and the children."

She opened the door uncertainly. "Why's the police bringing me food?" she asked.

Ricky laughed. "The police aren't bringing you food, young lady. Corsica's son Ricky is bringing you exactly what she told me to bring by. You got some place handy to store this? I figured there was no refrigerator here."

She just stood back and shrugged. "We live in this one room here, where there's heat from the wood stove."

"Good enough," he said, stacking the bags alongside her meager baggage against one wall.

She went back to the rocker with the baby in her arms.

"My mother can't get over here right away. This time of year there're lots of people need her and not enough of her to go around. So she told me to drop this by and she'll get here when she can. You need a few dollars to get you by?"

She just looked up at him in silent wonder. Ricky was about six-two, nicely muscled in his impeccable uniform, all the heavy police accouterments hanging from his belt. And handsome. So unbearably handsome. He grinned at her speechlessness and became even more beautiful.

"You need a couple of dollars to get you by?" he repeated.

"Um." She shook herself. "Um, no. Mr. Cussler took care of that. He gave me a little money. Which I fully intend to repay."

"Don't let it cost you any sleep. Old Sam is pretty well fixed." Ricky crouched, one knee on the floor, as he checked out the little girls and their worn-out baby dolls. "You ladies had your lunch yet? I brought some peanut butter and bread. And some bananas. How about that?" The little ones withdrew shyly and Ricky stood up. "Well, my mom will get over here when she can. Meantime, if something comes up, you can leave a message at the police department. You know where that is?"

She nodded. Her mouth was still slightly agog. She wondered what it would be like to have a man like this in her life. A man so strong and tall and clean and smart. A man on the right side of the law. It would have to be wonderful. And she could tell, just from this brief period of time with him, that he was safe. He wouldn't hurt. He would protect and not hurt.

There were women who had good men in their lives, she thought. She'd never been one of them and her mama hadn't, either, but there were decent men out there. Decent men, loving wives, happy, well-fed children. If she had to list the things she dreamed of, longed for, it would be that impossible combination for herself and her children.

"I'll check on you in a couple of days, make sure you're okay. Don't get up," he said, turning toward the door. When he got to the door he said, "Oh. If that Conrad shows up around here, would you let someone know? We'd like to talk to him."

"Who?" she asked.

"Well, me, the Chief, the police. We'd like to know where he was when the café was robbed."

"I don't think he did it," she said. "I mean, I don't say that because I'd make any excuse for him, but I think I'd of heard that old truck if he was anywhere near here."

"That right?" he asked her. "Bad muffler?"

"Almost everything on that old truck is bad. It makes a terrible ruckus."

He smiled that glorious smile again. "Thanks, Erline. That's good information. I'll pass it on to the chief."

Then he was gone. For the longest time she sat there in the rocker, holding her infant son against her chest and for the millionth time prayed that God would give her and the children a chance to escape from the dreary poverty and violence their lives had been.

June stood before her stove, stirring a pot of rich, thick chili. All seemed right with the world when she could get out of the clinic early enough to actually cook, lay a cozy fire, feel the baby move inside her and wait for the baby's father to come home.

The headlights from Jim's truck strafed the front of the house. Absently, she smoothed her hair and felt the roundness of her belly. "Daddy's home," she whispered.

The dog preceded him and June fell immediately to one knee to welcome Sadie, not at all surprised by how much she missed her when Jim took her with him. "Hey, my girl! How was your day? Were you very good? Did you entertain the twins?" Then she looked up at Jim, who had grime and sawdust all over his heavy sweatshirt. "You don't think you're going to take over my dog along with everything else, do you?"

"Look at her," he said. "She's grinning ear to ear. She likes riding in the back of the truck."

June gasped. "You didn't!" She had strictly

forbidden that.

"I didn't," he said. "Something smells wonderful. I didn't know you could cook," he teased.

She slapped his arm with a damp dish towel and a little cloud of sawdust puffed up. "I'm a better cook than you! Hey, you're dirty. Get a lot done today?"

"A real lot. It's damn near habitable." He pulled his shirt inside out over his head to capture the sawdust and dirt, and the sight of his bare chest took her breath away, like usual. Grace Valley was a town of strong men; June had grown up with them. But every time she saw Jim with his shirt off, she wanted to melt into his arms and never leave. She leaned against the counter, arms crossed above her swollen middle, and just gazed at him while he washed his hands and talked to her.

"I can see what Chris was thinking when he bought the place," Jim said. "It has great possibilities, and Chris is a good builder, a good carpenter. You should see what he's been able to do since some of us are helping him. He's taught me a lot. I don't know what kind of judge Judge Forrest is, but he's good with wood, and Chris is just that much better. We moved the boys into one of the bedrooms and did everything but lay carpet in that great room." She handed him the towel as he turned away from the sink. "Any news on the café burglary?"

"Not that I heard."

"Any word on that Davis guy?"

"Seems he abandoned his family," she said. "Sam said he called social services on their behalf."

"They're better off." He went to the chili pot and gave it a stir, took a taste. "Damn," he swore in appreciation. "Not bad for a gringo. Won't this give you heartburn or anything?"

"Naw. I have an iron stomach. Let's sit on the floor by the fire."

They filled bowls and put them on trays. June broke a French baguette in half and put it on a breadboard with butter and a knife, which she handed to Jim. She followed him into the cozy little living room and watched as he deftly lowered himself to the floor. Sitting cross-legged before the fire, he took a couple of giant spoonfuls of chili and yummed appreciatively.

June stood there in total consternation. She lowered herself to one knee, then two, but there was no way she could lower herself to the floor. Her stomach was just too big. When had that happened? She placed her tray on the floor in front of her, and attempted to brace herself with her hands, but there was a problem. She could reach the floor in front of her so she balanced on hands and knees, but when she kneeled upright and tried to reach for the floor behind her, her stomach became this ungainly giant mound that swayed out in front and threatened to topple her with its weight. She was back on all fours again, and tried the other direction. The result was the same. She thought about letting herself just drop to the floor, but realized that probably wasn't such a good idea.

On her knees, she wobbled to the couch, grabbed one of the larger throw pillows, then wobbled back to where her dinner waited. She applied the pillow to her butt, and with all the grace of a water buffalo, let herself drop the short distance to the floor. She immediately rolled too far to the left and had to catch herself before doing a complete backward somersault. When she sat upright, she saw that Jim was frozen, his unchewing mouth full of chili, as he watched this performance.

He slowly swallowed and said, "When it's time to get up, you let me know. Okay?"

"Yeah. Sure. Okay." She crossed her legs and reached for her tray, which she was going to put on her lap. Was. There wasn't really much lap there. But not to be discouraged, she simply picked up the bowl, took a dainty spoonful and said, "From now on, we'll be eating at the table."

"I guess so." He laughed. "Jesus, June, look how pregnant you are! Were you this pregnant this morning?"

"No," she said, making a face. "And I'm less pregnant right now than I'll be tomorrow morning." She took another bite. "And so forth." She rested the bowl atop her belly, and as he watched, it jumped slightly.

"Oh, man, did you *see* that?"

"Yes," she informed him.

"This is so fun," he said in a childlike way. This great, big, strong, dangerous man sat on the floor, laughing at her belly.

"You're a dolt," she told him, and ate her chili.

Deep in the night she was awake. At first she thought it was heartburn, but knew too quickly that it wasn't the chili. And it didn't feel like those harmless Braxton-Hicks contractions common in the last trimester of pregnancy. She wasn't even in the last trimester, just almost.

She got up, used the bathroom and went to the living room to sit alone in the dark for a little while, just to get a grip. She was too far along for miscarriage, not far enough for a safe birth. Her best guess was that she was approaching six months. And these were contractions.

She called John, described her symptoms and then woke Jim. He snuffled awake in the middle of a snore. "Jim, I have to go to the hospital," she said.

" 'S'okay. Wake me when you get back." He rolled over and presented his back to her. Sadie, on the bed again, snuggled in closer.

It took her a moment to realize he thought she was going out on a call. She tapped his shoulder again, more sharply. "Wake up. You have to drive me."

He rolled onto his back. "Why?"

"Because I'm having contractions. Labor pains. And it's too early for this."

That did it. He was on his feet instantly. He found his jeans, shrugged into them, got on shoes without socks and pulled his jacket over his undershirt. He picked up the truck keys from the dresser top.

Once in the truck he began asking questions. "What's causing this? Was it the spicy chili? The little bump to the floor? Are you working too hard? Should we have had the ambulance come? Should we call your dad? Does this happen often? Are you all right?

Can you feel the baby move?"

"Jim," she said, but she said it in her quiet voice. "Please don't talk right now."

"How can I not talk? Tell me what's happening!"

"Shh," she said.

She was deep inside herself. This wasn't something she had been formerly trained to do, but learned for survival as a doctor. When something threatened to topple her, cause her to collapse and render her unable to perform, she would have to control her emotions so completely that she was almost not in her own body. Usually this was a state she went into automatically when she saw a horrific accident, or maybe some mind-boggling violent abuse of a defenseless woman or child. Never did she think she'd have to protect herself from herself.

But, of course, that's what it was. If she allowed herself to think about what might be happening, the chances were excellent she could make it worse. What she wasn't thinking about was the fact that she was pregnant late in life with a baby that was probably a long-shot pregnancy. She was almost thirty-eight and surprised. She'd had unprotected sex far too many times for a physician, and there had never been a pregnancy. If this baby didn't make it, would there be time to try again?

And those were just the biological facts . . . how about the emotional ones? She felt this little baby girl move inside of her. She felt this baby's father's large and strong hand on her firm and hardening abdomen as they drove and she *wanted* them! Wanted them both with every fiber of her being. She could not let herself cave in to the weakness of fear. Not now.

"Just tell me . . . are you in pain?" he asked.

"Shh. No. Just drive very carefully. John will take care of everything. He's an OB genius."

"Okay, then," he said, and let her have her silence. But he kept his hand on her middle. He wished the baby would kick him, but she didn't.

John met her outside the ER with a wheelchair. He had on his game face. He wasn't going to let her see any of the justifiable concern over labor at six months, and she knew it. "Have a little tummy ache, do you? The way you eat, this is no surprise."

"Ha-ha. It's not a tummy ache. It's a uterus ache and I expect you to fix it."

"Certainly, June. Certainly." He wheeled her into the hospital. A couple of nurses waved as she passed. An ER tech said,

"Hang in there, June. You'll be all right."

"Sure. Thanks."

John stopped and looked over his shoulder to where Jim stood indecisively just inside the ER doors. John suspected he would never see this giant of a man look that meek again. "Come on," John said, and Jim nearly ran after them.

John must have phoned the OB ward ahead because they were all set up for an exam and ultrasound. He asked a few questions. Bleeding? Location of the cramping? Leakage of amniotic fluid? Then he spoke in a soft and comforting tone, explaining everything he was doing as he did it. "Nice heartbeat. No effacement or dilation. Big baby. Who knew you could grow a baby this big on bear claws?" Finally, he ran the ultrasound.

"June," he said, leaning over her and looking deeply into her eyes. "You're fine."

"What?"

"You're fine."

"I'm fine?"

"You're totally fine."

"But . . ." She grabbed his hand and pressed it to her hardening abdomen. "I'm having contractions!"

"That's not a contraction," he said with a smile. He knocked on top of the metal ultrasound monitor, making a loud rapping sound. "*That's* a contraction."

"What's this, then?"

"A little one. Practice. Braxton-Hicks."

"I'm a doctor!" she told him, outraged. "I know the difference between a contraction and a Braxton-Hicks."

He shrugged. "Apparently not."

Jim, who stood behind the examining table at her head, let his head fall till it reached her shoulder and he buried himself there, making a huge sigh of relief.

She, on the other hand, let the control go and a couple of tears slid out of her eyes. All she could say was "Thank God."

"Well, there is one thing wrong," John said.

Jim was upright, June was attentive.

"Show her," John told the nurse. She turned the monitor. With a pencil John pointed to the image, to a protuberance, on the image. A fairly large protuberance, at that. "The next town doctor isn't gonna be a girl. This is a guy."

"No way!"

"Way," he said. "A fairly common mistake. It doesn't often go the other way, but mistaking boys for girls? It happens."

She cried a little again. Tears of relief. "What can I say? I feel stupid."

"You're not stupid. Happens all the time."

"Well . . . then, I feel somewhat inadequate."

"Okay, that's a good place to start. Maybe now you'll let me be the OB on this case. Huh?"

Ten

June was fine and the baby was fine. There was no danger of complications as long as she took care of herself. But John did think it had presented a good opportunity to make a few changes that would benefit all involved, not the least being the baby.

First of all, he wanted her to work part-time, beginning with taking the next day off. All day.

"During flu season?" she protested.

"We'll get help. Susan is practically running the clinic these days. Your dad would love to see patients a couple of mornings a week and I think we could get some part-time help from some doctors from neighboring towns like Blake Norton or Dr. Lowe. We'll make it work."

"But if I'm perfectly fine . . . ?"

"Wouldn't it be nice if you stayed that way?"

He told her to go home, unplug the

phone, sleep in. Stay in bed late. Put on soft music. Finish a book she'd started reading six months ago and hadn't found the time to open since. Or how about her needlework? Susan had told him June was a master of petit point and quilting. "If all else fails, June, why not throw caution to the wind and make plans for the future? The baby is coming in three months or less."

Between Jim and John, there would be no argument. Jim took her home and put her to bed. Her body was tired, but her mind was awake and giddy with relief. She lay there, feeling the baby swim around, trying to picture a boy instead of a girl. She didn't find sleep until the very wee hours. And then, per custom, she was awake before the first streak of dawn.

Beside her the bed was empty, but a light shone from the kitchen and the smells of coffee and breakfast were delightful. Okay, she thought. This could be good. A little something to eat, a little reading, a little leisure time with the man I —

"Oh, good, you're awake," Jim said, interrupting her fantasy by entering with a tray. He was fully dressed, down to the boots that clomped into the room. He placed the tray on the bed and hurried out again. On the tray she saw eggs, toast, fruit and juice. The coffee had been for *him?* After the baby was born, she was going to drink seven pots of coffee in a row. She might have to forgo breastfeeding for that reason. "Here you go," he said, coming back to the bedroom with his arms full of things for her to do: her stash of needlework in the canvas bag that had an accumulation of dust on it; four unread magazines, specifically *not* medical journals; two books with markers in them after the second chapter; a cross-word puzzle and pencil. *Pencil?* Had he no faith in her?

"How long have you been up?" she asked.

"About a half hour." He kissed her head. "I have to go. The Forrests are expecting me. You want to keep Sadie for company?"

"You're leaving me? What am I going to do?"

He put his hands on his hips. "Relax. Enjoy a day off for once. Want me to put on some music for you?"

"Um, yes, please. My records. Frank, Steve and Barry."

He made a face. "It's really better if you spend the morning alone with those guys. I'll leave Sadie to keep you company."

"You say that like you're leaving your dog with me," she accused.

"Not at all, June. It's just that I've been

taking her to the Forrests'. The boys like her."

And that was how it began, with a nice breakfast, terribly bereft of sugar, Frank Sinatra doing it his way on her old stereo in the living room and a pile of diversions on the bed beside her. The last time she remembered a setting like this, she was nine, had strep throat and had to stay in bed long after the penicillin had kicked in. Then it was her mother who brought her quiet things to do. So there she was, feeling fine if restless. Even at nine she remembered feeling she shouldn't be still and unproductive for so long.

While Frank crooned to her, she picked up that long-unread novel. She'd have to just start over, she decided. She read three pages, then took her dishes to the kitchen and washed them. She went back to the bed, read three more pages, then lay her head back for a little snooze. She woke up feeling enormously refreshed. That's what she'd been needing! A nice, long nap! She checked the time — it was now eight-thirty.

Sadie, betrayed, sat staring at the front door, squeaking miserably. She did not like being left behind with an invalid.

June picked up her crossword puzzle and filled it in. She read three more pages of the novel, checked the petit point, but that was something you had to be in the mood for. She decided to shower, and for once she could do so leisurely. Take her time with her thick, wavy hair. Maybe have a good hair day for once. She could actually put on makeup!

All that was done by eight forty-five. And she had taken her time!

At nine she called the clinic. "Hi, Jessie. How's everything?"

"Fine, June. How are you?"

"Fine. How many patients do you have waiting?"

"Sorry, June. John told us you're not to be given any information about the clinic."

She felt her back stiffen and her cheeks grow hot. "Is that so? Well, does he know whose clinic it is?"

"Yes, he knows. Would you like to talk to him?"

"Yes!"

She was put on hold. On hold! Long enough for her to start to get her dander up. Finally, after actual minutes had passed, he came on the line. "This is Dr. Stone."

"And this is Dr. Hudson. Just what do you think you're doing?"

He moved the phone away from his mouth. "I win."

"Win *what?*"

"The 'how long can she last' bet. I was second earliest at 9:00 a.m. Susan actually thought you'd make it till noon because you've been complaining of fatigue."

"This is starting to piss me off," she muttered. "So, how many patients do you have waiting?"

"June, have a day off. We're fine here. Your father came in — he's going to spend the morning with us. Brought his own nurse, Charlotte. And the afternoon looks very light."

"I could make your hospital rounds," she offered.

"No."

"John, I'm bored."

"June, it's only nine."

"But I've already had breakfast, read, had a nap, a leisurely shower and primp and worked half the crossword. It's more stressful sitting around the house with nothing to do than working!"

"Then do something, just make sure it's not strenuous, fattening or stressful. Susan said for you to buy some wallpaper for the baby's room. Jessie said you should visit friends without your medical bag for once. And your dad said to get — Never mind what he said."

She knew what he'd said. "I hate this," she told him.

"You can come in tomorrow. Half day. Goodbye, June."

She seethed. It really fried her that Charlotte Burnham, her old nurse who was recovering from a serious heart attack, was allowed in the clinic with Elmer, but she, a perfectly healthy pregnant woman who'd had a few minor Braxton-Hicks contractions, was being ostracized.

"Well, *fine*," she said to no one.

She went shopping.

June had often wondered if she was missing a chromosome somewhere. Shopping had never appealed to her the way it did most girls. She headed for the coast towns — Rockport, Westport, Fort Bragg — in search of shops, department stores and strip malls that would cater to her new lifestyle. She then thought that maybe she should take the opportunity to buy some actual maternity clothes, maybe baby clothes, as well. But she *dreaded* it. She had absolutely no idea what she was supposed to do, what she was supposed to buy.

She went through four dress shops and a department store, fruitlessly, a glazed look in her eyes. She knew how to deliver babies, not clothe them. She could do an emergency

C-section, but which items to buy for a nursery was beyond her. In the largest department store she had browsed through, there were nine cribs alone! Not to mention all the other things — bumper pads, strollers, changing tables, high chairs, swings, car seats, mobiles, playpens . . . John thought this would relax her? It was nearly noon, her legs were beginning to ache, she was starving again and she thought she might cry. She was goddamn *sick* of crying! Why did *everything* translate to tears during pregnancy?

"June?"

She whirled around and found herself face-to-face with Nancy Forrest. She sniffed before a tear could actually wedge its way out of her eye. "Nancy. The last person I expected to run into!"

"Oh. Well, the physical therapist is at the house, the visiting nurse is due, there are four men there working — one of them being your Jim, as a matter of fact. And Chris is home so I could escape and run over here for more sheets and sheepskin to prevent bedsores." Nancy smiled a kind of sentimental smile. "Aw, shopping for the baby?"

That did it. First she'd thought she might *lose* the baby, then she'd been ordered to *relax,* an interminable torture, and now here she was trying to do something useful in motherhood and she was at a total, dense loss! Tears filled her eyes. "Shit," she said.

"June, what is it?" Nancy asked, a terrified look creeping into her eyes.

"If it turns out I know as much about taking care of a child as I know about shopping for one, this kid is doomed." Large tears spilled down her cheeks. "Plus, I'm *starving*. I'm *always* starving and I've been ordered to stop getting so fat!"

Nancy Forrest used June's cell phone to call her husband's cell phone. She told him that he'd simply have to see that the boys were taken care of through the afternoon. She had to do something very important for a good friend. When he pressed her for an explanation, she said she would explain later.

"First, we eat," she said.

Sometimes having an eccentric older sister could be tiring. Myrna called the clinic looking for Elmer when she couldn't find him at home or at the café or out helping the men at the Forrest house. She needed to see him, to talk to him about Thanksgiving.

"We'll have turkey," he had said into the phone.

"Don't be ridiculous! I know what we're going to eat. I have to tell you about someone who will be coming to dinner."

"Who?" he asked.

"That's why I want to speak to you. In person."

"Aww, Myrna . . ."

"Come at the martini hour, Elmer. And don't be late. I'll hold off until you get here."

Tiring, yes, but seldom dull, he thought as he drove up the long drive to the front of Hudson House. Sometimes Myrna would call him or June to the house to listen to a new book idea. Sometimes she'd have a scheme for a big party. And sometimes she'd be in trouble with the law. You just never knew with Myrna.

As he was pulling up, he caught sight of Harry Shipton just leaving the house, headed for his old station wagon. He waited for Elmer.

"She having a Tupperware party or something?" Elmer asked. This made Harry grin. "You're not here on some urgent pastoral mission, are you?"

Harry stuck out his hand for a shake. "If I were, I couldn't tell you, could I? And since I'm a man of the cloth and can't lie, I'd have to try to change the subject in such a subtle way you'd never catch on. Sorry I missed you out at the Forrests' today, Elmer. I had business down in the Bay Area. A family matter."

"I wasn't there, either," Elmer said. "John Stone insisted June have a day off, so I took some of her patients." He put a hand to the small of his back and gave a stretch. "Now I know why I retired. A lot of complaining goes with flu season. You had your shot yet, Harry?"

"No. I don't go in for flu shots much."

"You come in tomorrow and get one. On the house. You'll thank me later."

"If not tomorrow, maybe the next day," Harry said. "June's all right, I hope."

"Perfectly fine. But John's right to make her slow down now, before advanced pregnancy makes it imperative." He chuckled, that impish gravelly chuckle. "According to Dr. Stone, being forced to rest and relax had the effect of making my daughter rather gnarly."

He gave a short wave and trudged up the steps to Myrna's front door while Harry got into his car and started the engine. Elmer turned suddenly, only just realizing Harry had deftly steered the subject away from his sister's spiritual well being. He knocked on the door. Myrna opened it at once.

"Thank heavens," she said. "I thought

you'd never get here."

He looked at his watch. "It's only five-thirty!"

"You know I like to have my martini at five."

"Why didn't you have it with Harry?"

"Just come in, Elmer. Now that I've made up my mind, I can't wait to tell you about it." And off she toddled, toward the back of the house.

Hudson House, where they had grown up, was a remarkable place. As huge as it was, it was never drafty or difficult to keep at a moderate temperature. In summer it was cool and airy; in winter it could be toasty warm. He followed her into the large kitchen. A fire blazed in the hearth, some soup simmered in a pot on the stove — probably prepared by one of the Barstow twins before she left for the day — and fresh buns sat inside a warming basket on the counter. Myrna sat down at the small table in the breakfast nook. On the tray were two glasses with olives in them, a glistening pitcher of gin with a dash of vermouth and a bowl of Goldfish crackers.

"I'm joining you, am I?" Elmer asked.

"You might as well. Unless there's something else I can pour you?"

He sat down before his glass. "You must

think I'm going to need it." He couldn't wait to hear what she was going to lay on him this time.

While she poured, she said, "I'm going to have a gentleman guest over the Thanksgiving holidays. For an as-yet-to-be-determined length of stay."

That got his attention. Since Morton had departed some twenty years ago, he hadn't known his sister to have a gentleman friend other than at the poker table. Maybe he would have a small sip of that martini, after all.

She told him all about Edward, her long epistolary relationship with him, what good friends they had become and how they'd never managed to meet in person. She even explained how, at first, the mere thought of this visit had her overwrought. Though she was the type that nothing could get to her — at least on the outside — her nerves were fairly frazzled at the thought of a gentleman visitor. But now, thinking about it, she thought it was high time she began seeing men again.

Seeing men? Elmer thought. What was that supposed to mean? He didn't dare ask.

"So, I'm going to need a little help with this," she said. "I don't want to have to entertain Edward all the time, all on my own. He's going to come in just before Thanksgiving. He'll take a commuter flight into Rockport and we'll pick him up. Show him the town. Have a dinner or two to introduce him around."

Elmer noticed that his sister had two bright spots on her cheeks that might not be a result of either her martini or her rouge. Myrna was eighty-four, and if he wasn't mistaken, smitten.

"I want everyone to like him. Who knows how long he'll choose to stay on with me. We have so much in common."

Elmer glanced at the pot on the stove. "Does he cook?"

"I haven't any idea, but don't worry about that. I do. And Endeara and Amelia enjoy cooking, so he'll be well fed."

Elmer leaned toward his sister. "Myrna, dear, does this relationship hold the possibility of becoming, well . . . *physical?*"

She let out a burst of cackling laughter that caused her springy white hair to tremble. "Wouldn't that be a hoot! Why, Elmer? Did you want to have a talk with me about birth control?"

Elmer stood up. He was tired from his long day and he'd paid his dues here, listening to the details of Myrna's latest project. "I look forward to meeting your guest," he said, but he thought he'd do a little investigating first to make sure this gentleman was completely legitimate. Perhaps a quick call to his publisher or agent? "Does he play poker?"

She tilted her head. "I don't believe we've ever discussed it. . . ."

"Now, that would be entertaining. Speaking of poker, what was Harry doing here? You're not having a religious crisis, are you?"

"Don't be silly, Elmer. He just stopped by to say he can't play cards on Thursday. Some sort of family business is keeping him occupied in the Bay Area. He said he didn't think there'd be a problem with us using the rectory, but frankly, everyone is a bit too tied up at the moment, wouldn't you say? With you covering for June in the clinic, Sam and Judge trying to speed up the repairs at the Forrest house and . . . why, I'm going to have to have a few things done around here to get ready for company."

"I guess that's right," Elmer said. He twisted a few more kinks out of his back. "Harry's been a little down in the mouth lately. I hope he doesn't have a sick relative."

"He didn't say. He just needed a little advance on his paycheck and said he's sorry he's had to be out of town so much lately."

Elmer stopped in his tracks. He'd given Harry a small loan also. But Myrna was loaded, and that's why she took watching. She could be so trusting, so oblivious. For someone who did such damn fine plotting of mysteries, she never questioned the motives of friends and neighbors, nor even strangers. "You didn't give him a lot of money, did you?" Elmer asked.

"No, of course not. He said a thousand would tide him over nicely."

When Jim got home from his day of labor at Chris Forrest's house, he found June sitting on the couch in the living room with shopping bags and purchases draped over every spare surface. There were clothes for her, for the baby, blankets, towels, linens, toys. And she had tears in her eyes. "Look what I've done," she said, looking up at him.

He tried not to overthink the tears. There had been a lot of tears. He had been told that it was normal for pregnant women to eat too much, sleep too much and then too little, and have erratic emotions. "Well, since you've gone and done all this, you might as well have the baby." He lifted a bra that seemed to be falling apart with flaps instead of cups. He caught himself before saying,

"Oh, now this is attractive."

"Nursing bra," she said.

"Ah. That explains it." He splayed the cup with his spread fingers and found it, well, optimistic.

She sniffed and blew her nose. "I'll grow into it," she said.

"Do you mind if I ask why you're crying? And if you'd rather not talk about it . . ."

"Nancy Forrest took me to find all this stuff. After she fed me a huge, juicy hamburger that put George's to shame."

"I see," he said, but he wasn't even close to seeing.

"Growing up I hated her," June said.

Jim pushed aside some clothes so he could sit on the chair across from June, sensing this explanation wasn't going to be short.

"Go on."

"Nancy played with the little girls and I played with Chris, Tom and Greg Silva, who used to live here. Right there, we were total opposites. Then later, when we got to junior high and had more in common because I realized I was stuck with being a girl, she made a full-time job of trying to get my boyfriend away from me."

He leaned back. History. Women were very big on history. "I think she did, in fact."

"Oh yeah. You knew that. Well, she's been

through a lot lately, and I've only been barely nice to her. Like I'm holding some kind of grudge, which really I'm not. So today when I'm standing in JCPenney with tears in my eyes because I don't have a clue what to buy for myself or the baby, who comes along and rescues me? My lifelong rival."

"She's not your rival anymore, sweetheart."

"Oh, heavens, I know that! But it's more than that. See, I have some women friends who are very special to me. Like Birdie, my godmother. Ursula Toopeek. Jessie is like a surrogate daughter to me, and I've grown to adore Susan Stone. And that's just the tip of the iceberg. But Jim, I've never had a *girlfriend.* Not a real girlfriend you giggle with, barter secrets with, cry with, call the men in your lives dirty bastards with."

His eyebrows shot up. He thought he'd been doing very well as her man.

"Oh, not you. At least not yet." She gave him a tearful grin, dabbing her eyes. "It was kind of emotional for me. Here she has these banged-up, bedridden hellions at home who really need her attention, and I wouldn't say she got the best deal for a husband. Plus, she's exhausted and behind in everything. But when she caught me in this little crisis, she dropped everything and helped me." Her chin quivered and a fresh flood of tears emerged. In a hiccup of wet emotion she said, "I *love* her."

Oh, boy, Jim thought. There was simply no way a man could ever be adequately prepared for the many moods of a pregnant woman.

"June," he said. "I have to take a shower before I can think about dinner. Will you come with me? Scrub my back?"

"My stomach will probably just get in the way."

"It'll be okay," he said, standing and reaching for her hand.

"I'm getting a little hungry. Again."

"I'm not at all surprised. Let's take a shower, then we'll have something to eat."

When she put her hand in his, she knew it wasn't really cleanliness that was foremost on his mind. "You sure you know what you're getting yourself into?" she asked him.

Though she managed to surprise him constantly, he answered, "Yes. Come here."

He turned on the shower, made sure there were two towels on the door hooks, then slowly helped her out of her clothes. To his satisfaction, she helped him out of his. They dropped to the floor and were kicked aside.

"If I ever build a house," Jim said, surprising himself with the very notion, "it's going to have a giant shower with a bench in it."

"Good," she said. She kissed him while reaching around him with the soap, lathering his back. Then his front. Then his lower back . . . lower front. He took the soap from her and returned the favor till their bodies were slick as grease. "If we tried to do it now, we'd slip and they'd find our bloated bodies a few days from now."

"Doctors," he said. "The places your minds wander. Rinse," he said, still trying to hang on to her mouth.

Holding her was really what he was after, because he didn't quite know what to do with all the different emotions, levels of energy, various stages of nausea or ravenous hunger — and the tears. But he didn't have any trouble holding her. It had baffled him many times since her pregnancy became obvious that men would have trouble with this part, being with a pregnant woman. The Madonna complex or some damn thing, where a guy suddenly couldn't touch his wife sexually because she was now the mother of his child. It eluded him; he'd never found June sexier. He'd never been more hungry for her. But conscious of the small life between them, he knew how to be extraordinarily gentle, which drove her enticingly mad.

Jim had always secretly known he had this side — this lovingness, this patience and gratitude — but there weren't many places to show it when chasing drug dealers undercover. If he lived to be a hundred, he could never adequately thank June for letting him into her life and accidentally getting caught with his child. All this was new, and it was refreshingly pure, sweet and miraculous. Without her, without the baby, he might never have known this side of his being, his life. When he thought of the coming years, with this woman, in the beauty of her town, he couldn't believe his luck. He probably didn't deserve it, but he'd take it just the same.

He made love to her tenderly. She sighed with satisfaction at the end. He said, "I love you," when his breathing evened. Then she curled up in his arms, naked on the bed. There was one towel under them and he pulled the other over them.

"That was very nice," she said. "Very, very, very nice."

"You're welcome."

"But I'm very hungry."

He hoisted up on an elbow. "Is this where I offer to go out into the woods, shoot a deer, dress it and roast it on a spit for you?

My queen?"

She liked the way he teased. "How about if you just rustle us up a sandwich?"

"I can do that. BLTs. Or egg and cheese on toast. With . . . are you ready? Soup. Last time I went to the market, I loaded up on soup. For damp, dark, romantic nights like this."

"You are the perfect man."

"I am."

"Jim? Are you upset that we're not married?"

He got a panicked look on his face. "You aren't going to throw up, are you?"

She gave him a shove. "No. Just answer."

"No," he said, grabbing her and pulling her tight. "Just as long as you don't kick me out."

" 'Course not. I just don't want to get married yet. I want to know you better. I want to feel secure about it. Because when we do it, I want us to say 'forever,' mean it and have a good shot at pulling it off. Is that okay by you?"

He smiled at her. Then he kissed her nose and said, "Very okay, June. You just tell me when you think you know me enough."

"Do you agree with that? About saying 'forever' and being sure?"

"I do."

"Will you tell me when you think you're there?"

"Sure."

"Good," she said.

"June?"

"Yes?"

"I'm there. You go ahead and take your time."

ELEVEN

By the time the carpet was installed in the Forrest house, the kitchen was nearly finished. And the boys were out of their hospital beds and sitting in wheelchairs, well enough to begin home schooling. The junior high sent a tutor out three afternoons a week. They were bright, a factor that no doubt contributed to them getting in trouble so often, and would very likely not miss even a semester of school.

Sam paid a visit to the county assessor's office and learned that the abandoned house he'd appropriated, illegally, for Erline and the children had actually been repossessed for back taxes. It was a lot for a house of such poor quality, but with one quick trip to the bank, he became a landlord. No one knew this. Not even Erline. But it became suspect as Sam continued to work on the house, making it more sound and comfortable. He solicited help from his friends, new and old.

"Why are you wasting your time on this old shack?" George asked. "Throwing good money away, if you ask me."

"This young woman and her children need a fresh start, and they have to be warm and fed to get it." Plus, Sam kept thinking, if he hadn't been fooled by that young Conrad, maybe the little lady and her children would still be in a shelter in Rockport. A place with central heat, plumbing that worked all the time and subsistence for groceries.

"But you're going to sink your money into this firetrap and then she'll just move out and leave it sit vacant again," Elmer argued.

"We aren't completely sure about that, now. Maybe she'll stay, make a home for herself and the children," Sam said — and Sam hoped. He'd come to think of Erline as a quality girl who deserved a break.

"You taking another shine to a younger woman, Sam?"

"Oh, Doc, you can believe I've learned that lesson. I just want to lend a hand."

"What if someone comes along and claims the property?" Jim asked, coyly.

"Why would anyone want to do that?"

As the month of November progressed cold and rainy, Jim Post grew more content, and it was not lost on his new friends. He never talked much about the life of law enforcement he'd retired from, but he did mention that until now he hadn't had the luxury of this kind of time. Nor had he felt needed in this way. Needed by June, but by lots of others, as well.

Life was changing for June, within and without. She slowly came to realize what John had attempted to do for her by insisting she reduce her work schedule. In addition to guarding her health, he wanted her to take a moment to enjoy this time in her life before it was gone. He wanted her to take the time to contemplate growth, which seemed almost daily, take time to spend learning about Jim, who would be with her from now on. Soon enough she would be as hassled and harried as any working parent, and as John knew, it would only get more so with each passing year as their child or children became more active, more demanding, more *expensive!*

June was restless at first, especially since Jim was busy helping around town, having lunch with the guys at the café and so on. It had been a good twenty years since she'd had time on her hands. She began to use it to visit with friends, both the old and the new. She spent more time with Nancy

Forrest, and the friendship suited them both. And she spent more time with the quilting circle, who came together to quilt for the women in town who needed them. Nancy, Jurea, Erline, Leah.

Behind June's back the Graceful Quilters were stitching up a storm for her and Jim, and for their baby.

As the cold rains turned to sleet and, farther up the mountains, snow, townsfolk filled the wood stoves and hearths with logs and stove pots with hot soup. They huddled against the darkness of winter and warmed to the idea of holidays — the bright spot in an otherwise dour time of year. Spirits began to slowly rise in anticipation of family, food and fun.

But there was one person who didn't get cheerier as the season of Thanksgiving grew near. Harry Shipton carried his burdens in solitude, or so he thought. He grew increasingly depressed, finding it harder and harder to smile through his unhappiness. Even his sermons became less uplifting.

Harry had only been at Grace Valley Presbyterian for about six months, but the town had taken to his upbeat and humorous nature immediately. It was such a nice change from their last preacher, and they embraced him. But by late fall, clouds covered his demeanor and it was obvious he was deeply troubled. He wasn't even making it to weekly poker, when they had weekly poker, and it was well known Harry loved nothing better. He was clearly miserable, but no one knew why. The usual café crowd talked about it.

"I think it might be a sick family member, somewhere near the Bay Area," Elmer conjectured. "He goes there often, and he's been needing money."

"I've asked him if there's anything I can do to help out, but he insists there isn't anything wrong," Susan Stone shared.

"We should call the presbytery," George suggested. "Ask them if they know what's wrong with our preacher."

"No, George, you must never do that," June warned him. "Not unless you think he should be counseled or removed. No, we have to find another way to see if we can help Harry. We don't want to lose him. Everyone loves him here."

"Then we'll have to pay very close attention, see if he drops us a hint as to what's wrong. Has he mentioned the name of this family member?"

"Not a word. But he has mentioned having an ex-wife. Should we call her?" Susan asked.

"I don't know," Elmer said. "What if she's bitter?"

"What if she makes trouble for him with the church?" George asked.

"Harry has mentioned being on good terms with her," June said. "But I don't think calling her is the answer. Not yet, anyway."

"Let's just keep a close eye on Harry for now," Elmer said. "If anyone gets a notion as to what's wrong, I'm willing to do whatever I can to help. I'm willing to bet there's a town full of those willing."

Elmer had no idea how close his words came to the answer.

Grace Valley resembled other cities and towns in the dichotomy the holidays presented. On one hand, there was a sense of coming together, a feeling of celebration. Families and friends united first to give thanks, then to exchange gifts and tidings. On the other hand, it was the worst season for depression and domestic problems.

But even those people most down on their luck were making optimistic plans for the season of joy. Erline and her children were going to join Jurea and her teenagers for the very first turkey Clinton and Wanda would have. The oven was still new to Jurea, but she loved it dearly. She asked for lots of advice from anyone who would give it, and as a surprise, Harry Shipton brought her a sixteen-pound frozen turkey. He stood, gangly and grinning at her door, his arms full of plucked bird, and said, "Jurea, this is for you and your family. Happy Thanksgiving."

She wept for an hour.

Jurea's life had been hard and she didn't expect much from it, so she never complained. But once she'd been brought out of the woods with her children and embraced by the town and the church, her life had changed in so many wonderful ways that she had trouble believing it wasn't all a dream.

She sent Wanda next door to get Erline and the babies, to show them the turkey. Erline was likewise moved to tears, but fortunately she didn't take up all day with weeping. "I don't have a workable kitchen," Erline said, "but I can help you with some things like potatoes. I used to do the potatoes for my stepmother when I was a young girl. Both the white and the yams."

So the women got down to the nitty-gritty of planning out the food. They asked Harry to come to dinner, but he disappointed them by saying that he'd be visiting extended family in the Bay Area, back in time for an evening Thanksgiving service for those residents who could push back from the table and lumber over to the church.

This would be the first Thanksgiving for Leah Craven and her five children after the death of her abusive husband. Even though they were clearly better off without him, holidays were not easy. It was a strange confusion, and the Craven family didn't exactly understand it, but while they gave thanks there would be no fighting and hitting on one of the holidays that almost guaranteed it, there was also a cloud of sadness. So when there was a knock at the door and Leah looked out to see Harry Shipton's old station wagon in front of the house, she swung open the door optimistically, hoping Harry would have some helpful and supportive words for her.

"Hi, Leah. This is for you," he said, presenting her with a twenty-pound frozen bird. "I hope you don't already have one."

Leah kept better control of her grateful tears than Jurea had. But the truth was, she was worried about the meal. There was so little money, just what the garden could earn in summer and what she and Frank earned at the café.

Harry had to decline yet another invitation.

The pastor drove around the town and rural area of Grace Valley delivering a few more turkeys. The congregation bought them and a small committee came up with the list of families who should get them, but they left it to Harry to deliver them. Everywhere he went he was met with pure joy and gratitude. Not only that, people were always happy to see him. He was drawn into their homes, embraced with the love they had for him, and he a newcomer at that. At every home he was begged to come to dinner. There was no mistaking the genuineness of these offers, of this outpouring.

He only wished he deserved it.

June, who for the first time she could remember, had time to plan in earnest for a holiday, also had a friend to get it ready with. Nancy Forrest had a new kitchen and a white thumb for baking. The women spent the Tuesday afternoon before the holiday meal baking pies and homemade bread.

"You'll never know what a treat it is for me to look around your new home and think about what Jim might have done. This is a whole new life for him," June said.

"What was his life like as a cop?"

"I'm learning about that a little at a time," June said, avoiding the truthful parts that were actually secret. "He was just a kid when he started back in Wisconsin, first in a little rural village, then in Madison, where he grew up. He said it was all he'd ever wanted to do, but once he'd put in twenty years, he was ready to move on."

"To Grace Valley of all places?" Nancy asked as she rolled out dough.

"Oh, you know that story, right?"

"I'm not sure. . . ."

"He was camping out in the woods with friends when one of them got hurt. Accidentally shot. Jim brought him into town, saw lights on at the clinic, and while I picked a bullet out of his shoulder, we fell in love." She smiled sentimentally. "Jim fainted."

Nancy had stopped rolling. "Well, jeez. Isn't that romantic."

"I thought it was."

"But what made him decide to stay here?"

"He didn't stay here, he went back to work," June explained. "He visited a couple of times, told me he just about had his twenty years in, but really, I didn't have any expectations." Nancy made a dubious face. "Okay, I might have *had* them, but until I told him I was pregnant and he came back and said he was here for good, I wasn't sure that would happen."

"And you're happier than you ever expected to be?" Nancy asked.

Just as June was about to answer, the front door opened and Chris walked in. He wore a ski jacket over his shirt and tie and carried his briefcase. He smiled and said, "Hey, ladies," but didn't hang around to talk. He passed right through the living room, headed for the back of the house. Maybe he's going to see the boys, June thought. Or to change clothes.

She looked at Nancy and saw her eyes glued to the empty space that had marked Chris's passage. She bit her lip, troubled. Then she looked at June and said, "Excuse me a sec," and, wiping her hands on a dish towel, followed him.

By the time she came back, June had the rolled-out crusts lining four pie pans. Nancy had a look on her face that made June think maybe she should leave.

"Problems?" the doctor asked carefully.

She shrugged. "It's not the end of the world."

"Um, should I . . . I could put these pies in and leave, come back and pick them up tomorrow?"

"No, let's finish. You can watch me drink

a glass of wine." She forced a smile. "Next time we're alone, I'll tell you all about my husband and his current crisis," she whispered.

"He's having a crisis?" June whispered back.

Nancy leaned across their work space to get closer to June. "June, this is Chris Forrest. You remember him. He's been having one crisis after another since I met him in the eighth grade."

Which made June laugh, which made Nancy laugh, which, before long, had them laughing hysterically at the laughter as well as the subject. June had to hold on to her stomach while it shook. Then June's hand went suddenly to her startled mouth and, stricken, she said, "Oh! I think I peed my pants!"

The highlight of the Thanksgiving holiday for the Hudsons, and quite a few curious townsfolk, had to be the arrival of Edward Mortimer, the first known suitor for Myrna Hudson Claypool in twenty years. Elmer and June were comfortable that Morton Claypool had just wandered off and was most likely deceased by now, but there were still quite a few residents in Grace Valley who thought Myrna might have done him in. Imaginations had run wild all over town not long ago when bones had turned up under Myrna's rhododendron, and very likely fell in disappointment when Myrna was absolved of any wrongdoing.

But this guest, Edward, was being met with much enthusiasm. He was coming by bus from San Francisco on the busiest travel day of the year. Elmer drove Myrna's big Caddy to the Rockport bus station while June and Jim, as support staff, went in Jim's pickup. The bus depot, usually a fairly quiet place, was brimming with people traveling to and fro for the holiday.

Myrna was decked out in her cashmere coat with the fox-tail collar and one of her very favorite hats, a black velvet with a wide brim, gold lamé band and a poinsettia. Her wiry white hair was tucked neatly underneath and her cheeks and lips were rosy with rouge and excitement.

June had her arm looped through Myrna's and whispered, "How are your nerves?"

"As solid as a rock, thanks to you, dear."

"Me? What did I do?"

"You should know. You simply wouldn't take seriously all my ridiculous fretting. Why, it's like I've known Edward all my life. You know, for writers, sometimes knowing each other's work is more intimate than what is shared by husbands and wives. It's intellectually intimate."

"Goodness," June said, giving silent thanks that she wasn't a writer. She stole a glance at Jim, who stood at her side, and her breath caught. It was a feeling she never hoped to replace with intellectual intimacy. She reached for his hand.

Myrna was oblivious. "It's true. In all the years I spent with Morton, we were never as intellectually close as Edward and I." She chuckled conspiratorially. "I wonder, if Morton had stayed, if I'd have ended up having an affair with Edward."

"What rubbish," Elmer said.

"Rubbish to *you,* maybe," she returned contrarily. "But don't think I haven't thought about it lately. You see, dear, Morton was a love, but he was dull. And Edward, while years older than Morton, is extremely stimulating."

"Is that right?" June asked out of politeness. "Look, the people are getting off the bus. You're sure you'll know him? There wasn't a single photo on any of his book jackets."

"I'd know him with my eyes closed," she said. "Plus, he promised to wear a red carnation in his lapel."

Seven or eight people disembarked, then

240

there was a break and no one came. Then another six or seven, then no one. For a long time afterward June asked herself what would have happened if there'd been no red carnation. What would they have done? Finally, after about twenty people got off the bus, there came this very slight, very neat-looking man of eighty-six in a rather old-fashioned but tidy navy blue pin-striped suit, white shirt and red tie, dark felt hat with a black satin band, and wearing a red carnation. And it was none other than Morton Claypool.

"Dear God," June said in a breath.

"Jesus Christ in heaven," Elmer concurred.

"What? What's the matter?" Jim asked, as the little man drew near.

Finally the man stood before a speechless Myrna, slowly removed his hat and bowed. He smiled. "My dear," he said. "I am home at last."

June was stricken with disbelief, but finally tore her eyes away from Morton to glance at her aunt. Myrna's lips were pursed and her cheeks redder, if possible. Her hair seemed to spring loose from under her wide-brimmed hat.

"That's what you think!" she said, then turned on her heel and stomped off.

■ ■ ■ ■

"This is what we usually refer to as a fine kettle of fish," Elmer told Morton.

Elmer drove Jim's truck with Morton as a passenger, his bags tossed in the back, while June drove the Caddy, Myrna sitting in the passenger seat in a monumental pout and Jim in the back seat. Myrna would not even consider having Morton in the same vehicle with her. She'd fled to the Caddy, got in, slammed the door and locked herself in while the others all stood around and tried to figure out how to shuffle drivers and passengers.

"She didn't appear especially happy to see me," Morton said.

"You've always been a gifted observer," Elmer said. "Morton, what the devil were you thinking?"

"I was thinking of coming back to Grace Valley," he said. "Now that I was convinced Myrna wanted me."

"Where the hell have you been?" he demanded.

"Mostly in Redding. But I did treat myself to a little traveling."

"But why did you stay gone so long? We looked for you! We were worried!"

"Piffle," he said.

"What?"

"I said 'piffle.' You didn't look. No one looked. Not at all."

"Well . . ." Elmer didn't quite know what to say. No one had looked until very recently, and by then the trail had gone cold. In fact, Myrna insisted that no one look for him. In double fact, she hadn't even noticed he was gone until *months* had passed.

"I bet no one even noticed I had gone until years had passed," Morton said.

Elmer felt himself blush. "That's just not true," he said. It wasn't *years*. "My sister quite naturally thought you'd walked out on her. Left her. Her reasoning was very simple, if you'd been hurt or killed, your employer would have called her. But when she checked with the paper company, they said you'd been showing up at work regularly."

"Humph," he said. "I imagine no one in your family will *ever* admit how long it was until someone called them."

"Now, see here," Elmer said, getting a little miffed himself. "Are you going to pretend to be angry at all of us? It's possible that Myrna waited a bit too long to call your employer, but think of her feelings, man! She was abandoned! And it turned out you were quite well, working away, not even bothering to phone her!"

"That's not exactly so, but I'm not going to defend myself any further. I was invited for Thanksgiving and I've come. If no one wants me around after that, I'll go back to my little apartment in Redding. No hard feelings."

"No hard feelings?" Elmer echoed, astonished.

"Not on my part," he said.

Elmer sighed deeply. "You know all those books in which the husband was killed off?" he asked.

"I should. It was originally my idea."

"Well, it could become a reality. She's pissed."

In the Caddy, there was a similarly emotional conversation, but that's where the resemblance stopped.

"You had absolutely *no* idea?" June asked.

"What do you think?" Myrna countered.

"But now, in thinking back, did nothing trigger suspicion?"

"That Morton, he always did have a sneaky, underhanded streak. You have to watch those quiet, dull ones."

June drove quietly for a spell while Myrna sat way across the seat, seething. "Imagine,"

June finally said. "The very man who suggested that you write book after book killing off the husband was *your* husband! Tell me, when you were being investigated by the district attorney for suspicion of murdering him, did he say a word?"

"Not a peep!"

"What balls," June said with a short laugh.

"He's a blithering coward! A boring one at that. Didn't I always say so?"

"You did indeed, and you were completely wrong, weren't you."

"What in the world . . ."

"Auntie, I don't know the exact reasons for all this, but essentially your husband went away and began writing you letters. The man you didn't have all that much use for wooed you in print and won your heart. You said yourself, you were intellectually closer to 'Edward' than Morton. You spent more years adoring him through the mail than you ever did when he was right under your roof!"

"And now I despise both of them, regardless. I wonder, is that old shotgun of my daddy's still in the attic?"

"Hoo-boy" was heard from the back seat.

She pulled off to the side of the road, put the car in Park and faced her aunt. "Auntie, listen to me. I know you're miffed, and maybe you have a right to be, I don't know —"

"You don't *know?*"

June folded her hands over her rapidly growing stomach, peered down at her tiny but formidable aunt and lifted one brow. "Auntie, you didn't realize for six months that Morton was gone. It's possible he left because he was feeling just a tad neglected."

There was a sound from the back seat. It was something like a backward sneeze that dissolved into a clumsy fit of coughing. Or else it was a poor attempt at disguising unintentional laughter.

"He should've spoken up if he needed something," Myrna said. Then she glared over the seat at Jim. She made him redden.

"Be that as it may, I'm certain both of you bear some responsibility for this mess. He's here, it's a holiday, a *family* holiday, and we're going to make the best of it. I don't know how this whole thing will turn out in the long run. Morton might choose to go right back where he came from. He seems to have made a good life for himself, writing. In the meantime, we're going to be civil. And kind. Aren't we, Auntie?"

She huffed and looked out the window.

"Aunt Myrna? Aren't we?"

She looked back at June. "This is going to

take some doing."

"Whatever it takes. Right, Auntie?"

"I suppose you have a valid point. We probably both contributed, although my contribution was slight and my retribution could be vast."

"Aunt Myrna," June warned.

"I can be civil. I can *attempt* to be civil."

"There. You see? We might as well have an enjoyable holiday. I've been baking for days. I've gotten good at it." June turned back to the steering wheel and put the car in Drive. "Think of it this way. We're blessed that Uncle Morton is alive!"

"Humph. We'd be *blessed* if he were under the rhododendron!"

TWELVE

When June opened her eyes on Thanksgiving morning, the rare northern California sun was shining and there was the distinct sound of birds. She loved this, waking up on her own instead of by the phone. Lazing around in the morning while other doctors made the calls and staffed the clinic. In the back of her mind she heard John's voice just as the baby gave her a sound kick. "Don't get used to it!"

Ah, yes, breast-feeding every two hours. Twenty diapers a day. Potty training, Mommy and Me swimming lessons, preschool, soccer, piano lessons, ballet . . . Oops, it's a boy, remember? Okay, revise that to soccer, piano, football.

It was cold in the bedroom so she gravitated toward the heat beside her, but she had to kick Sadie out of the way. Jim was spoiling the dog. Sadie, the wayward slut, now thought she was Jim's dog and only went with June as a last resort.

"Hmm," he hummed, feeling her stomach kicking against his back.

"We're going to need a piano," she whispered.

"Before breakfast?" he asked after a long moment of silence.

She giggled. "All children take piano lessons," she informed him.

"Ah. So we have a few weeks, then?"

She giggled again, but it made her want to pee. This child had been sitting on her bladder for at least the past month. She was afraid to laugh, cry, sneeze or cough. Jim started to turn over. "Don't move!" she instructed hotly. "I have a bladder situation!"

Jim froze. It occurred to him that this was the sort of dialogue couples should have after years of marriage and not mere weeks of living together. Yet it all felt so oddly natural and sweet. "June, did anyone ever tell you that you're at your romantic best first thing in the morning?"

She laughed in spite of her better judgment. "You're tempting fate."

He wiggled his back against her rollicking stomach. She made a panicked sound, rolled away and dashed for the bathroom. Sadie barked at her flight, thinking it might be playtime.

In a minute she was back, comfortable and with freshly brushed teeth. She jumped back into the bed and this time snuggled into his embrace. Then she thought about Myrna and Morton. Although a very nice evening at Hudson House had been planned, last night hadn't been the festive occasion hoped for. The Barstows, stunned by the revelation of who Edward Mortimer was, served up their predictably inedible dinner open-mouthed. The only two people at the table who ate were Morton and Myrna, and they did not speak to each other. At dinner's end, Elmer took Morton home with him and a spare bedroom was fixed up.

When June and Jim were leaving Hudson House June said to her aunt, "I hope we can do a little better at Thanksgiving dinner than we just did."

And Myrna had replied through clenched teeth, "Doesn't he just sit at the table as if he hasn't been gone a day?"

Now June snuggled against Jim and said, "Don't I have the most interesting life of anyone you know?"

He sighed. "Can't we just stay here today? Make some grilled cheese and tomato soup?"

She hoisted up on an elbow and looked down with amusement. "Come, now. You've chased down hardened criminals. Surely you're up to today."

He shrugged. "I don't know. It's all pretty weird."

Thanks to the Barstows, who must have stayed up pretty late on the phone, the word was out about Morton. Of course, they only called women they knew, but the women quickly filled in their husbands, who made sure all bases were covered. Gossip in Grace Valley was a time-honored tradition.

June made it a point to get to her father's early to help with the cooking, and to help with the transition — or whatever it was — between Myrna and Morton. But by the time she got there Morton had already been called on by Sam, Judge Forrest and Birdie, George Fuller and Tom Toopeek.

"News travels fast," June said to her father.

"I'm surprised CNN isn't here," Elmer returned.

June noticed that Elmer had really worked up a sweat in the kitchen. His bald head was gleaming and there were sweat stains on his shirt. "Is this upsetting you?" she asked her father.

"What? Having my dead brother-in-law

reappear after twenty years? Having the town at my door while I try to stuff the god-damn turkey? Having my eccentric older sister out at that haunted house of hers, try-ing to remember how to load our deceased father's hundred-year-old shotgun? Naw," he said, shaking his head. "Just another day in paradise."

"Maybe I should take your blood pres-sure," she suggested.

"No, you don't. Right now I'm just a little irritated. I don't want to be scared to death on top of that."

"Sit down," she said, pushing him into a kitchen chair. She opened a window, letting some of the oppressive heat out. She fished around in the cabinets until she produced a single aspirin and a glass of cabernet. "Cook's cure," she said, fixing him up. "Jim and I will take over the dinner."

He took his aspirin, a sip of the wine, and said, "Great timing, June. Everything is done for now."

"Good. Then, you relax. For now."

Jim was bringing in June's baking, load after load. Four pies, dinner rolls and candied yams.

"So," June whispered to her father, "what have you found out?"

"That he didn't have amnesia and he's

very happy to see everyone."

"That's all? That's it? Come on! I know if Judge and Sam were here they asked him why he left? Why he's been away so long?"

Elmer inclined his head toward the living room. "Suit yourself," he said to his daughter.

She found Morton seated in Elmer's favorite chair, probably the main cause of his sweaty brow and rosy cheeks. Morton was such a tiny man. He seemed even more so now than she remembered. But then she recalled that Myrna and Morton had always been thought a cute couple, both of them so tiny and frail-looking. And, as it turned out, wiry as steel cords.

"Hello, Uncle Morton," she said, sitting down in the chair opposite him. "How are you this morning?"

He put down his paper and smiled at her. He wore his pin-striped suit pants, but over his white shirt and tie he had on a red cardigan. Neat and tidy. His feet barely touched the floor, his legs were so short. She thought maybe he stood about five feet and two inches to Myrna's five feet in her shoes.

"Good morning, dear June," he said, folding the newspaper onto his lap. "How wonderful you look. When Myrna said you were expecting after so long a wait I knew I had to get back here to see you and your father. He's very excited, you know."

"Thank you, Uncle Morton. Now, before Aunt Myrna arrives, do you mind if I ask you a question or two?"

"Not at all, my dear. Not at all."

"First, the obvious, what caused you to leave?"

"Oh, my." He looked upward as if the answer could be encased in the ceiling. "It certainly wasn't any one thing. I had grown unhappy in my work, I suppose you could say. And retirement was looming. Now, there are two ways to face retirement, as I've learned. As an opportunity for a new beginning, or as the end. It all seems very simple now, but I admit, June, at the time I grappled with it."

"You haven't quite answered," she pointed out to him.

"Well, I suspect I was depressed. In the way you medical people diagnose."

"Did you see a doctor?" she asked.

"No. No, no. I simply looked for a new beginning. And Myrna was such a wonderful help in that!"

June was dumbfounded. "Wait a minute. She didn't appear to know where you had gone."

"True. True. It's really not so very complicated. I went on one of my sales trips as
usual, and I wrote her a fan letter, telling
her how much I have always loved her work.
And how it had long been a dream of mine
to be a writer, but I didn't get much encouragement from the people who knew me. I
left a post office box and she wrote me back
immediately, telling me I must reach for my
dream and never allow anyone to dissuade
me. Why," he said, smiling at the memory,
"it was so refreshing. So delightful, that
instead of coming back to Grace Valley as
usual, I simply wrote her another letter. And
another, and another." He leaned toward
her and reached out his old and trembling
hand to touch hers. "Frankly, I thought she
knew it was me. It was months before she
mentioned that her husband had abandoned
her." He clicked his tongue against his teeth.
"She was put out, to say the least."

"Uncle Morton! And you didn't tell her?"

"I guess you know the answer to that," he
said.

"Not very gentlemanly, Uncle Morton."

"Perhaps not. But I don't think she dis-
likes the way things worked out for her.
Those books about the dead husbands —
genius! Can you imagine my thrill at seeing
her on talk shows? And she must take credit

255

for encouraging me in my own writing career, for I couldn't have done it without her!"

"But, Uncle Morton, you could have done it so much better had you just come home to Hudson House and —"

His face, marked by the passage of eighty-six years, melted into an expression of sadness. "But there's the rub," he said softly. "It was Edward Mortimer she mentored. She told Morton Claypool not to be absurd."

June was stunned silent. She knew her aunt very well, and while Myrna would never be deliberately cruel, she did have this no-nonsense side of her that could be terse. Too matter-of-fact.

So that's how it had been. As Morton approached retirement, feeling useless and perhaps used up, maybe a little depressed in the shadows of his famous novelist wife, he'd expressed a desire to start a writing career of his own. Myrna tossed it off as a ridiculous notion and Morton was injured. So he wrote to her and found a whole new woman at the other end of his letters, a woman who didn't find him absurd, but rather talented and exciting.

"How is it we couldn't find a trace of you? Even through the social security rolls?"

"Why, I can't say. Did you have the right number?"

"I thought so," she said with a shrug. "Could we have gotten it wrong?"

"Perhaps so, June. I haven't had a problem getting my checks. They come every month to Edward M. Claypool. Writing is not as lucrative for me as it is Myrna."

"Edward M?" she asked.

"Edward Mortimer Claypool, though I've always gone by Morton."

She stared at him, her mouth parted in consternation. So that was why Myrna didn't know. She finally recovered herself. "I bet you signed that very first letter Edward Mortimer, didn't you?"

He looked down. "Imagine my disappointment . . ." he said softly.

"When Dad and I tried to locate you, we were looking for Morton Claypool. We didn't know any Edward! Did Aunt Myrna even know that was your full given name?"

"Perhaps not, June. We never even had a joint checking account in twenty years. I introduced myself to her that first day as Morton and that's who I was to her. Always."

"Oh, Uncle Morton, you must explain this to Myrna."

"I think she may be a bit too upset with

me to listen just now. If she doesn't send me packing too quickly, I'm sure we'll get to the bottom of it." He smiled suddenly. "I have no hard feelings, after all."

"You might have to give her a little time, Uncle Morton. I can't guarantee you Hudson House, but Grace Valley is your home as long as you want it to be. You have family and friends here, after all."

"That's very kind of you. Quite a few of them have already visited today. Nosy buggers, aren't they?"

"They are," she laughed.

"I haven't attempted to explain to them because, you see, I wouldn't want to bring any embarrassment on Myrna. I saved the explanation for you. And when she's done being furious with me, perhaps we'll talk about it."

June grimaced, remembering the stony silence at dinner last night. "Do be patient," she said. She prayed her aunt Myrna wouldn't stand them up for turkey dinner.

She was not held in suspense for long. Myrna arrived in early afternoon. Though she wore a serious and aloof expression, only June knew that she also wore her very best cranberry chiffon cocktail dress and favorite hat and gloves.

■ ■ ■ ■

The Toopeek household teemed with family. Lincoln and Ursula had had seven children, all of whom were educated through college, had married and had children of their own. They hadn't all returned to Grace Valley for this holiday, but four of them had, making a total of twenty-six people under one roof. The food was unbelievable, the laughter contagious and the chaos of sixteen children enough to bring the roof down.

In the midst of this, Tom crept away to his bedroom and reappeared in his uniform. He asked his wife how much time he had before dinner and she told him it would be hours yet. "But please don't get yourself hung up unnecessarily," she pleaded.

"Of course not," he said, kissing her.

"You're running away from the noise, aren't you?" she accused.

"You're on to me." He laughed, but inside he was filled with the happiness of having three brothers and a sister and their families with him.

Tom and the deputies were on call, but no one was going to keep the police department open unless they had some trouble they couldn't easily diffuse. Tom was optimistic. He felt in his bones that it would be a calm night. His father had said that later that night a peaceful harvest moon would rise.

Tom drove his Range Rover out to Rocky's roadhouse. There were only two pickups outside. Both had gun racks with nothing in them. Inside the bar was dark. Rocky stood behind her counter drying glasses with a dish towel. At one end of the bar sat Cliff Bender, a crusty old woodsman who rarely socialized with anyone. He also rarely drank alcohol, but this was a special occasion. He was probably giving thanks of a sort. On the other side of the room were two men, MacAlvies.

Tom stood before the table. "Vern. Ben," he said.

"Chief," they both intoned, looking up from their mugs.

"How about dinner? You have plans?"

"Yeah, Chief. We planned on drinking dinner," one said. The other laughed.

"George cooked again this year and I'm trying to drum him up some business. I'll drive you over, have a cup of coffee and piece of pie while you eat, then bring you back here. Hardly put a dent in your drinking time."

"What you think, Vern? Interested in food?"

"That George," Vern said. "He can't screw up a turkey too bad."

Tom took that to mean yes and went to make his offer to Cliff. That didn't take too much arm-twisting, either. "Rocky?" he asked.

"No thanks, Tom. I'll just enjoy the quiet."

George had put up a sign in four churches around the valley: Free Thanksgiving Meal. He did this every year. While his mother-in-law tended the turkey at his house, George and his family served a meal to anyone hungry. Not everyone in the café that afternoon was too poor to fix their own meal, but most were. There were men, women and children who were having a hard time keeping life together in the cold of winter. They were rounded up by preachers, social workers, cops, firefighters, shelter operators, neighbors and friends. Tom made it his routine to go to the only bar in the valley and make sure those old boys had a belly full of decent food before they wasted the rest of the day in drink. They had a much better chance of holding their liquor after a solid meal. In fact, they might just get sleepy and go home.

The café was full of people Tom had never

seen in town, never seen before. Sam was having a cup of coffee, so Tom slid onto the bar stool next to him to visit a spell.

"I heard a roar just west of here and someone said there were thirty or so Indians out there, cooking and eating," Sam said.

"Not quite thirty," Tom said with a laugh. "Not everyone could come this year."

"Ah. That's why it was quieter than usual."

"You want to come out? Sample some of my mother's pies?"

"Sorry, Chief. I have plans of my own. I just wanted to stay close in case anyone needs help at the station." He smiled. "And, too, I want to see that grin on old George's face. I think this might be the happiest day of the year for him. Nothing gives that boy a rush like feeding people who need to be fed."

While the MacAlvies and Cliff enjoyed their turkey dinner, Tom took advantage of the time to run by the Craven farm. There was something about holidays and domestic abuse that seemed to go hand in hand. Even though the central abuser in this family was dead and buried, Gus Craven had left a legacy in five young sons.

Tom saw the curl of smoke from the chimney and the soft lights shining from within, though sunset was at least an hour away. When Tom's booted foot hit the first step on his way up to the porch, he heard the crack of an ax. He froze, listening. It came again, and a few long seconds later, again.

He followed the sound around the house to the back. There he spied Frank. It didn't escape him that Frank, the one who most often tried to protect his mother from his father's violence, had a mean streak of his own to contend with. It was obvious as he split log after log, the sweat beading on his forehead despite the chill in the air, that he was trying to work off a temper.

Tom leaned against the house and watched. Maybe this was a technique learned in some of the anger-management sessions the boy was having with Jerry Powell, the local counselor. When you feel it coming on, chop wood. Or was Tom getting this mixed up with his own youth? Lincoln had a lot of wood-splitting set aside for his own boys.

Jeremy Craven, age thirteen, stuck his head out the back door. "Frank? Ma says it's 'bout ready."

"Yeah," he said, putting another log on the stump. That's when he saw Tom leaning against the corner of the house. He stopped with the ax in the air, paused there, then let it fall and split the log. The young man, though still too tall for his frame, was getting some nice shoulders and biceps on him. "What you doing here, Chief?" he asked.

"Just thought I'd stop by," Tom said. But they both knew why he was here. Checking on things. Letting Frank know he was never too far away.

"Why, Tom Toopeek," Leah Craven said, coming out the back door while wiping her hands on a dish towel. "What in heaven's name you doing all the way out here?" Then, without waiting for an answer, she said to her son, "That's gonna be enough wood, son. Thank you."

Enough wood to last till spring, Tom thought.

"You having a nice holiday, Leah?" he asked.

"We sure are, Tom. Awful nice of George's family to take over the café today so that we might have our family holiday together. Will you come in for coffee?"

"Thanks, Leah, but didn't I just hear Jeremy announce dinner?"

"It's close, Tom, but I'd be honored if you'd step into the kitchen while I fix up the last of the trimmings."

"I've got my own dinner waiting. And half

264

the state of California at the table."

"Lincoln was in the café the other day saying you had brothers and sisters coming."

"Three brothers, one sister, all married with children. One day your table will boast even more than that," he said, meeting eyes with Frank. The hard glint was finally working its way out of Frank's eyes. "Can I help you stack up some of that wood, son?" he asked.

"It'll keep," Frank said.

Tom knew better than to ask about his anger-management therapy, but Frank didn't know he knew better, so he waited tensely. Then Tom said, "I couldn't help but notice, Frank. You're getting a pretty impressive set of pecs there. You been working out? Or you get those muscles chopping wood?"

Leah laughed softly. "He's been working out, all right, Tom. He's got his work at the café, does most of the farm chores, and without his split logs, we might freeze to death."

Frank looked away, a slight stain charging his cheeks. But there was also a little lift at the corner of his mouth.

"Take care, now," Tom said, turning to go.

"You, too, Tom. My regards to the Toopeek family."

"Regards," followed a soft male voice.

In homes around the valley, people bent their heads over tables full of food and gave serious thanks. At Chris Forrest's house, with his sons up in wheelchairs at the dining room table, he thanked God for their lives. In a house refurbished and rebuilt by his friends and neighbors, he was a man forever changed. Yet not changed enough. He prayed for strength.

At Leah Craven's house, where the gift of a turkey sat on the first dining room table she had ever had, her children looked on hungrily while she insisted they bow their heads and thank God for their bounty. She silently prayed her sons would be spared the legacy of abuse and that one day they would bring wives and children to her table.

And at Jurea Mull's house two tables sat dressed. Sam had brought a card table and folding chairs to add to the kitchen table Jurea already had. He fished out some old linens that hadn't been used in years and made them a gift to the Mulls. Then he helped Erline cart the little ones and all the gear that went along with them to the Mulls' house next door. Just as they prepared to carve the turkey, there was a knock at the door.

When Jurea opened it, she gasped in wonder and covered her mouth. Charlie MacNeil, one of the counselors at the Veteran's Hospital, stood there with Jurea's husband, Clarence.

"We thought it might be nice if Clarence could have a meal with you and the children," Charlie said.

She embraced her husband lovingly. She had only seen him once a week, and very briefly each time. His action to return the embrace came very slowly, but it came.

"He's a little buzzed," Charlie said, "but he said he feels pretty good today."

"I feel pretty good today," Clarence repeated.

"He's getting better every day," Charlie said.

"I am, Jurea. I am."

"Mr. MacNeil, will you come in to dinner?" she asked.

"I can't, Mrs. Mull. My family's waiting. But I'll come back for Clarence in a few hours, if that's okay."

"You take your sweet time," she said, touching her husband's face and arms and shoulders. "God is so good to us today."

Grace Valley Presbyterian wasn't as full for

the Thanksgiving candlelight service as it was most Sunday mornings. The crowd was modest, in fact, which some would say was a blessing. Jurea Mull and her children stayed at home to have every possible moment with Clarence before Charlie came to pick him up, but Sam helped Erline take the little ones. It was only Erline's third service in the valley, and to be honest she had started going for the free nursery that was provided. If the candlelight service had been her first, it might have been her last.

June, Jim, Elmer, Myrna and Morton attended, because Myrna had said, "Get your coat, Morton, and let's get this over with. Let the town see you're not buried in pieces in my garden. Yet." June and Elmer had exchanged nervous glances until they saw a large grin break onto Morton's face. In that particular tug-of-war the adversaries were equal, as it was just beginning to become obvious.

Tom Toopeek and his brothers John and Carl attended with their parents while the wives stayed at home with the million or so children at the house. Truth to tell, the men were not just good sons, but grown men sick of the commotion and looking for a way out of doing cleanup after the turkey.

John and Susan Stone were there with

their daughter, as was ex-clinic nurse Charlotte Burnham and her husband, Bud. The
Barstows were present, sitting in different
pews, and Birdie and Judge were there, as
was Jessie and her father.

Harry Shipton seemed to be looking at
his toes all night. When he did look up, it
seemed he was on the precipice of some terrible grief. A few of his congregation had
been worrying about him, anyway, and now
his behavior made them think that the family member in trouble had perhaps passed
on. Then came the sermon, and they were
sure.

"On this day of Thanksgiving, let us each
take stock of what the Lord has so generously given us and not only thank Him, but
endeavor to deserve His bounty. It's true
that most of us are not capable of great
works or charitable contributions that will
change the world. There are those among
us who don't even have the wherewithal to
be of much help to one another. If that be
the case, brothers and sisters, then let us
look inward and see what we can do for
ourselves spiritually, to deserve the Lord's
bounty. If there are amends to make, let's
take the opportunity to make them. If there
are bad habits to change, better ways to
adopt, then give thanks that there is another

day to do so. And if there are debts to be paid, let's at least make an accurate list of accounting and thank God there is another day to work, another week, another month. And if there is no work to do, then let us give thanks there is an able body to look for work.

"And if all is lost, pray God gives us the will to carry on. Let us pray," he said, and bowed his head.

"Not much of a sermon," Elmer whispered to June.

"I think Harry's depressed," she returned. "Maybe he has Seasonal Affective Disorder. It's been so cloudy and dour."

"He's from the Bay Area, June. He knows all about clouds."

As the pastor bid everyone good-night, he was asked so many times if he was all right that he found himself apologizing for the sermon. "I had hoped it would be uplifting, but it was just the opposite. I'm going to have to try harder!" He laughed at himself, but there was no humor in his expression at all. It was completely forced.

"Harry, is that family matter getting worse? You got some relative real sick?" Sam asked him.

"I'm afraid so, Sam," Harry said. "I don't know if he's going to make it. Pray for me?"

"You bet your life, Harry," Sam said. "Let me know what else I can do to help, hear?"

"That's all, Sam. Just your prayers and good faith."

THIRTEEN

When the Thanksgiving leftovers were down to the gizzard and a hardened pie crust, Morton said to Elmer, "I suppose I should think about going back to Redding."

"Not without checking with Myrna," Elmer returned, though in truth he was tired of having a roommate.

"I'm not inclined to pressure her into asking me to stay on in Grace Valley," Morton said with a slightly injured air.

"That's not what I was suggesting," Elmer said. "Call her up and say exactly that same thing to her and see how she responds."

Morton did so. He had no expectations whatsoever. With Myrna, it was best that way, for to call her unpredictable was an understatement.

"If you leave, it won't be long before someone is digging up my yard again, looking for you."

"The climate is a trifle . . . cool here."

"Oh, Morton, you've always been so high maintenance," she said, but in fact it was she who was a lot to deal with. "Do you want to stay? I never bothered to divorce you because I assumed you were dead. Since you're not, you might use that second-floor porch in the back for writing. Where you used to take your pipe. But it's up to you, I won't grovel."

"Grovel?" he asked. "You've barely been civil!"

"I have a little pique to work through. If you don't have the patience for it, then you might as well go now."

Morton hadn't even bought a return ticket. He was, if nothing else, an optimist. Elmer drove him out to Hudson House, where he reclaimed that back porch and told Myrna he was having his belongings, modest though they were, shipped from his small apartment.

Then Elmer set about the cleaning of his house, delighted to have it to himself again. He phoned June and told her the reunion had taken place and that never had he known two more peculiar people than his sister and her estranged husband. "They're a sideshow," Elmer said. "And I hope she doesn't give in to temptation and put something in his tea."

■ ■ ■ ■

When June's eyes opened lazily on Monday morning her first thought was that she couldn't remember the last time she'd taken a long weekend off, not to mention a holiday weekend. Those were usually the worst. But she hadn't heard a peep out of John. Either it had been a very quiet weekend or John had gotten assistance elsewhere. Though she had hastened to tell him she was available, he had only to call.

She had to confess she felt better rested than ever before in her life. Not only had she worked just three afternoons last week, but it appeared Jessie had lightened her load even further by reducing her usual number of patients when she was in the clinic. And they seemed to be managing just fine. Without her.

With a sigh, she sat up and dangled her legs off the side of the bed. Well, the time off had done her good. She'd managed to make a number of purchases for the baby, including paint, wallpaper and a chair rail for Jim to use in redecorating the room that was to be the baby's. She'd had time to finish the two novels she set aside months ago. And she was definitely up to speed on her baking and had had some quality time with her family, including evenings and nights with Jim, settling into a very domestic routine.

But enough was enough. It was her town. Her clinic. Her patients.

She went to the kitchen and peeked into the living room to where Jim sat in the easy chair beside the fire, his steaming coffee cup on the table beside him, his newspaper in his lap and one dangling hand dropping over the side to pet that traitor, Sadie, who stayed close to him as though he might get away otherwise. For the millionth time she said to herself, *This can't be happening. This just isn't real.* But it was real. He was real and he was there. He was unconflicted and calm, taking everything in her complicated life, in her complex little town, in stride. He was not intimidated by the rigors of pregnancy nor by her slightly anxious elderly father nor her wacky aunt and uncle.

In all those years she thought she'd lost out on the one chance she had to marry happily and live in Grace Valley because she let Chris get away, little did she know she was saving herself for this, for Jim. Had she known and been offered a clear choice, would she have had the strength and wisdom to do it?

She went to him. When he saw her coming he tossed the newspaper to the floor and made room for her on his lap. She curled up there, her arm around his neck. He growled bearlike, nuzzling her. "I weigh a ton," she said, but not too apologetically.

"A lot of woman," he said. "But not too much for me yet."

"How are you so good?" she asked, marveling.

"It's the company I keep. What are your plans for the day?"

"I'm going to go to work, whether they like it or not. And I'm going to leave you alone so you can paint and paper the baby's room."

He rubbed her belly. "Do I have to do that today?"

"No. Why?"

"I just want to make sure you're not going to come home all pissy if that room isn't ready today."

She frowned. "Do it in your own time, as long as the baby doesn't have to smell paint and paste."

"You got it, sweet cheeks."

When June got to the clinic, everyone remarked on how well she was looking, and they acted surprised to see her. "I thought you were only working a few afternoons a week," Jessie said.

"You must be feeling better than ever. You look fantastic! But we're all caught up here, so you can have the morning if you like," Susan said.

"Now that Morton's not underfoot, I don't have much else to do," Elmer said.

And finally John weighed in with "Shouldn't you find something more relaxing and less taxing to do?"

So it was with great deliberation that June called an office meeting for noon. Maybe they had been right and she'd needed some time off, because she was now her old self again, much in possession of confidence and resolution. They came, as instructed, to her office and stood around her desk, looking down at her. She folded her hands atop her desk, looked up at them — John, Susan, Jessie, Elmer — and said, "You're the best. The absolute best. You were right, I needed a little break, if for no other reason than to get used to the idea I am having a baby and have a partner. Someone I have enjoyed getting to know better. But now you have to listen to me. Now that I know there are ways we can adjust if I need time off for medical or even personal reasons, I'd like you to let me back into the schedule without any more plotting or conspiring to keep me away. Because I'm a little emotional sometimes. And if I think I'm not needed —"

"Oh, no, that's not it!"

"Nothing could be further —"

"It's only a temporary solution!"

"It's just not the same without —"

They all protested at once, but she heard each one. She put up her hands. "I know, I know, your hearts are definitely in the right place. While I can, I'd like to see patients. And I want to share on-call duties with John and maybe help a little before the Stones are at each other's throats again."

To that Susan smiled, and there was no mistaking it — the Stones were once again romantically on track. "Don't you worry, June," she said, and slipped her hand behind John. She slapped a little jump out of him.

"Nevertheless," she said. "Now, go. Get lunch while you can. And Jessie, build a little more equity into our schedule. Aren't you studying for finals?"

"I am, June. No problem there."

"You'd better get A's, that's all I can say."

They started to file out, and June, shaking her head with amusement, bent to the task of writing in a chart. Then she heard her father clear his throat and she looked up. "Dad?"

"It's time for you and I to have a talk, too," he said. "I think I've been very patient."

Though she knew exactly what he wanted, she said, "What is it?"

"Marriage. Has the subject crept into your dialogue with the father of my grandchild?"

"Of course it has, Dad."

"And . . . ?"

"The fact is, we're very comfortable with the way things are."

He frowned. "What idiocy is that talking?" he demanded. She could tell he was trying to keep anger from his tone, but it was sneaking in. There was no confusion. He wanted them married. Period.

"Dad, sit down." He did, but not happily. "I don't want to defy you or hurt you or make you in any way embarrassed. But I'm very independent, and so is Jim. I know my limitations, and since I share the parentage of this baby with Jim, we'll parent together. No problem there. But we're just not ready to make a lifetime commitment. Despite the fact that I'm pregnant, we are really in the early stages of getting to know each other and, well, we're going to enjoy the process. Do you understand?"

He looked at her for a long time over the rims of his glasses. His bushy eyebrows bounced up and down a couple of times and his bald head grew pink. His expression was not one of understanding. "You're just full of crap," he finally said.

The days were getting shorter, entering into December. The rains were steady and the river behind the café was swelling, rising. George and Sam spent a lot of time out back-marking its progress. That could've been one reason there were so many locals taking their meals in the café. Every winter and spring they stood ready lest the Windle overflow. South of them the Russian River flooded almost every year. Flash floods sweeping suddenly over roads and through gulleys without warning took property and lives all over California. This winter the unseasonably warm days far outnumbered the cold. Snow in the mountains melted, began to run down the mountainsides, then froze up again. This condition was bad for flooding.

Frank Craven had his classes down to mornings so he could work every afternoon. It was partly the weather, partly the time of year and partly being tired all the time, but he was morose. He washed dishes, swept floors, hauled trash and was learning to do a little short-order cooking on the side, but he was thinking about that last counseling session he'd had with Jerry Powell. Not his anger-management group, but his one-on-one.

"When you get angry like that, do you talk to a family member? A friend?"

Frank had smiled cruelly at Jerry. "I got no friends, Doc," he said. "You oughta know that."

"How would I know, Frank?"

"Why am I here? Because I get in fights! I get in fights because my dad beat us all up for my whole life and finally my mom killed him. You think there's anyone in Grace Valley wants to hook up with someone like me?"

"I don't know, Frank. Maybe it's not the history so much as the attitude. Maybe you keep people back with all that rage."

Yeah, he was thinking, sweeping up behind the grill and the ovens. People better stay back. 'Cause if they stay back where they belong, they don't get hurt.

The shadows outside were getting long. Most people were home for dinner. Leah waited tables all day, then went home to be there for the younger boys before dark. When the weather was wet and cold, George took Frank home. When it was decent George might let him go early and he rode his bike the five miles.

George didn't keep regular hours at the café. Rather, it served the town in a way. He'd watch to make sure the regulars either had their meal or weren't looking for one. He'd check to see if the lights were off in the clinic, church and police department, then he'd lock up. If there was a town meeting, a big game or a town fair, George would make a bunch of extra pies, put on the coffeepot and open up for business, because he was pretty much the only game in town. Summers he stayed open later. In winter, when people were driven inside by the dark and cold and wet, George went home unless he was needed. Tom and June, and now John Stone, all had keys to the café in case they needed anything, like a big load of ice to tend to emergencies.

There were only two people in the café besides Frank and George, and they were close to leaving. Sam and Harry Shipton had had some dinner, their plates almost empty when George gave them each a second cup of coffee. Frank grabbed the trash from the biggest compactor and dragged it out behind the café in the soggy, wet night. He heard a cat wailing a high-pitched scream. Cats fighting in this weather? Not too bright, he thought. He heard it again, but it sounded more like a woman than a cat, so he looked around, but didn't see anything. The rushing of the swollen river behind the café made it hard to hear anything clearly.

He opened the door to go back inside when he heard it again — children crying and someone yelling — so he let the door fall closed and sprinted down the street, past the church and around the corner. He didn't even think about what he was doing, he was simply compelled to find out who was yelling. His shoes hit each mud puddle with a huge splash that wet his jeans up to his thighs, but as he heard that sound — a sound familiar to him — he ran faster. Two blocks. Three.

There it was. Jurea Mull and her son were yelling and banging on a door they couldn't get open. In front was that old broken-down truck he'd seen at Sam's station. It was him, the guy they all believed had robbed George. He'd come back, and by the sights and sounds, he was making trouble at the house where Sam had put up the wife and kids.

Frank felt his heart hammering in his throat. All the beatings came back to him and he remembered how his daddy, once tanked up, didn't care how small a kid was. His mom had taken the brunt of it all those years, keeping him away from the kids. Frank's legs moved so fast down the street back to the café he could've set a new record. He crashed inside, slamming the door against the wall.

"It's him!" he said to the men within. "That guy that robbed the till! He's back, he's beating on his family, sounds like." Then he grabbed the only thing handy and took off again. He wielded a large umbrella.

Frank could hear the footfalls behind him and knew that the men had come to help. When he got to the house he yelled at Jurea. "Get back! I'll kick it!"

"No!" she screamed. "There're little ones! They might be at the door!"

He hadn't noticed that Clinton wasn't there till he came back with a crowbar. Clinton limped up on the porch of the little house and, without a word, applied the crowbar to the large plywood square that covered the window. Once a few nails were loosened, he grabbed the wood, gave a tug and tore it off the window frame, exposing the occupants inside.

Something happened to Frank. He began drifting in and out of reality. At first he saw Conrad, skinny in his baggy pants and thick-soled shoes, with his young wife up against the opposite wall while the little children huddled in a corner away from them. Then suddenly Frank saw his father beating his mother. The two little girls became five little towheaded boys, shivering in fear, cowering from Gus Craven. But reality shifted again and Frank saw himself beating a woman while the babies cried and clung to one another. He stood frozen. He looked through that open picture window as if it were a movie screen that showed him the past, the present and the future all at once, the images shifting.

While he stood, not knowing quite what he saw, Sam and Clinton crawled through the window and grabbed Conrad, pulling him off his wife. Conrad yelled at them to mind their own business, that she was his wife. Frank had heard that very thing so many times growing up while Tom Toopeek or the deputies dragged old Gus out of the house.

Erline, her face bleeding, ran to her children to comfort them. That, too, was the same. Was there no other script for these beaters and their families? He heard the familiar sound of a siren and realities blended again as he feared they would take away his daddy, then feared they wouldn't, then *knew* in his heart they were coming for him!

He felt a gentle but callused hand on his face and saw it was Jurea wiping tears from his cheeks. "There now, son. It's going to be all right now. You can see she ain't hurt real bad, the babies are okay, and now the police is —"

Frank, in a state of panic, turned away from her and ran.

Ricky pulled up in front of the house and got out of his car. He glanced at the fast-departing Frank Craven, ready to give chase, when Sam yelled from the porch, "Ricky! In here!"

Within the little house he found Clinton, a large boy and plenty able despite being an amputee with a prosthetic leg, sitting on top of the wriggling Conrad while Sam crouched over Erline, trying to assess the damage. Harry was rocking the baby. It took Ricky only a second to replace Clinton with a pair of handcuffs. "What's up with Frank Craven?" Ricky asked.

"Don't know," Clinton said. "Was Frank who brought help. Mama and me, we heard that old truck pull up, then heard Erline scream for help."

"That boy had tears all down his face," Jurea said. "I think what he saw scared him to death."

Ricky jerked Conrad to his feet. What

Frank saw, he's seen too much of, he thought.

"I think we ought to take this young woman to the hospital," Sam said.

"I'll be all right. He didn't hurt me that bad." She looked up at Ricky. Her lip was three times its original size on one side and her nose was bleeding. "It probably looks a lot worse than it is."

Ricky frowned blackly. An abusive marriage had sent his mother, Corsica, first seeking shelter for her and her only son, Ricky, then eventually getting her degree in social work so she could help women in the same straights. There was a reason Ricky was his mother's best deputy and assistant. "Give me one minute to put this guy in the car and we'll take care of Erline."

Grabbing the handcuffs on the chain that held them together, he lifted upward, putting the strain on Conrad's shoulders, and steered him toward the now-opened door. Except Ricky was a little bit off and Conrad's head nearly hit the door frame. Ricky had to pull him hard right to keep him from hitting it.

"Hey! You son of a bitch!" Conrad shouted. "You did that on purpose!"

"If you'd stop squirming around, this would be easier," Ricky said. "Here, let's try that again."

This time he did hit the door frame and Conrad let out a wail.

"Jesus," Ricky said. "I'm all thumbs." He pushed him through the door. "I'm awful sorry, Conrad," he said, steering him out the door successfully. But then poor Conrad, completely of his own accord, didn't see the step and tripped, landing right on his face. He rolled over and glared up at Ricky.

Ricky shrugged. "Hey, accidents happen, pal." Without much concern for gentleness, Ricky got him to his feet again.

Just as Ricky was putting Conrad in the back of his police car, George came down the street, half jogging, half walking. George had a pretty good gut on him and, it was fair to say, was not in nearly the shape seventy-year-old Sam was in.

"Did Frank go back to the café?" Ricky asked him, shoving Conrad in and slamming the door.

"No. I locked up. He's not here?"

"He took off like a scalded dog. Where you think he went?"

"Got me." George shrugged. "I'll look around for him. Maybe call Leah, make sure he's okay. Why you reckon he ran off?" George asked.

"He might've been upset with what he saw — young woman with little children getting beat up. He's got a history with that."

"The poor kid," George said. "You gonna arrest this scum?"

"Oh, yeah. Consider him arrested."

"You like him for the burglary of the café?" George asked as they were going back into the house.

Ricky stopped short. *"Like him?"* he asked. "George, you been watching *NYPD Blue* again?"

His face went a little red. "Bet he did it, though."

"Very likely," Ricky said, but he couldn't help chuckling.

Erline didn't appear to be badly hurt, but you could never tell when there was more to an injury than there appeared to be. Ricky agreed that she should go to the emergency room and be looked over, so Sam was designated to drive her while Jurea watched the children.

"He wanted money," Erline said as she was leaving. "He just wouldn't believe I didn't have any."

"But you let him in," Ricky said.

"I didn't think he'd hurt me," she said.

"He has before, hasn't he?"

"Yes," she admitted.

"What about today was different, then?" he asked her.

She shrugged her shoulders. "I was stupider than usual," she said.

Frank ran, and while he ran there was a movie reel of beatings going on in his head — those he had endured, those he had dished out. The tears streamed down his cheeks as the face of the victim and aggressor changed. He saw himself as the small boy who shrank away from his brutal father. He saw himself at the bus stop, pummeling a kid for saying something that pissed him off. He saw his mother trying futilely to ward off Gus Craven's fists. He saw himself as he slapped his girlfriend across the face.

There was a demon inside of him and it had come from his father.

He ran past the café, down the street, past the police department and turned off Valley Drive. He was running for his life and he was so scared.

A dim light shone deep within the little yellow house where Jerry Powell lived, where he kept his counseling office. There was nothing welcoming about that light. In fact, it looked as if no one was home. A walk led to the side door where he kept his office and saw his clients for counseling, but Frank threw himself against the front door and began hammering. It was a long time before lights started to come on in the house. Finally Jerry opened the door.

"Frank?" he asked.

"God," Frank cried. "I just saw the worst things! You gotta get me out of this!"

Calmly, slowly, Jerry led Frank around the front of the house to the office doors. He tried to keep his personal life and his professional life separate. He didn't mind that clients often came to the door of his residence, but each time he would take them to the office. It was there that he worked. It was one of the ways he managed to keep what he heard at work from giving him nightmares.

They sat down in chairs opposite each other while Frank described hearing the screaming, getting help to free the young woman from her abusive spouse. Then he described the changing shapes and identities as he saw, or imagined he saw, his father and himself. And himself becoming his father.

"Am I losing my mind?" he asked Jerry.

"No, Frank. Finding it."

Jerry and Frank spent a long time talking about his reaction being the turning point he'd been needing. Once Frank saw the total picture of the cycle of abuse and understood it on an emotional level, there was true hope he could overcome it. Frank had been damaged by abuse, and part of the long-term effect was his inbred helplessness to rage.

"And that means I can't control it," he said in a defeated tone.

"No, Frank. It means that, until you understand what makes you vulnerable, you can't control it. But now, knowing what you know, understanding what kind of life you *don't* want anymore, now you have as good a chance as anyone."

Tom joined Ricky at the police department to interrogate Conrad, who was now in custody.

"What brings you back to the valley, Conrad?" Tom asked him.

"My wife," he said.

"She's not your wife," Ricky said.

"Common law," Conrad said. "Them's my kids. At least I think they are." And he grinned meanly.

"So? You come back just to knock her around?"

"Jesus . . ."

"Well? I don't think I get it —"

"Money! The old man gave her money!"

Tom and Ricky looked at each other, then back at Conrad. "Did she give you money before, Conrad?"

"Before what?"

"The last time you came to town?"

"What time? I just came today. All these years I took care of her, gave her whatever money I had, you'd think she could give me a couple a —"

"No, Conrad, the last time you came to town."

"*What* time?" he asked, agitated. "I told you, I just came today! What are you *talking* about?"

"We think you were here before. A couple of weeks ago, maybe."

Conrad's expression changed and a slow smile spread on his mouth. Even though he'd spent years trying to kill off his brain cells, he hadn't succeeded in becoming totally stupid yet. He realized what they were getting at. Something had happened in town, some crime, and they were going to lay it on him. He started to laugh. He laughed till he had to hold his sides.

"Sure am curious about what's so damn funny," Tom said.

"You are! You think you're going to hang something on me and you are just shit outta luck! I been in jail! I been in jail for almost three weeks! At the county!"

FOURTEEN

Harry could see from the parsonage when George arrived at the café. He didn't have a stitch of food in the house, naturally, and he was starving. Being unable to sleep all night made him all that much more aware of his lack of food and his gnawing hunger. He gave George just enough time to get the coffee on.

"Good morning," Harry called into the café. "Am I too early?"

"No! Come on in! I was just making myself some breakfast. Can I throw on a couple of eggs for you?"

"That would be wonderful, George." He leapt up on a stool at the counter. "I could eat a horse. I didn't sleep a wink all night, worrying about Erline."

"I called Sam last night — she's back at home."

"Thank God! But what worries me is that young man, coming back, hurting her again."

George brought Harry a cup of coffee. "I think he's going away for a while. Don't you, Harry?"

Harry shrugged and looked into his coffee. George took a thoughtful sip, then turned back to his bacon and eggs, giving each a flip onto a plate. The toast came up right on schedule, and in what seemed mere seconds, he put a plate in front of the preacher.

"Besides, Harry, I'd bet anything he took what was in my till."

"You think?" Harry asked, looking up.

"Who else?"

"Indeed," Harry said. He buttered his toast. "Maybe it was someone real needy, George."

George just shrugged and got his own breakfast. "It wasn't losing the money that upset me, Harry. It wasn't enough to get upset about. I'd've given just about anyone who asked for it two hundred bucks. Maybe not that Conrad fella, I admit. But then again, if he'd of asked real nice and promised to get some food laid in for the wife and little ones, I'd of probably given it to him. If he'd asked real nice." He messed up his eggs with his fork and dipped his toast into the yolks, taking a big, sloppy bite. "It's just that I'd give almost anyone a loan, a meal, a job. You know? I open the café early, stay late and try to take good care of people. So why they got to go and wreck the damn door? Now it's more than the money, it's the hardware and time and all sorts of things."

The bell on the door tinkled as Leah came in, shaking her slicker outside the door to remove the moisture from it. "Morning, Pastor. Morning, George."

"Leah, how's old Frank doing this morning? He going to be all right?"

"He's fine, George. It shook him up a little, seeing that mean young fella beating on his wife." She stashed her coat and got a cup of coffee. "The truth is, it reminded him of his daddy, and it threw the fear of God in him. Frank has a hard time controlling his temper. It terrifies him to think he can't help but turn out as mean as his daddy was, God rest his soul and forgive me."

Harry smiled a sweet smile and touched Leah's hand. "Leah, when you asked, it was so. And I'll give a little extra time in my prayers for Frank, since you worry about him."

"I have to say, Harry, that most reverends wouldn't be so easy around a woman once tried for murder."

"We're none of us perfect," Harry said.

While he ate his breakfast, a meal he wouldn't offer to pay for and that George wouldn't bill him for, he felt he was at the end of his rope. He didn't know how long he could go on letting the people of this town down like he did. He was dishonest with them and they had no idea. He knew he didn't deserve their respect, but they gave it unflinchingly. Here was a good woman, who had killed only in defense of her own life and her children's, standing before him with shame, when it was he who should be shamed before her.

"You're awful quiet this morning, Harry," George observed. "You still worrying yourself about that family member in trouble?"

Harry stirred his coffee. "I guess I am, George."

"Are you sure there isn't some way I can help out?"

"I'm afraid not." He tried not to say any more, but he was helpless. "It just gets so expensive, running down to San Francisco so often. . . ."

"And you, on a fixed income," George said, reaching into his pocket. He peeled off two twenties. "Things'll turn around for you, Harry. You'll see," he said, slapping the money on the counter.

Despite his best effort to resist, he took it.

Tom Toopeek was the next patron to arrive and the sun still wasn't up on the day. "Morning," he said. "George, I don't think you're going to take this as good news. It wasn't Conrad Davis who robbed the café."

"No?"

Tom shook his head. "Turns out he was in jail in Humboldt County on a possession charge. He couldn't make bail so he served just under a month. They got crowded and let him out early because he'd behaved himself. He was locked up when you got robbed."

George just scratched his head. "Then for the life of me, I can't imagine who'd of done it."

"Don't you have a whole mountaintop full of drug farmers just east of town?" Harry asked.

"True," Tom said. "But it's doubtful any of them would break in and steal money."

"Why's that?" Harry asked.

"They don't exactly need money," Tom said. "They're busy making money illegally, and drawing even more attention to themselves is not what they're looking to do. And there're others back there, too. Mountain people, dropouts, the like. But if they were to break into the café, it would more likely be for food." Tom looked around, as if taking inventory, but no one else was there. "Only regulars know George keeps a couple hundred dollars in the cash drawer at night."

"I hate to think about that," George said. "If it's a regular, then it's a friend."

"Dear God," Harry said.

Nancy Forrest looked out the kitchen window and saw Jim's truck outside the detached garage. And Chris's car was still parked out front. He wasn't going to the office again today. She began to wonder if he even had an office anymore.

As much as everyone in Grace Valley seemed to know everyone's business, there was one thing that no one seemed to know. Chris just didn't work very hard. When he did work, he didn't make much money. He always had an excuse, either he was just getting started or the economy wasn't good or he'd just moved. The reality was that he didn't have many skills, and he did have a few handicaps.

In the years they had lived in San Diego, Nancy had been the primary breadwinner. She'd worked her way up from a secretary to an administrative assistant, working for the senior vice president of a brokerage firm. Her salary and benefits were enviable.

Chris, on the other hand, was an independent insurance agent in a little neighborhood office. He had a few good clients and the occasional new one would stumble in off the street. His schedule was spare, leaving time for things like tennis and golf, and general goofing off. Nancy had never caught him in actual affairs, but she'd caught him in a few flirtations. And he had an endless knack for puttering.

When they had separated some months ago and Chris came back to Grace Valley, he found an independent insurance agent in Rockport who offered him a little space in his office. He very generously gave it to him cheap for the first six months while Chris settled in and built his clientele. But, as usual, the clientele didn't build, the rent went up, Nancy left her job to return to Grace Valley to care for the boys after their accident, and now they were just about out of savings. Still, Chris was out in the garage instead of trying to find work. He was building some kind of table for an old school chum, Greg Silva, while he simultaneously helped Jim fashion a cradle as a surprise for June. If it weren't for that cradle, she would dump all these woes on June, like girlfriends do.

Having this sense of community again

gave Nancy a feeling of optimism, a hope that they might actually belong here once more. But they couldn't do it without income, and Chris didn't seem in any hurry to find a job with benefits. Nancy had wisely taken a leave from her job in San Diego, which kept their benefits intact and gave her something she could go back to, because there wasn't work here for an office administrator.

She hated to think about it, but she'd probably have to go back to San Diego with the boys as soon as they could travel.

This wasn't entirely Chris's fault. He wasn't lazy. He had dyslexia and paperwork was hard for him. And there weren't many things he was trained to do; his education had been spotty at best. He would get easily frustrated, and rather than have a temper over it, he would just drift on to something else and lose interest.

As she looked around the house she was reminded that one of the few things Chris didn't lose interest in was building. Well, that and gardening and sports. He might not be any great shakes as a breadwinner, but he was good around the house. And though he hadn't been real attentive to discipline, while the boys had been laid up with their injuries, Chris had been a good companion to watch football with.

It was just too bad they had to eat.

She poured two cups of steaming coffee, told the boys she was stepping out back for a minute and went to the garage. She knocked on the door with her foot. "It's me," she said.

The air was cloudy with sawdust when she entered. Chris was standing over an eight-foot-long pine table that was sanded down to a satiny finish. Jim hovered over a maple cradle that rocked slightly on its base as he buffed the top.

She handed each a cup of coffee. "Thanks, honey," Chris said hopefully, as if to say "You're not mad anymore?"

"That's really beautiful, Jim," she said. "Are you sure it's your first piece?"

"I never did anything like this until I helped Chris with the house. I think I've caught the bug."

To Chris she said, "You're not going to the office today?"

"Not today. I'm just going to see if I can get the first coat of stain on this table. Don't worry, honey. Greg's going to give me three-fifty in labor."

She smiled a wan smile. He'd spent the better part of a week getting to this point. It didn't take a math whiz to know that, even if he could find constant work in the field of furniture building or house refurbishing, at that rate of pay they'd starve to death.

"I'll try not to spend it all in one place," she said, trying to keep the sarcasm from her voice.

"Nancy, I'm going to be done with this pretty soon, but can I leave it here? To hide it from June until the right moment?"

"Of course, Jim," she said, running a hand over the smooth side. She remembered that she and Chris had been their happiest when they were waiting for the babies to come. They'd been married awhile, had already suffered a miscarriage, and had had some serious ups and downs. But when the twins were about to be born they were filled with hope and optimism and love.

It had been a long time since she'd felt that way.

The rain came down in steady sheets all day. On the coast of northern California there were reports of mud slides and a couple of houses were lost, but in Grace Valley it was just one big soggy valley.

Rainstorms in that part of the world were like sheer-descent waterfalls. The mountains and tall trees kept the winds to a minimum and there was very little cloud-to-ground lightning. An identical weather system on the East Coast or in Texas would blow and billow and crash and boom, making itself felt in a major way. Around Grace Valley the water just kept running out of the sky in a constant flow, quietly soaking the ground and filling up the rivers, ponds and ravines. But just because it was relatively quiet and still, it was no less dangerous. When the groundswell reached critical mass, there could be landslides and floods. Roads could wash out, bridges could collapse and low areas could fill up and trap unsuspecting motorists.

The inclement weather kept the patients in the clinic to a minimum, and during a lull in the action, June and Susan dashed across the street for a coffee break. They found the usual suspects — Elmer, Sam and, of course, Leah and George. Elmer was talking about driving out to Hudson House to check on Myrna and Morton. Hudson House was on high ground, but the grounds were still a disgraceful mess of mud left by the sheriff's department. "I want to make sure neither of them is thinking of driving and that no one is bailing out there."

"You sure you aren't going there to make sure Morton isn't missing again?" George asked.

"Last I heard, they were getting along just fine," Elmer said.

"Call and ask her if she needs anything before you drive all the way over there," June advised him. "When I last talked to her, she said she'd told the Barstows to stay home and stay dry. I don't think anyone is shopping from Myrna's household."

"Good idea," he said.

George was the only one who noticed the car that drove slowly down the street in front of the café, but his staring caused the others to turn. It was a nice car, a fairly new BMW. Inside a woman hunched over the wheel and peered left, then right, then crept along down the road. Leah went to the front window to see where the car went. She turned and reported to the group, "She parked at the church and got out. Anybody know that car?"

"I never saw it before," Sam said. He'd be the most likely to know a car from the valley.

"She's gone into the church. Maybe someone from the Presbyterian office? Up here on church business?"

Silence prevailed while everyone waited.

"She's still in there," Leah said, leaving the window. "She must have some business with Harry."

Conversation slowly went back to the weather, to Myrna and Morton's shaky reunion. George whipped up some hot chocolate for June and Susan. Before long the door to the café opened and the woman from the BMW came in, shaking off her umbrella outside the door. She went to the counter to order a cup of coffee, but she didn't sit.

"If you'd like to find a table or booth, I'll be glad to bring it to you," Leah said.

"Thank you," she said. She found a booth near the front of the café where she could look out the window toward the church. When Leah brought the coffee, the stranger had shrugged out of her coat and fluffed the thick white cowl of her cashmere sweater, which set off the sheen of her coal-black hair.

Leah put down the coffee and added a slice of apple pie. "George says it's so cold, no one's come in to eat his pie. Have a piece so it won't go stale."

"Tell George thank you," she said, smiling, taking the pie.

She was an attractive woman of perhaps thirty-five. She had a scrubbed, wholesome look about her and her clothes were of very fine quality, but not fussy. She took a sip of her coffee, gazing out the window at the rain. She took a bite of the pie and turned to look into the café. She was a little startled to find everyone staring at her. They didn't just look, they stared. June and Susan had actually turned in their chairs. The woman looked at the front of her sweater to see if perhaps she had spilled something on herself.

Elmer cleared his throat and everyone recovered. June laughed softly and said to the woman, "Our apologies! We all belong to the Presbyterian Church and noticed you went there first. That makes you a curiosity."

She smiled at them. "I can understand. I grew up in a small town. I was hoping to find the minister at the church, but he doesn't seem to be in."

"Are you from the church office?" June asked.

"No. Actually . . . Well, Harry and I are friends," she said, and seemed somewhat uncomfortable. "I just wanted to drop in and say . . . hello."

A quiet moment passed while she looked into her coffee cup. Then June got up, crossed the floor with her hot chocolate in hand and, without asking permission, sat across from her in the booth. "Where are you dropping in from?" she asked.

"I'm sorry?" she said, but of course she had heard the question.

"I asked where you're from."

The woman's eyes were dark and very round, lined by heavy black lashes the same color as her hair. Her skin, by contrast, was ivory. She was extraordinarily beautiful. "I drove up from Sebastapol. My name is Brianna Shipton," she said. "I'm Harry's ex-wife."

"Oh!" June said. She stuck her hand over the tabletop. "June Hudson. I'm one of the town's doctors. And that's my nurse, Susan. My father, Elmer, or Doc, if you like. He's another of the town's doctors, mostly retired. And Sam Cussler, owner of the gas station you passed coming into town." As each person was introduced, they stood and came over to Brianna, offering a handshake. "Susan's husband John is another of the town's doctors. It might seem we have an awful lot of them, but it's not true. My dad is trying to retire and I've gone to part-time because of the baby. And, well, that's the clinic over there, which is why we eat here. You've already met Leah, and that's George back there." He waved. "I don't know where Harry is, but it's a safe bet you'll run into him here at mealtimes. As far as I know, he doesn't cook for himself much, especially with the café right next door."

"Harry's very special to us, Mrs. . . . um, is it all right to just call you Brianna?" Susan asked. She squished into the booth beside June.

"Of course. Yes, of course. And despite our divorce, he's special to me, too."

"He's mentioned that you remained good friends. Was he expecting you today or is this a surprise?" June asked.

"Oh, I didn't tell him I was coming," she said. Again she looked into her coffee cup, gripping it with both hands. "I was hoping he'd be here."

"I saw him at both breakfast and lunch," George called from the grill. "I saw that old station wagon of his drive by after lunch. He might be visiting someone from the congregation."

"He's been called to San Francisco a lot lately," Elmer said.

"Seems some family member is having trouble of some kind," Sam informed her. Then, as if he wanted to suck back the words, he said, "I hope I didn't talk out of school, ma'am. You know small towns. We all know too damned much about one another's lives."

"I understand," she said, smiling. "So you think he'll be back this afternoon?"

"Depends on if he went all the way to the Bay Area again," Elmer said. "That's quite a drive."

"So, he has a family member there?" she asked.

"Would that be you, Brianna?" Susan asked. "Sebastapol's close to —"

"No, I haven't seen Harry in a long while. But I've talked to him. And . . . well . . . I've been a little worried about him. Does he seem all right to you?" she asked, looking around at the faces that now surrounded her.

Elmer pulled a chair from one of the tables and sat beside the booth. "Tell the truth, young woman, we've been a mite worried ourselves. Me and Sam here, we play poker with Harry and —" He stopped when he noticed that shock penetrated her eyes, causing them to grow astonished for a second before she could recover herself. "I think you're looking at Harry's closest friends, Brianna, and yes, we've been concerned, too."

"Have you noticed anything odd about him lately?"

"Well, other than the fact that he seems distracted. Sad about something . . ."

"Has he been borrowing money? Because that's why I'm here. He asked me for a loan," she said. "And I'm about the last person Harry would ask for a loan."

"Preachers never did get paid right well," Sam said, hoisting a hip on a nearby table.

"His pay is not the problem," Brianna said. "I don't know how close you all are to Harry, but I don't have many options. The roads aren't good and I have a long way to go. I don't think I should stay till after dark. There have been flash floods south of here. But Harry's in trouble and someone has to do something."

"What is it?" Elmer said.

"Are you sure you don't know? You play poker with him."

"He hardly ever wins," Elmer said with a shrug. "My sister has almost always won, since we set up our table years ago."

"Well, there you go. If you care anything about Harry, don't give him any more loans. Believe me, it does him more harm than good."

They looked at one another, still confounded. "Miss, we don't play much poker around here these days. If we make it regular, it's only once a week, and it's penny ante."

"Poker's not his only game," she said. She slipped her arm into one sleeve. "And I don't know of any family members in the

Bay Area, but there's a track." She slipped her arm into the other sleeve. "I love Harry very much, I always have. There just isn't a more wonderful man alive. But Harry has a problem. Harry gambles . . . and he rarely wins."

You could have heard a pin drop. Everyone was frozen in their places.

"I wasn't sure what I was going to do," she said. "I thought about calling the church office and telling them that it's gotten bad again. They've gone around with Harry on this before. I thought maybe I'd beg him to get help. Now I'm going to go back home. I took the afternoon off to drive up here and I have to get back. I have papers to grade."

She looked as sad as Harry had. Resigned. Angry, too.

"I thought he had trouble balancing his checkbook or managing his charge account," June said. "Gambling never occurred to me."

"Oh, you know. The minute I told you I saw the dawning in all your eyes. You know it's true, you've all been loaning him money. And I'll bet his poker mates see a rather unnatural gleam of excitement in his eyes when the cards are cut." She fished around in her purse for a couple of bills, leaving them on the table. "I just hope you're really his friends and not a bunch of folks from town who are going to rake him over the coals." Tears glistened in her eyes. "He really is the most wonderful, loving, giving man I've ever known. He just thinks one of these days he's going to win big."

She wriggled out of the booth. Elmer had to slide his chair back to let her pass. He stood, as did Sam.

"It was nice meeting you all," she said softly. "Good luck," she said.

No one spoke or even moved for a long spell. They silently watched her leave, pop open her umbrella and dash to her car. She started it up and drove back down Valley Drive the way she had come.

Finally Elmer said, "We never have had the best luck with preachers, have we?"

The former preacher for Grace Valley had been a shameless womanizer. When warnings didn't alter his behavior, women like June and Susan took action to stop him. The old men in town like Elmer, Sam and Judge tended to think him ridiculous in his flirtations and therefore harmless. But women like Susan and June, who suffered his clumsy advances regularly, grew more than a little weary of the disrespect. They stopped him in a very final way — they boycotted the church. Angry, the pastor and his family left.

The townsfolk couldn't believe their good fortune when Harry came to them. With his humor and easy disposition, Harry fit in at once. When weekly poker couldn't be held at Judge Forrest's house because his son and grandsons were visiting, Harry offered the parsonage right away. He laughed and played with them as much as prayed with them. He was easy and fun, and had such a wonderful carelessness about him that it made things always seem less dire, more gamelike. Of course, that was his problem as well as his most endearing trait. But they loved him. How could they not?

When that old station wagon Harry drove came growling into town late that night, the lights were all still on at the café. Inside were a few people — June and Elmer, Sam, Judge and George, of course. Susan had gone home to her family, as had Leah, and it had been discussed that, although Myrna was certainly an integral part of the group, it wouldn't do to bring her out late on a rainy night.

Harry couldn't resist stopping by, he was feeling so good about everything. He'd had a good day, and for once quit while he was ahead. "What's the occasion?" he asked as he burst into the café. He was stopped short by the grave expressions they wore. "What's the matter?"

"Come on in, Harry. Have a cup of coffee," Elmer said.

"You look like you've been waiting for me," he said.

"We were about to give up and go home," June said. She felt like crying. She didn't know how this was going to turn out.

As George was delivering a cup of coffee, he passed by the back door and flipped on the Closed sign.

Harry swallowed.

"Harry, we met Brianna," June said. There was no point beating around the bush.

His eyes registered the gravity of the situation. "Brianna Shipton?" he asked weakly.

Nods all around. "She drove up here to be sure you were all right. She's been worried about you."

"Has she now," he said, sipping coffee.

They held their collective breath. They'd had plenty of time to talk and compare notes. They all had made substantial loans and gifts of money to Harry. They'd added it up. They knew his ex-wife was telling the truth. But what would Harry do? Deny it?

"We've been worried, too," June said. "But you knew that. We all, each one of us, asked

316

what was wrong and how we could help. Now we'd like to ask again. How can we help?"

He quietly sipped his coffee, then put down the cup and stood. He put his hands in his pockets and looked at the floor. "There's nothing you can do," he said solemnly. "It's entirely up to me."

"Something tells me you're not up to this. Alone, at least," Sam said. "Son, life is hard in the best of times. Sometimes we need our friends. Sometimes —"

Harry held up a hand. "I'm sorry to have abused our friendship. I'm sorry to all of you."

"Then it's true, Harry?" Elmer asked. "You have a problem with gambling?"

He shrugged. "Not exactly," he said, his smile wan. "I have a problem with losing." He turned to go.

He was almost to the door when Judge called him back. "Harry, we're all friends here. Don't you want to talk about this?"

He reached the door and looked back at the somber group. "Thanks. I know you mean well. I can't tell you how much I ap-preciate — There isn't anything to talk about. Not tonight, anyway."

With his head down, hands plunged into his pockets, he slowly crossed to the church in the rain. He left the station wagon sitting in the café parking lot.

"I don't like how that was left," June said. "I have a bad feeling."

"Who among us has a good feeling?" Elmer asked.

"Let's wrap it up," Sam said. "Nothing more to be done tonight."

"We should have put this off till morning," Elmer said.

"But, Dad, this isn't about us. It's about Harry. Our only part in his drama is to tell him we know he's in trouble and ask how we can help. What he does with that is up to him. By my way of thinking, if you're a friend, you tell him as soon as you know. You offer your help as soon as you can." She took a breath. "What else could we have done?"

"There's one thing doesn't sit right with me," Sam said. "If Harry'd said 'Yeah, help me,' what would we have offered?"

No one said another word; no one could answer that one. That they'd be willing to do anything wasn't an answer if you didn't have any idea what to do. They turned off the lights and locked up the café.

In the morning the station wagon was gone. When George opened up the café he found that an envelope full of bills had been

318

pushed through the mail slot. There was a list of who was owed what and a very brief note. "I'm sorry I let you all down. You'll be better off. Harry."

FIFTEEN

As word of Harry Shipton's departure spread through Grace Valley, spirits sank in a profound sense of loss. His problems were talked about, but with sympathy, sometimes even empathy. The deacons ran the church, collected the tithe and paid the bills. Members of the congregation took turns reading from scripture, choosing hymns and delivering short sermons. But no one called the presbytery down state. No one wanted a new minister to entrench himself there and thus close off the possibility that Harry, who had apparently lost his way, might find his way home. This was not a decision by consensus, but rather an action arrived at spontaneously.

At morning, noon and evening various patrons of the café would murmur the question, "Has anyone heard from Harry?" Or, "Any pastor sightings?" After the inevitable answer of no they would chat about where he could be and what he might be doing.

There were two people who held secrets. One was June, for she had immediately located and called Brianna Shipton. She hadn't been hard to find in the lovely little town of Sebastapol, just inland of Bodega Bay. June wanted to know if Brianna had heard from Harry, and she admitted she had not. Of course June told Brianna what they had done. "As we were honorbound to do," June said. "Once knowing, we couldn't . . ."

"You couldn't pretend you didn't know," Brianna acknowledged.

"Have you any idea where he might have gone?"

"It would be so easy if Harry had ever hung around a racetrack, but the fact is he favored off-track betting, private and somewhat dangerous high-stakes crap games, and lately, Internet gambling and day trading. He could be holed up somewhere at an Internet coffee bar."

"You don't think — After what we . . . ?"

"That he'd go on a major bender? Oh, June, I can tell you're not an experienced co-dependent or enabler. Frankly, I think that's the most obvious scenario. And maybe the least tragic possibility."

Those were the fearful words June harbored in her secret soul, because a part of her worried that Harry might be despondent enough to take his own life. His note was ominous — "You'll be better off." Perhaps others were likewise concerned, but no one was willing to jinx the situation by speaking the fear out loud. And June didn't tell that she'd contacted Brianna.

The other secret-holder was George, and for George to have a secret meant a monumental force of will. Everything George heard or saw or read about he told. He had the loosest lips in town. But he would never let this slip. In the envelope full of cash, his name was at the top of the list in the amount of two hundred and forty dollars. He recopied the list in his own pen and threw the original in the trash. On top of the discarded list went the coffee grounds and eggshells, obliterating it forever. He remembered peeling off two twenties from his wad of bills in his pocket, but the two hundred could only have come from one place. The till. Harry must have robbed him. It was just too hard to believe. If Harry had robbed him, Harry had been a desperate, driven man with demons George couldn't imagine.

George didn't know the law well, but he suspected that if he told Tom, Tom would be forced to arrest Harry. And things were already bad enough.

But during this time, a pall cast over the valley or not, there seemed to be no stopping the constant drizzle that the occasional cold snap would turn into sleet and ice. There was no way to slow the approach of Christmas. And the heir apparent of the town doctor was showing his heft. June was waddling like a duck, a very pregnant duck.

A group of women met in the basement of the church to assemble Christmas boxes of necessities, ranging from mittens and scarves to canned goods and nonperishables. "I can't even get up to the table," June complained.

"Funny, you *look* like you've been up to the table," Susan teased.

"She looks like she's been knocked up to the table," Nancy said, making them all laugh, and Jurea flush. "Don't complain to me," she added. "You should have seen me fifteen years ago. Twins, remember?"

"Oh, that reminds me," Julianna Dickson said. "I meant to tell everyone. We're pregnant again."

This would be number six for the Dicksons, and all the women gathered squealed and hugged and carried on except June, who sank into a chair and had a strange look on her face. All she could think was, Julianna's babies come so fast! She hadn't made it to the hospital once! It was a miracle John and June even made it to the Dicksons' orchard for the last one.

"June?" Julianna finally asked.

"I thought you were going to stop," she said.

"I thought I was, too." Julianna shrugged. "Oops."

"What's really funny is that Julianna and Mike were in this huge feud," Mary Lou explained to Nancy. "They weren't even speaking."

"We made up." She shrugged again, then her face lit up with a big smile. "I'm thinking of picking another fight with him. He makes up very well."

Hoots and catcalls followed from everyone except Jurea, who hid her grin behind her hand. It sounded not at all like one would think a bunch of churchwomen would sound. Then all eyes fell on Susan, whose delicate skin was charged with a red blush. "John and I were fighting, too. It was the same feud," she explained. "One night at cards the men were talking about working women. John said he didn't want me to have to work. At one point he said he just wanted me to be able to relax at home — with all the cooking and cleaning, et cetera." There was a chorus of moans.

"And Mike said he was glad I didn't want to work," Julianna added. "I wonder what he thought I was doing with five kids!" Another chorus of moans.

"I guess that blush means that John really knows how to make up, too," someone remarked.

"Well, if you want the truth, I'm a little late." The rush of excitement shifted to Susan, but she tried to hold them back. "Don't! I'm trying not to get my hopes up! We quit trying a long time ago because . . . I wouldn't be surprised if this is just another false alarm."

"Heavens, is there something in the water around here?" Nancy asked.

"You haven't heard about the high fertility rate of Grace Valley?"

"I want to know more about the fight. What made you decide to make up with your husbands?" Nancy asked.

They looked at one another. "Groveling," they said in unison.

A great deal of good-natured poking at the male of the species followed, along with laughter that had June holding on to her stomach and gritting her teeth. She ran to the bathroom twice, which sent the women into howls of laughter.

Nancy and June shared an umbrella on the way to their cars. When they stopped at Nancy's car, she turned to June and hugged her. "Thank you for letting me in on that crowd. I needed to laugh."

"You better look out," June warned. "Half of us seem to be pregnant."

"I wouldn't worry about that," she said, a sadness creeping into her eyes.

"Things will get back to normal," June promised. "Don't you have at least one boy up on crutches?"

"That's not the problem, June. It's Chris and me. We've been at odds for years. I had hoped coming back here would help, but I don't think this has turned out to be the answer. For me, anyway."

"Nancy, there must be something you can do to get back on track. You should see someone."

There was no money for that. There was no money for anything. So Nancy forced a smile, gave June's hand a squeeze and said, "It'll work out. Don't worry."

"Nancy," June said, grabbing her hand. "What's the problem. Enough skittering away from me. We're friends, right?"

"It's a little embarrassing, June."

"You don't have to be embarrassed."

"It's money. In San Diego I was the major

breadwinner. I had a great job with great benefits. I had to take a leave of absence to come up here. And as much as I'd like to stay here, with my new old friends . . ."

"What about Chris and his insurance business?"

"He's all but given it up," she said. "He never did much with it, anyway."

"What *is* he doing?" June asked.

"Well," Nancy said, crossing her arms over her chest. "Now that the house is pretty much finished, and nicely at that, he's in the garage building things. Building things to sell."

"And . . . ?"

"I wouldn't call us Forrest Furniture, Inc., just yet. I think he sold a table."

"Oh, boy."

"It was a nice table," she said meekly.

The Graceful Quilters were in full holiday swing, not limiting their works to only quilts, but also tree skirts, place mats, basket liners, table runners, wall hangings and everything Yule. Time was bearing down. The quilters now met at Birdie's, now twice a week, trying to catch up.

"I want us to make something special for Jurea Mull this year," June said. "If I could, I'd wrap that woman in solid gold."

"Why is that, June?"

"I just helped Susan and some of the other women from church put together boxes for Christmas, and who was there, working? Adding her own knitting and canned goods to the mix? Jurea! She should be getting a box, but she is oblivious to that fact. Instead she's worried about who might be hungry!"

"She looks after the little ones next door, as well," Corsica said. "That young woman has nothing to cook with, so Jurea makes sure she has hot meals as often as possible. Sam had a stroke of genius when he put her in that house."

"Have you looked in on her lately?" June asked.

"I haven't personally, but I have angels who keep me posted. Sam and Ricky both look in on her and make sure they are safe and warm there."

"We have to do something about toys. Do you imagine those children have ever had toys?"

"The volunteer firefighters have been told there is a need there. They're doing rebuilt toys again this year," Birdie said. "Now, toys remind me of babies, babies reminds me of pregnancy, which reminds me that my god-daughter is not yet married."

June looked up. "That was subtle, Birdie."

"Wasn't it? I had a dream last night, dear. And in it your mother was slapping me senseless for letting you get away with this for so long."

"How far along are you now, June? Seven months? Eight?" Philana asked, possibly to divert the conversation.

"Right," June said. "Seven or eight, no one's sure. Especially me."

"Jim seems a wonderful man," Birdie said. "I wouldn't say this in front of Nancy, but since you didn't marry my son, I think you did just fine with this Jim. What kind of man helps a virtual stranger rebuild his house?"

"There were a lot of neighbors in on that, but you're right, Birdie. He's good catch."

"And you plan to catch him . . . when?"

"My father doesn't hound me this much, and do you know why?"

"Because Elmer is a coward?"

"Because he knows of this stubborn streak I have, since I probably inherited it from him. And he knows that the more he hounds me to get married, the longer I'm likely to put it off."

"Coward," Birdie muttered, stitching.

"If you don't mind my asking . . ." Ursula began, letting the question trail.

"It's not very complicated," June said. "Neither Jim nor I have ever been married, we're both dangerously close to our forties and we think taking time to get to know each other better, to settle into the idea of a lifetime commitment, is prudent now. We're a little set in our ways."

"And so? This taking of time?" Philana couldn't help herself.

"It only means that if we don't soon discover some enormous incompatibility, we'll probably get married. But there's no hurry. This baby will not be without parents. Loving parents, I might add."

There was quiet for a moment before Birdie said, unhappily, "Hardly the point."

On they stitched, the subject temporarily dropped. But only temporarily. Birdie chirped about June's best interests several more times while they quilted.

Myrna put a CD of soft music on the stereo while Morton, as she had returned to calling him, put a log on the fire. Then they sat on separate divans with their reading lights above them and read their exchanged manuscript pages, those that had been written that day.

This was the new routine, which had been blended from the old. Myrna got up in the morning and had her muffin and tea while Morton had his coffee and bagel. She went into her den to research, read and write while Morton went upstairs to the room that had been his twenty years before. His writing was being done on a yellow pad because his computer had not yet arrived, but his handwriting was impeccable and Myrna almost hated to see it converted to type. One of the Barstows came to the house to clean — the word should be used loosely — and prepare lunch.

It was lunch that reunited them. They would chat about their morning of work while eating a very small meal of soup, then back to their corners they went.

Myrna had never liked five o'clock so well, for that was when she would meet Morton in the sitting room for martinis and crackers. They often entertained a guest or two — Elmer might drop in, or her dear friend and attorney, John Cutler.

A new part of the routine was that Morton cooked dinner. His meals tended to be a little more bland than Myrna liked, but they were perfectly nutritious. He claimed a sensitive palate, saying he was not up to the fancy and often experimental meals that Myrna and the Barstows concocted. He was a genius with a chicken breast or salmon fillet, though. And he was as tidy as could be, doing all the cleanup afterward.

Then they would retire to the parlor, fuel the fire and have their reading. With poker suspended indefinitely, Myrna would be bored to tears if not for this little domestic routine she had with Morton.

"Morton?" she said.

"Yes, my dear?"

"Have I mentioned how delighted I am that you've returned to Grace Valley?"

"I believe you have. And have I said how pleased I am to be back?"

"I think you've mentioned that. But Morton, I have a serious question, if you don't mind."

"Not at all, dear."

"You've been reading my pages on a nightly basis, and you've given me some good suggestions here and there, but do you find that, now that I'm experiencing this contentedness, I've lost my edge?"

"Not at all, dear. In fact, I was just looking over this chapter and marveling at the perfectly wicked dismemberment you've performed on this philandering husband. Why, it makes me want to sleep with one eye open!"

She smiled happily. "Thank you, Morton. I don't think anyone has ever quite appreciated my darker talents with the enthusiasm you have."

"It's my pleasure, my dear."

June was in the clinic with a slate of patients to see. Just before beginning she made a quick call to Nancy. It was one of the most welcome new customs of her new world — a close girlfriend with whom she shared daily news, inevitable woes, gossip and everything in between. They were two women of the same age, with histories they knew, each mothers, though at vastly different stages. There were so many issues to which they related. They talked every day, often more than once.

"What's on for today?" Nancy asked her.

"It looks like a possible flu, two sore throats, one back strain, an infected toe . . . ew, I hate those . . . baby with croup, and . . . oh-oh, teenager with swollen glands, lethargy, low-grade fever —"

"Mono," Nancy diagnosed.

"You're getting good at this. Damn, I miss the prenatals. John and Susan do all the prenatals now. He was OB-GYN before a second residency in family medicine. What are you up to?"

"Rockport," Nancy said. "I need groceries. And now that the boys are getting around better and have somehow managed to mysteriously grow in spite of broken bones and bedrest, I'm in search of sweats and comfortable clothing for them to wear. Plus, I want to stop by Chris's old office and see if any paperwork has miraculously appeared on his desk."

"How are things in that, you know, department?" June bravely inquired.

There was a pause. "Here's something you and I have to get used to, June, old buddy," Nancy said, a very slight catch in her voice. "There isn't that much more time to dicker with this situation. I can make it through Christmas. I might be able to make it till your baby comes — it's a goal of mine. But before too much longer, I'll have to go back to San Diego and earn a living."

This wasn't news to June, but it still made her wince in discomfort. She said, "But I just got you!"

"Funny, isn't it?" Nancy laughed hollowly. "Rivals if not enemies all through school, despising each other long distance for twenty years, and practically best friends in our middle age."

"Practically?" she returned.

"I didn't want to presume."

Presume, *presume!* she thought. "Middle age?" she asked.

"Well, much as we hate the image that brings." Nancy laughed. "What if I said *almost* middle age?"

"That might be a little easier to swallow."

"All right, then. You have patients and I have shopping. We'll catch up later."

June sat awhile at her desk and thought about Nancy trying to hold it together economically long enough to be in Grace Valley for the baby's arrival. It suddenly meant as much to June as her father being there, as much as seeing Aunt Myrna holding the baby.

June had money. She hadn't been spending her modest income on Caribbean cruises or Vegas vacations. She'd barely been able to get a weekend off since coming home to Grace Valley! She'd been putting a little aside for a rainy day. And there was Jim, pulling in his retirement income. But Nancy was proud. She'd never accept charity.

Judge and Birdie likewise had a little money, and Judge would get a pension from the bench. June was sure they'd want to help keep their only son, his wife and their kids in Grace Valley, especially now that they were getting older, closer to Judge's retirement. But June was also sure that Nancy wouldn't allow it even if Chris would.

She rang up her dad and asked him if he'd take part of the morning for her.

"You feeling all right?" he asked.

"Great. I want to run out to the Forrest house and take a look at the boys. Nancy says they're getting around better. But only if you don't have plans already. . . ."

"It's so wet, I think even the fish have drowned by now," he said. "I'll be over there in half an hour."

It was a day June thought she'd never see. She was about to go out to the Forrest house, make that *sneak* out to the Forrest house, and talk to Chris behind Nancy's back. How far they'd all traveled to get to this point! A year ago if his name was mentioned, all she felt was that slow burn creep over her, residual anger that he'd jilted her while she was away in her first year of college and run off with her arch rival and nemesis. Now all that mattered to her was that they find a way to stay in Grace Valley, because friendship was so dear.

The car was not in the drive at the Forrest house, so Nancy must have gone to her shopping. June parked up close and knocked at the door. It was a long time before the door was opened by one of the twins. "Brad?" she asked.

"Brent," he said, teetering on crutches.

"Wow!" she exclaimed. "You're doing awesome. How long have you been on crutches?"

"Couple of weeks now," he said, and smiled.

"Your mom said you'd graduated to the wheelchairs, but —"

"Okay, well, you don't have to say anything. We're only supposed to use 'em with the physical therapist."

She frowned, but a slight smile crept through. At least they were giving it all they had. All of this was a major change from the hellions that had first come to town. As her grin broke through, so did his. "You know why you're not supposed to do this without him, right? Because a fall now could be devastating."

"I'm good," he said. "I'm really careful, too."

"Your mom isn't home?"

"Grocery shopping. Dad's out in the garage, building."

"I'm sorry I missed her. I talked to her this morning and she said she was going into Rockport to shop. I thought if I hurried out here, I might catch her. Go along." This was probably an unnecessary lie, but just on the off chance Nancy said, *June? What was June doing here?* she wanted to head her off. "I'll say hi to your dad, since I drove this far. But first, I'm going to make sure you get back to your room safely."

Brent looked at her huge belly doubtfully. "No offense, but if I start to fall, what are you going to do about it?"

"Maybe I'll get under you real fast so you have a big fat mattress to bounce on. Huh? Let's just go. I'm stronger and more agile than I look."

That done, June left the house. She stood on the porch and listened to the whistling hum of a power tool — saw or sander or the like — coming from the detached garage. She set off across the yard, her boots sinking through the matted grass into the soft earth. They'd gone through three years of near drought conditions with fear of forest fires, only to have the situation remedied with more winter rain than they'd had in ten years.

She knocked the mud off her boots as she rapped on the garage door. The tool stopped. "Who is it?" Chris asked.

"It's me. June. Got a minute?"

"Hang on a sec, okay?"

She heard him rummaging around in there, moving things. "It's pretty wet out here, okay?" she called.

"Hang on a sec. Gotta . . . ah . . . move some stuff to let you in."

More scrapping and moving and rustling.

Finally one of the large double doors opened to a fantastic workshop. June hadn't been in the garage before, but she could tell it had been renovated. Transformed. The floorboards under the dust from sawing and sanding were new and polished. The shelves and cupboards were recently built, and tools hung from newly installed Peg-Board. The faint hum of a dehumidifier could be heard now that the power tools were turned off.

Chris led her to a chair completely covered by a tarp. "Here," he said. "You're kind of wet. Nancy's old rocker is under this tarp. I fixed it, but I don't want you to get water on it or I'll have to sand it down and refinish it."

"You have a lot of stuff in here," she said, taking it all in.

"A lot of it's borrowed. Hal Wassich fixed me up with the circular saw and table, John Reynolds loaned me the dehumidifier from one of his furniture stores that closed down and Lincoln Toopeek insisted I borrow some of his fine-finishing tools. Dad bought the sander so we could finish the cupboards in the house. I got a shop vac from Sam — he says he's been meaning to clean up the station, but he just never gets around to it. And I had Nancy ship some of my things from San Diego when I first bought the house."

June's eyes fell on a pair of cherry-wood chairs with three legs and V-shaped backs. Very sleek and dark and artistic. "Chris," she said, surprised. "Those are gorgeous!"

"Yeah. Thanks. Sarah Kelleher said there's a gallery in San Francisco that'll take 'em. I'd rather build furniture that's useful than artsy stuff, but you do what comes to you, you know? So, I'm working on a sideboard that's going to have some leaded glass on the top. Sarah's going to do the glass and bring it over. She says it's okay to pay her for it when the sideboard is sold. I've already had one offer."

He indicated a piece of furniture, six feet long with cupboards and drawers, the front carved in a beautiful design.

"The glass will provide a five-inch ledge around the top. Sarah does leaded designs and stained glass. It was her idea. She saw my chairs and said she'd love to work with someone that could put her glass on wood pieces."

June could hardly close her mouth. She was silent and rocked slowly.

"It is beautiful, isn't it?" he said.

"Chris, how long have you been doing this?"

"Like this? I just started. But I've always been good at fixing things. And I built a couple of pieces over the years. You could count on me for the best shelves in the neighborhood. The best garage cabinets. I built the boys their first bunk beds and chests. But that was all weekend stuff. Lately, I've been doing this all the time."

"Can you support a family like this?"

He laughed, but without much humor. "In about ten years, I think."

"What about your insurance business? Can't you keep it up and do this part-time?"

"I should," he said, and she saw the light go out of his eyes. "I should, that would make sense. But I just can't anymore. It's like I feel right about what I'm doing for the first time in my life."

"But Chris —"

"You can't imagine what that's like, June. You always knew what you wanted to be, where you wanted to be it. You never struggled. . . ."

"That's not true! I had no idea I wanted to be a doctor!"

"No, you were going to be your dad's nurse. And then in the first quarter of college you said, What the hell, I'll go all the way and be a doctor. And it worked." He paused. "Nothing ever worked for me. I could hardly pass in school, what with being dyslexic. Even when I thought I was getting all the answers right, the test would come back with an F on it. You can't imagine the frustration."

"But you said you finally got help for it!"

"June, it doesn't go away. You learn how to deal with it, but it doesn't go away. It remains a struggle. Sales was the only thing I could ever get away with because I like everyone. So I sold a little insurance here and there, but the paperwork killed me. And I'd lose interest all the time, get distracted, find myself taking an afternoon off for golf, go home early. . . ."

Chris leaned his hip against the worktable that held his circular saw and June sat in the tarp-covered rocker, slowly creaking back and forth. Neither spoke. She looked around the workshop and admired the fine finishing touches inside this old garage.

"Jim helped me with a lot of this," he said. "In the house. Out here."

"I didn't know he could do this sort of thing," she admitted.

"He can't." Chris laughed. "I mean, he *couldn't*. At least from scratch, on his own. But when I told him what to do, he did it *perfectly*. I think he likes woodworking. Carpentry."

"Yeah?"

"Yeah."

They fell quiet again for a few moments, he thinking, she rocking.

"I feel right now," he finally said, "like I'm in the right spot. Sam says I need to take his spot on the fire truck. Tom says he can hook me up with search-and-rescue training so I can volunteer at that, too. The boys, they're real anxious to get back to school here. They don't want to go back to the city. My folks, they don't want us to go." Then he grinned. "I've got good insurance!"

June did not grin. "Nancy's my friend now," she said. "I know this is none of my business, but . . . she's worried about money."

"I know she is," he said, hanging his head. "I've never been as good as her in that area."

"Chris, this is beautiful stuff, but you have to find a way to pay the grocer."

He looked up and gave her a half smile. "She's gonna be good and pissed when she finds out you stuck your nose in this."

"Don't tell her, then," she said, feeling instantly guilty and horrible. "If it comes up, tell her I stopped by and said hi, but don't . . ." She trailed off. "I can't believe it myself, but we're friends. Close friends. We laugh till we pee — I pee faster of course.

We complain about our men —"

"She complains more, of course."

"She's had hers longer," June said, shrugging. "She wants to stay for my baby. I want her to. She says you're running out of money."

"Sort of," he admitted.

"Sort of? What the hell does that mean?"

"There's a little left. Retirement from that investment firm she worked for — we haven't touched that. We still have the house, not that much of a house, but you don't need much in San Diego to make a couple of bucks. She took a leave, you know. So she can go back. It's more than money, June. It's a little tough for Nancy to give up that big paycheck, that 401K, those stocks. She can't get used to the idea that it just doesn't cost as much to live here. I bought the house for nickels, used my personal retirement savings — IRAs — to fix it up. There's still time to sell the San Diego house, pay back the IRAs and start over. But," he said gravely, "there's no country club. Nancy's boss gave her a complimentary club membership, mainly so she could arrange functions for him and the company, but still . . ."

"But she said she likes it here! She wants to stay but feels she can't! Oh jeez, I'm so damned confused."

"Maybe she ought to sell the insurance while I build the furniture, volunteer at the high school in the wood shop and on sports teams, get into the search-and-rescue and volunteer fire department . . ."

June stood up. "I'm just stupid. I shouldn't have gotten into this. This is between you and Nancy. I hate it when people get into my business, tell me where to meet men, when to get married. . . ." She rubbed her forehead wearily, then looked at Chris, who still lounged back against the table. "Don't tell her I brought this up, okay? And talk to her about it. Work it out so you can stay here, raise your boys here. Because I love her like a sister. And I find you . . . tolerable."

"Tolerable?" he asked with a sharp laugh.

"Barely."

"You know, I've been wanting to tell you . . . Now don't get all offended and huffy. But I wanted to tell you, you're gorgeous pregnant. Have you noticed how nice and full your face is?"

"Oh, jeez!"

"No, really! You look good . . . thick like that."

"I'm going to have to kill you!"

He smiled lazily. "That was a tolerable

good compliment, I think."

She shook her finger at him. "Work this out, Chris. I mean it!"

Sixteen

Rain turned to snow and back to rain. The long tradition in the valley was to hope for a white Christmas, which they had about once every twenty years. "White Christmas? Oh, I thought you said *wet*," was the standing joke. Despite everything, lights went up on the clinic, café, police department, church and The Flower Shoppe.

Sam probably should have learned his lesson by now, but he had another idea. He tried to repress it, but it wouldn't go away. His late wife, Justine, had operated the flower shop and it seemed such a shame to have it sit idle, especially during a holiday season. Justine's father, Standard, owned the huge flower fields and greenhouses west of town. He shipped to flower shops all over the country. He was the father of five daughters, Justine having been the youngest, and he saw the shop as some kind of security for them. Work and independence, should they be so inclined. But each of the daughters married and went her own way, leaving only Justine to run the shop.

Sam and Standard shared a few common traits, or perhaps what they shared was the absence of a few traits. They weren't young, they weren't all that sentimental and they didn't have much use for waste.

Sam went out to Standard's flower fields and found him in one of the greenhouses, up to his elbows in peat moss. He hovered over his special orchids, snipping, clipping and misting. The greenhouse was kept as warm as the tropics and two of his employees, Garcia and Ramirez, had their own chores nearby.

"I put lights up on the shop," Sam said to Stan.

"Justine woulda liked that," he replied, without taking his eyes off his work.

"I hate seeing it sit idle."

"Don't we all."

"There're a couple of women in town. Neither one the artist Justine was, that's sure. But they're poor, honest, in need of work, and if I'm not mistaken, sharp enough to learn."

Standard's attention was snagged. "Learn *what?*" he asked suspiciously, looking up.

"A little flower arranging, maybe?" Sam

suggested.

"You gonna teach 'em?" But he hadn't even asked who they were. He was more curious of the plan than anything, which made Sam smile.

"I thought maybe your girls could help out. Just enough to get that store open again. And maybe that would help out all around. There're people who need arrangements for the holidays. There's you with that shop sitting empty like that. And then there're those women in need of work. . . ."

"My girls don't even live around here," Standard pointed out.

"I know. But they aren't that far away, either. Besides which, there's four of 'em, Standard. Can't we snag the attention of one or two to pay a visit? Teach 'em a little something about the flowers?"

"You think that's all it would take? A few days of teaching?"

Sam shrugged. "Probably not. But it wouldn't take all that long to see if there was any hope it'd kick in. One of the women is Jurea Mull. If you think about it, it's pretty amazing what she's been able to do without resources, having been back in the woods all these years. Why, she's barely learned to operate an oven and she managed a Thanksgiving dinner, turkey and all!"

349

"Well, I don't . . ."

"Señor Roberts?" Ramirez interrupted. "Beg pardon, *señor,* but there are many from these gardens who have skills in the arrangement of the flowers. Señora Ramirez is very good, too, and now the children are grown it is easier for her to take such time. It would be good to sell the flowers in town again, I think."

Standard looked at Ramirez over his shoulder. He lifted a bushy salt-and-pepper brow and frowned.

"We know Señora Mull from the church, *señor.* She's the woman with the —" His hand brushed down one side of his face.

"I know who she is!" Standard snapped.

Sam put his hands in his pockets and smiled. Standard had been through a lot, sure, but his disposition had always been that of a grump. Few knew what Sam knew, that deep down was the soft heart of a man who'd lived in a house full of women most of his adult life.

"Seems like there'd be a lot of people around who could show Jurea and Erline what to do with the flowers. Mrs. Ramirez is a good idea. There's always Sarah Kelleher. Ever thought of her?"

"She's not a florist! She's an artist! Statues and the like."

"Aw, I bet that's a talent that cross-pollinates," Sam suggested. "I could go talk to her. See if she shows an interest."

Standard threw down his clippers and yanked off his gloves. "You know what we ought to have done long ago, Sam? We ought to have gotten you steady work so you could stay out of people's business."

But he'd had a passably pleasant look on his face as he said it. And Sam decided to go ahead and turn the heat on in the shop.

Nancy Forrest had just finished getting the boys their lunch and was cleaning up the kitchen when she happened to notice a truck pull up to the garage. A closer look out the window revealed it to be Sarah Kelleher wearing heavy work gloves and carrying long, covered strips of something into the garage. But Chris wasn't there; he'd gone to run some errands and hadn't mentioned that Sarah would be by.

Nancy threw a jacket over her shoulders, pulled her rubber boots over her shoes and dashed out the back door, sloshing carefully across the wet and mucky yard.

"Sarah?" she called as she got closer.

"In here," the woman called back.

Nancy went into the garage and found the older woman opening up the soft blankets that covered what she'd been hauling to expose the most beautiful leaded-crystal designs she'd ever seen. Nancy's pace slowed as she approached this art almost reverently. "Oh, my goodness," she whispered. "Sarah, that's incredible. I didn't know you were working in glass."

"I've been trying some things out the last couple of years, but nothing really gelled until I saw some of Chris's work. Did he tell you about our project?"

Nancy frowned. She really didn't want to hear about it. But out of politeness she asked, "No, what's that?"

"He's building a buffet and this glass will serve to edge the top. It's going to be magnificent."

Nancy gently touched the intricate glasswork with tender fingers, but inside she was so disappointed she could cry. He just kept going further and further with this building nonsense. As if it wasn't bad enough they were running out of money because he wasn't going to work, now he was spending more and more on his supplies.

"I'm glad you're home," Sarah said. "I made some cookies for the boys."

"How sweet," Nancy said. "Come in and have a cup of coffee."

"Just a very quick one, I have so much to

do." She then looked around the workroom as she peeled back her heavy gloves. "The cradle is finished now?"

"Seems so," Nancy said.

"And the dining table? Gone?"

"Yes, last week Chris said."

"The gallery owner who took his chairs is very excited. I realize he'll take a large percentage in the sale, but it's still going to impress you. Wait and see," Sarah said.

Nancy couldn't keep the disappointed grimace from her features. "Sarah, I don't mean any disrespect. I understand that you're a very well-established artist. But Chris isn't, and we could use a little grocery money from real work instead of all this tinkering."

Remarkably, Sarah smiled. She was a roundish woman, stunningly beautiful in a way that was both nurturing and sensual. She shook her head at Nancy. "My dear," she said patiently. "You call this *tinkering?*" She touched the top of the piece that would become the finished buffet as if giving it her seal of approval. "Let's have that coffee."

Sarah wasn't able to tell Nancy anything she didn't already know. Yes, Chris seemed to have a talent for woodworking, building, refurbishing and, if you stretched it a bit, artistic design. Yes, it was a business difficult to become known in and even more difficult to make a good living with. Yes, it seemed to make him happy and it seemed to Sarah that he had a better chance at success than many. And sure, a nice 401K or pension was handy, but one of the things Sarah liked best about the culture of Grace Valley was that most people loved their work and planned to do it till they dropped.

"You never hear George talk about how anxious he is to close down the café, or even give it to one of his kids," Sarah said. "Doc . . . I mean to say, Elmer Hudson, still sees patients, he just gets a little more fishing in than he used to now that John's here. Myrna writes, Hal Wassich is up at dawn every day to work his farm, and my Daniel and his sister have no desire to shut down their stable any more than I plan to stop painting and sculpting."

"I agree that work is a virtue," Nancy said. And I wish Chris would do some, she kept herself from saying.

"People around here seem to take more stock in making a difference than making a dollar," Sarah said.

But at the end of the day, Nancy liked things like a cushy balance in the checkbook, a savings account that reached out at least several months ahead of some unfortunate unemployment, and forget working till you dropped, she liked pensions!

That evening after dinner, when the boys were made comfortable in their beds, traction finally a thing of the past, she put that jacket back on, slipped into the rubber boots once again and took two cups of coffee out to the garage where Chris was back at work. He took a cup, thanked her with a peck on the cheek and went back to the slow rhythmic buffing of hardwood.

Nancy perched on a stool and watched. She'd meant to come out to talk, but instead she held her tongue for once and just thought. Chris had always been a dreamer. It was one of the things she'd loved about him since she was a girl. He was athletic, artistic, easygoing to a fault and frivolous.

As he buffed a beautiful shine into the wood she realized that she hadn't seen his face as relaxed as it was right now. If he spent evenings looking over work from the insurance office, he often grimaced.

"Johnny Toopeek called today," Nancy said. "He wanted to know if the twins were well enough for visitors. Kids from school want to come out over Christmas vacation to visit them."

"Really? That's great!"

"They seem anxious to get back to school.

I think a lot has changed for them because of that accident," she said.

"I know it has. For me, too."

"You know, it occurs to me that you came back here for all the wrong reasons, and not all good came of it, but in the end it seems to be the best place for you and the boys. They were up to their necks in trouble in San Diego," she said.

"They were here, too, for a while. The boys and I have a lot to atone for. But the good news is, there are lots of ways to do it that won't hurt a bit. Did I tell you that in the spring I'm going to train for the volunteer search-and-rescue team?"

"I think you might have mentioned something about that. And volunteer fire department, too?"

"Only if I can manage both. I don't want to overcommit. When the boys are fully upright, I'm sure they'll have school things —"

"Football is out, Chris," she said with finality. They had suffered multiple fractures and didn't have a spleen between them.

"Boy, no kidding," he said with a laugh, surprising her. "Even though it never occurred to me when I was in school, there are things like band and choir, drama, debate and things that don't require pads and helmets."

She sipped her coffee quietly for a moment, then said, "Yep. You and the boys seem to have found a good place for yourselves."

You don't just turn the heat on in the flower shop and open for business, especially when the two principals operating the business have never so much as had fresh flowers in their own houses. Fortunately, that wasn't really the point. Sam's idea had long-term implications — if it worked. If it didn't work, well, it never hurt to try.

With a couple of pieces of painted plywood and a carpet remnant, a squared-off play area was fashioned in the workroom of the shop. Sam went to the Goodwill in Westport and loaded up on toys that were clean and repaired. It being Christmastime, they were in short supply. He bought a bunch of picture books and a couple of baby dolls and baby-doll bottles.

Then he went to Jurea and Erline with his proposal. He said the shop had been his wife's and her father's, and there was no one to run it. It sure would help everyone out if Erline and Jurea would try to learn to make flower arrangements to sell at the shop. There were a few people, he said, willing to show them how. And he knew they wouldn't be ready to fashion bouquets for the church or take on wedding contracts anytime soon, but Christmas centerpieces weren't that hard to make. And the whole town would be grateful if they'd just give it a try.

The women went to the shop together, and when Jurea saw the little play area all set up for the little ones she said, "Mr. Cussler, you don't fool me one tiny bit."

Five days later, with the help of Flora Ramirez, two of Standard's daughters and Sarah Kelleher, the shop opened for business again. Standard had stocked the place with poinsettia plants and Sam had unpacked ornaments, decorations and knickknacks Justine had put away last season. As word spread, people stopped by and purchased arrangements for their parties and family dinners. The plants were as lush as Standard was famous for, and if the centerpieces weren't as professionally done as Justine's might've been, they were at least as lovingly prepared. And while people might still have some reservations about Erline, Jurea had become beloved by them all. Jurea, a woman who had so little, seemed to always have so much to give.

June bought a large arrangement made of

pine, juniper, red carnations and holly, with two big red candles in the middle, for her office, and planned to go back in the coming days to make purchases for her house and her dad's house. Just as she was about to go back into the clinic, she saw Sam's truck slowly pass. In the back was a Christmas tree.

She left the arrangement with Jessie and headed out again, this time in the direction Sam's truck had gone. It wasn't far. Sam's truck was parked in front of Jurea's house. With her hands in her jacket pockets and the hood up over her head, June appeared to lead with her stomach these days. As she watched Sam drag a bushy tree out of the back of his truck, she was reminded of Santa, if Santa were fit. With that shock of white hair, tanned face and shoulders a forty-year-old man would envy, Sam looked like a Christmas commercial for a fitness center.

He leaned the tree against the truck as June neared. She could see that he had another right underneath and a couple of cardboard boxes that she imagined would contain lights and ornaments unearthed from his cellar.

He turned and looked at her. She smiled as she looked at him.

He nodded toward her stomach. "You gonna make Christmas?"

"Oh, yeah. And then some."

"Looks iffy to me," he said, grinning.

"Sam, I heard about all you did." He shrugged. "You're about the nicest man this town has ever known."

He shrugged again. "What else am I going to do with my time. Huh?"

It was nearing closing time when Ricky Rios came into the café for a cup of coffee. What made this event odd was that he wasn't wearing his uniform. Ricky was on duty so much of the time — as were all the valley police — that to see him without his uniform was strange indeed. Of course, he still drove the squad SUV because, like Tom and Lee, it was the only vehicle he had.

"Can I get you anything else?" George asked him.

"No, just this. You're getting ready to close up, aren't you?"

"No rush, Ricky. You take your time. Have some pie."

"Thanks, but I was just wondering if I could talk to Frank." The boy's head popped up from behind the grill where he was busy with dishes and cleanup. He had a nervous and bewildered look on his face that made

Ricky smile. "Just wondered if I could give you a lift, Frank. I wanted to tell you about a couple of groups for young men that might interest you."

"Why?" Frank asked.

Ricky shrugged. "Because you're a young man?" he posed as a possible answer.

"I got my bike," he said.

"We'll throw it in the back."

"Go on, Frank," George urged. "Ricky don't bite."

"Not real hard, anyway," the deputy said.

Frank just muttered something under his breath while he wiped the grill down.

"What was that, son?" George asked.

"I said, if I have to!"

George shook his head. "He's just contrary, Ricky. Sixteen. You know."

"I know," Ricky said.

A little while later they were under way, the bike stowed in the back of the squad car, Frank slinking down in the front seat like a criminal. Ricky glanced at him and had to struggle not to laugh out loud. What misery! What energy it must require to maintain all that gloom and negativity.

"Lighten up, will you, Frank?"

"What?" he asked.

"I'm not taking you to jail, for God's sake. I'm just giving you a ride home. I wanted to tell you about this group out of Paradise that I belong to. Big Brothers. I thought if you signed up, and if it's okay with your mom, maybe I could be your big brother?"

"Why?" he asked, sitting a little taller and straighter, but totally perplexed.

"Well, there isn't a group in Grace Valley because there aren't enough big brothers or enough kids who would sign up. But if I'm going to have another brother, I'd like it to be closer to home for me. Plus, we have a lot in common."

"Like what?"

"Well, I had an abusive father, too, so I know what that's like."

"Oh, yeah?" Frank returned sarcastically. "And I suppose your mother knocked off your father, too." He sunk into the seat again, but he felt bad. He had no idea what made him always react that way, as if he was constantly enraged. And he always screwed things up, too. Like this thing with Ricky. Frank was interested, but a part of him just couldn't believe Ricky would really want to be his big brother. So he reacted as if unworthy, hoping that Ricky would just go away quietly and Frank wouldn't face the risk of proving inadequate.

Ricky acted as if he didn't know what Frank was getting at. "Our situation was a little different, and I was a lot younger. My parents are Mexican. I was born in California, so I'm naturalized, but my mom wasn't legal. My dad put her in the hospital a bunch of times, so there was no doubt he was going to kill her eventually. We had to run away and hide. There was this group that helped people with places to stay and changed identities and all that. We moved around for years. I don't think I ever went to school in the same town two years in a row. But by the time I was in high school, we were finally safe, my father had been in jail a couple of times, and we settled just down the road in Paradise. My mom got her education and citizenship." He looked over at Frank. "But it was hard. I know what it's like."

Frank looked at him but didn't say anything.

"I know what it's like to be mad all the time, too," he said. "And I also know the damn craziness of it being Christmas, and even though you still hate the son of a bitch, you wish he was around sometimes. Doesn't make any sense, does it?"

"Does everybody know that about you?" Frank asked.

"I think so. We never tried to hide it, my mother or me. That's why she likes working in Child Protective Services, where she can help."

"Wow," Frank said. One of the hardest things for him was that everyone *knew.* Wherever he went, he felt that people looked at him, thinking, There goes that kid who's jackass father used to beat up the whole family till his mother killed him. "Everybody knows about me. About my family." He looked over at Ricky. "I mean, there was a *trial.*"

Ricky didn't respond to that. It was beside the point. If they got together in this program, there would be plenty of time to talk about that stuff, to meet with other big brothers and their little brothers and share experiences and, better still, share solutions to their coping problems.

"There're lots of guys like us," Ricky said.

They rode together quietly for a little while. Sometimes not talking with someone can be as important and revealing as trying to talk it all out. Frank had been with people who understood his situation, like his mom and George. Like Tom Toopeek and the counselor, Jerry Powell. And then there was that anger-management group, full of pissed-off teenage boys just like him. But this was the very first time he was with a guy like Ricky — a guy he secretly thought was awesome — and they had come from the same place of pain! That gave Frank hope he could end up having a cool life after all. He had started to think that wasn't ever possible for him. He thought he was doomed.

"So, what do people in this brothers thing do?" Frank asked.

"Mostly we like to keep it simple and just have fun. We have some organized sports in summer — softball, soccer and volleyball. But everyone's busy, so there's no pressure. We might catch a movie, get together with some of the guys and go to the lake, whatever we want. I want to get you in the program as soon as possible because I really think your little brothers are going to need that, too, as they get a little older." He looked over at Frank and grinned. "You have any idea how many times, growing up, I could have used a big brother?"

"Man," Frank said, overwhelmed. "Life is just one big piñata after another."

"I guess that's a good thing?" Ricky asked, feeling every bit of thirty next to this kid.

"Yeah, it's a good thing," he said. And then he smiled. A rare thing for Frank.

Christmas Eve started out with the usual damp air and threatening skies, but with the temperature dropping, there was every possibility for snow. When John called June and asked her if she had time to dash over to the clinic to put some sutures in little Robbie Gilmore's chin, Jim insisted on riding along in case she ran into trouble. "It's slick out there," he said. "I'm not taking any chances on Christmas Eve."

She never saw it coming. Even when she pulled into town and there were cars everywhere, she still didn't get it.

"Drop me off in front of the café," Jim said. "I'm going to see what's going on while you put your stitches in."

"Well, wait a minute," she argued. "I want to know, too!"

"Do your stitches first!" he ordered, jumping out of the truck.

Pouting like a punished child, June parked behind the clinic. With all those cars and trucks in the church and café parking spaces, she couldn't tell if the Gilmores had arrived or not. She went into the clinic, turned on the lights, and scribbled a message on a sticky note. She stuck it on the unlocked clinic door. "I'm at the café. June."

Although June knew she was loved, she was always a little naive about how much. She knew the townsfolk appreciated her, as they appreciated her dad and John Stone, but she had trouble grasping that there was a difference. June was *their* girl, born and bred in Grace Valley. Her patients were her lifelong friends, her town and its people her first priority no matter what, whether she was in love or lonely, whether she was feeling great or ill, no matter what. And they knew that, and did not take it for granted.

So when she walked in the café, they got her.

"Surprise!" they shouted.

Her hands went to her face to hide her open mouth, then to her stomach to guard the baby from the shock of it.

She had never seen the place so full. There were streamers and balloons, presents everywhere and absolutely every person she loved.

Jim separated himself from the crowd, pulling a woman toward June. "June, honey, I have a surprise. This is my sister Annie."

June was so stunned, so touched, all she could do was say, "Oh!" and reach for the woman to hug her. They'd spoken on the phone a couple of times, talked of wanting to meet, but there had never been so much as a whisper of a plan.

"And here is her husband, Mike, and daughter, Tracy, and this one we call Mo because he's Mike Junior."

"Mo?" she asked.

"Yeah," the fifteen-year-old said, grinning. "For Mo Mike."

For some reason, she hadn't thought about something as obvious as a baby shower. It hadn't crossed her mind. There was so much else going on, what with Christmas. And there were other things to divert her attention, like Morton's return, like Nancy and Chris having their problems. And there was Harry, she remembered.

How had they done this? she wondered as she was led to the place of honor. So secretly, without giving off a single hint? How had Jim gotten his family here without going to the airport? Clearly there were conspirators and co-conspirators galore.

The presents went on forever, but there were two gifts that stood out in her mind. One was the quilt, lovingly designed and sewn by her circle of friends. It depicted in beautiful appliqué blocks the life of June Hudson: a baby in the arms of her mother with her father looking on; jumping rope with what had to be Tom Toopeek and Chris Forrest each holding an end; a twelve-year-old girl in an arm cast standing under a large tree with a tree house in it and two boys peeking out the windows; June in her cheerleading uniform with pom-poms; a med student carrying books with a stethoscope around her neck; and finally, in the center block, June standing at the forest's edge with Jim. A story quilt, lovingly created by her dearest friends.

The other gift waited for her at home and she wouldn't find out about it until much later.

They celebrated, ate cake and filled the back of the truck with gifts for June and the baby. Jim and Mike took all the new things plus the out-of-towner's luggage back to June's to unload and set up the baby's room as a guest room and lay out sleeping bags in the attic loft for the kids. June and Annie went to Elmer's to work on Christmas Eve dinner.

"I've never seen my brother look happier," Annie told June.

"Well, if you had known me before today, you'd be saying the same of me." They put both leaves in the dining table and began putting out plates. "This is the best Christmas I've had since my mother was alive."

"How long has she been gone, June?"

"Nine years now. But it still seems like yesterday."

"We lost our mom about a dozen years ago. And our dad not long after, so I think I know how you might feel."

"Annie, are you okay with the fact that Jim and I haven't married?" she boldly asked.

Annie shrugged. "I haven't given it a lot of thought. I understand you haven't really known each other all that long. Not a year yet, is it?"

"That's right," June said gratefully. At least here was someone who understood the basic reason for patience. "I'm having a little trouble getting my dad and my godmother, Birdie, to understand. But they're older. . . ."

Annie laughed softly. "Don't worry about them, June. The one you have to figure out how to explain this to is your son or daughter."

June froze. Something leaden weighted down her arms and legs. "Son," she said quietly.

Then, as if on cue, Mo burst into the house through the kitchen door, Tracy on his heels. Their jackets were covered with the damp glistening of snowflakes. Their faces were flush with excitement, eyes aglitter and cheeks charged red. "Mom!" Mo yelled. "It's snowing! Doc says it only snows about once every twenty years on Christmas!"

"That means good luck, doesn't it, Mom?" Tracy asked.

Annie put an arm around June's shoulders and said, "Definitely!"

June held on to her swollen stomach.

Through dinner Jim's family was entertained with town and family stories, from the barely returned Morton Claypool to the ghost at Angel's Pass rumored to have helped motorists in trouble over the decades. Though it was late by the time they all made the journey back to June's, no one was tired in the least, not even June.

Jim had something to show her, and took her by the hand to the bedroom where the cherry cradle sat next to her side of the bed. "You *made* this?" she asked, stunned.

Right behind them in the doorway, Annie said, "You *made* that? You did?"

"Yes," he answered.

Mike pushed through the door. "Hey. *You* made that? You?"

"Yeah. Me."

Tracy and Mo shoved in. "Whoa, Uncle Jim! You build things? You?"

"Come on, you didn't do that!"

"Jeez! I did, too! I had a little help, but I did it myself!"

"Wow." His doubtful family laughed. "Who knew?"

"It's beautiful, Jim," June said. "So beautiful."

"You'll have to excuse us," Annie said. "Not only has he never done anything like hang wallpaper or build furniture, he's been living out of a suitcase for about twenty years."

"Well, I'm not living out of a suitcase anymore," he said, and pulled June into his arms. "I'm all domesticated!"

Sadie, a little excited by the teenagers, barked her approval and madly wagged her tail. "Go, Uncle Jim," Mo cheered.

Deep in the night, finally abed, June and Jim lay close and whispered. "It was the best Christmas Eve of my life," she said. "I wish my mom were here."

"She's watching, don't worry. Mothers are not only tenacious, they're very nosy."

"Then you better put some clothes on," she giggled.

"Forget it. I'm not moving."

"I love your family," she said. "Annie's the best."

"She's bossy."

"I love her. I like it when she bosses you."

"It's a conspiracy."

"The kids are awesome. Whoever heard of

such nice, funny teenagers? They don't even fight!"

"Yes, they do. Just wait."

"Mike's a jewel."

"He's a good guy. . . ."

They lay there listening to the sounds in the house. Sadie had abandoned them to go up to the loft where the teens were camped. They lured her with doggie treats, then put her between them where she shamelessly rolled onto her back so they could rub her stomach. Every so often there would be a thump and a giggle from up there.

"Do they ever sleep?" she asked.

She was answered with a snore, so she began to doze. She was having a pleasant dream in which a youngster in his early teens with the same curly brown hair Jim had was talking to her in the kitchen of her little house. She was somewhere between imagining life with her son and dreaming about it. And then the young man said, "What do you mean you didn't know Dad very well?" and her eyes flew open. She bolted upright in bed.

"What was I thinking?" she said aloud.

"What? What? What is it?" Jim asked through groggy semiconsciousness.

"Jim, we have to get married!"

He shook his head sleepily. "What?"

"We have to get married right away!"

He would never understand pregnant women. "What brought this on?"

"Teenagers," she said, starting to get out of bed. He grabbed her hand and pulled her back. Bright-eyed, she stared at him. "Jim, what are we going to tell our son about why we didn't get married?"

He frowned at her for a moment. It was like it was her job to keep him off balance. Confused. She drove him crazy sometimes. And he was mad about her. "We'll just tell him the truth, that by the time his mother was ready, it was Christmas Eve, we didn't have a license and the town preacher was on the lam."

She considered this half seriously for a moment and then grabbed her pillow and whacked him in the head with it.

SEVENTEEN

June's family and friends gathered at Hudson House for Christmas Day, where presents had mysteriously appeared for Annie, Mike and the kids. It seemed that Jim had been planning this with his sister for quite a while. Elmer, June and Annie did all the cooking, in fact brought all the food, and the Barstows were invited and treated like special guests. Mo and Tracy kept Myrna busy showing them the house and her millions of collectibles all day long. They appeared at Christmas dinner in full costume, Tracy in a ball gown and feather boa, Mo in an old tuxedo and top hat.

When they all gathered at the table for the Christmas feast, Jim clinked his glass and stood. "I have an announcement and a toast," he said. "First, for all ye of little faith, June Hudson has consented to be my wife at the earliest possible convenience." Cheers went up around the table, and everyone,

one at a time, got up and made their way to kiss and congratulate the couple. When they all settled back in their chairs, he said, "I would like to toast family, large and small, old and new —" he looked down at June "— carefully planned and out of the blue!"

Around Grace Valley, families celebrated in their own personal ways. At the Mulls', Clarence was present again. This time he came for Christmas Eve and stayed over for Christmas Day. It was obvious he was much improved and he talked of coming home permanently very soon.

Erline and the little ones were at the Mulls' table for dinner, but didn't overstay, for at her house — her very first house — there was a tree with presents for the children, and it was a great comfort to be there, warmed by the wood stove. Sam checked in, bringing yet more gifts, and so did Ricky Rios, bringing a greater gift than she could have dared hope for. Corsica had managed to get a voucher for electricity repair and appliances for the house. With a home she could heat, work she could learn and friends whose generosity she could never possibly repay, her life had officially turned around.

Sam took his holiday meal with Standard Roberts and his daughters. The Toopeeks were just their family without visiting aunts, uncles and cousins, but even on their own they were a formidable group. Leah Craven was able to put a nice meal on the table and a few welcome gifts under the tree, thanks to a Christmas bonus from George. George, of course, provided free meals for both Christmas Eve and Day. There was nothing that made him happier. And the Stones celebrated with the Dicksons, a very loud and happy affair.

Judge and Birdie were with Chris, Nancy and the twins. The boys were getting around well in both wheelchairs and on crutches, and they were getting antsy, too. Their cabin fever was evidence of their improved health. Another month would have them back at school.

Late on Christmas Day, when Judge and Birdie had gone home and the twins were settled in front of a video, Chris migrated back to his wood shop. Nancy followed. She found him sanding down a coffee table. She wondered if someone had ordered that from him or if he had just decided to whip one up and see if it could sell.

"I thought I might find you here," she said. "Can't you even spend Christmas with us in the house?"

"I spent Christmas with you. All day."

"Can't you put this aside for one day?" she asked.

"Why?" he asked. "What difference does it make? You're not going to talk to me, anyway. I might as well be out here."

"It just drives me crazy," she said, running a hand through her thick brown hair. "I can't deal with it."

"It?"

"This," she said, sweeping an arm wide, indicating the workshop. She'd tried to think of it in terms of what was good for Chris, but she kept coming back to what was good for the marriage, the family. It seemed so irresponsible to her that she couldn't take him seriously.

"I remember a time you really believed in me. It was a long time ago, but I remember."

"Chris, I still believe in you. It's just that —"

"Nancy, do you still love me?" he asked her.

"I'll always love you, Chris," she said, the sound of tears creeping into her voice. "But how can you just blow off your job for . . . for . . . *this!*" She took a steadying breath, trying not to cry. "Do you even have a plan?"

"Yes, Nancy, I have a plan. It's to take one day at a time and take every job related to building that I can get. Is that enough of a plan for you?"

She couldn't believe he was proposing something as ridiculous as that. Just go day to day? Pick up odd jobs? "What if there's another accident, Chris? What if someone gets sick? Where's the medical coverage going to come from?"

He wiped his hands on a rag and leaned a hip up against his worktable. "The kids are making great progress. Pretty soon, you could get a regular job. We'd be all right."

"I could never make the kind of money here that I made in San Diego!"

"Fortunately you don't need to. I got this house for just about the cost of renovation, which I used my IRAs for. It's almost paid for. And around here people barter for things all the time. Plus, come spring, I plan to get a good-size garden going and maybe get some chickens or even a cow. . . ."

"Oh, Jesus Christ," she swore, completely beside herself. Returning to the small town of her childhood was one thing, but becoming a subsistence farmer, living from day to day, was another. Was she supposed to milk the cow, gather the eggs, pull up a few carrots for lunch and then trot off to her job as a waitress at one of the oceanside bars? What was to become of all her suits? Her

379

pumps? Her tennis clothes? This was Nancy Forrest, who had risen to the executive assistant to the senior vice president of a large brokerage firm!

Chris had turned back to his sanding, taking long and meticulous strokes. "It's a different kind of life here, I know. But damn, Nancy, it can be good. These people aren't a bunch of hicks. They're talented. Professional. Smart. Your new best friend is a doctor. We could be happy here."

"Not if we're always hungry, Chris."

"We won't be hungry."

"How do you know that!" she shouted at him. Why was he so dense? Did he think he could just keep sanding things and everything would work itself out?

"Because life is simple here. If we sold the San Diego house, we'd have a couple hundred thousand to put by and —"

"Chris, you dope! We were living on about eighty grand a year in San Diego!"

"That's just it, Nancy, you bigger dope," he yelled back. "It doesn't take that in Grace Valley! It doesn't take half that!"

"But Chris, I like making money, even if you don't. I like the challenge of a difficult job. I like to be busy, to be in a position of accountability! I don't know that Grace Valley has any of that for me!"

He just looked at her for a long time, his hands still. "Well, Nance, that's something you'll have to work out for yourself. Because, see, here's something I just barely found out. San Diego was way too much for me. No one there would ever have appreciated a couple of chairs, a sideboard with leaded-glass accents. No one needed me to lend a hand there. It was all about working to earn a buck, then another buck, then another.

"But don't get me wrong, Nancy. I don't think Grace Valley is a good idea because here I can work with wood, have a garden and chickens and volunteer. I think it's a good idea because it might be the best place for the boys. Now, at least. Now that I almost lost them."

It was impossible to argue with that. Of course it was a good place for them. It was clean and wholesome and pretty safe, considering. "But what will we use for money when they want to go to college?" she asked.

"I don't know, but I bet it'll work out somehow."

Give it up, she told herself. He's always been like this. He never worried about the money too much, he left that to her. And he didn't worry about earning it much, either.

"I took a leave of absence from my job. I

have to make a decision about whether or not I'm going back."

"I wish you wouldn't," he said. "I love you."

"You do? You really do? You can blow off a paying job for this and still say you love me?"

"Actually, I love you more now than I did last year. I finally realize what a bad husband I was. What a bad father. You know why, Nance? I wasn't happy. I was miserable. Every day was another rotten day of insurance . . . and because I wasn't happy, I was a screwup. Because I never felt good enough, I was a self-fulfilling prophecy." He smiled a melancholy smile. "Now that I've found something that makes me feel good enough, makes me look forward to each day, am I going to lose you?"

Tears gathered in her eyes. "I don't know," she said in a whisper.

June stood in the doorway of the nursery. Two walls were painted yellow, the other two hung with yellow-and-blue wallpaper with carousel ponies dancing on ribbons . . . or so it seemed. Jim had managed to finish and install the white plantation shutters for the window, and she wondered how much help he might've gotten from Chris.

The crib was in place, but all the others things — from shower gifts to Christmas gifts — were scattered about. Lots and lots of clothes. Little-boy clothes. She felt a pang. She was thrilled about her son, and left with a longing for a little girl. She wondered if she would feel so if she hadn't thought for so long that this was a daughter.

"I can wash the clothes and put everything away for you while you're at work," Annie said from behind her. Then she felt her future sister-in-law's hand on her shoulder. "Or I can leave it all as it is and help you with it tonight."

It took her a moment. "Leave it for later," she finally said. She had to go to work until at least early afternoon, but she didn't want to miss any more of this process. And then a sudden tightening caught her attention and her hand went to her swollen abdomen. "Whew," she said, amazed.

From behind her Annie reached around and felt the hardened mound.

"Braxton-Hicks," June said.

"A pretty solid one," Annie said. "You sure about that?"

"Worse than sure. I already went running to the hospital once, certain I was in early labor. John hooked me up to a monitor and ultrasound. I felt pretty stupid. I'm a doctor. I should know better."

"When are you due, exactly?"

"We're not sure. I wasn't paying attention. But judging by the progression of the baby, it looks like early February."

"Just a month, then," Annie said, smiling. "It's always nice to get to the point that the baby can come perfectly safely."

"I could use another week or two," June said, though in truth she'd grown tired of wetting her pants with every sneeze or laugh. And her lower back was beginning to ache. "I'd like to get married."

"All that holding out," Annie said, "only to be in a big hurry."

"Well, I thought I was being rational. I didn't know I was being an idiot. I've noticed that pregnancy kills some otherwise healthy brain cells."

"In case you were wondering, you don't get them back, either. Your son will be sure to remind you of that often. So, when is the big day?"

"I thought we'd better dash off to Lake Tahoe or Reno, have a Nevada wedding quick, but that's not intelligent. One, I'm not up to the long drive. Two, my town is obviously as into this as I am. They won't be happily excluded. My being married is not nearly as important to most of them as being invited to the wedding. So Jim and I are going to drive to the county courthouse today at lunchtime and get a license. Then we thought we'd get a preacher from Rockport to come over here on New Year's Eve. We'll open up the church, have a little party after."

"New Year's Eve. Nice idea. We have to get back on the second."

"No one ever has anything fun to do on New Year's around here. Maybe it'll start a tradition."

"A marrying tradition. How long are you planning to work?"

June shrugged. "Well, if I don't know when I'm due, how do I know when to quit working? I feel perfectly fine, except for the backache, swollen ankles, weak bladder, heartburn and this broken rib from someone's foot. I guess I'll quit when my water breaks."

"Oh, you young moderns," Annie said, shaking her head.

Later that morning June made a phone call that she never in her wildest dreams thought might take place. She called Nancy Forrest and asked her for two favors. "First, will you help me find a dress to get married in? A nice cream muu-muu, perhaps?"

"Sure." Nancy laughed. "We'll get you

fixed up. Pregnant women are much better taken care of by the designers than they were when I was imitating a water buffalo."

"Thanks. And another thing. If you're free on New Year's Eve, would you be my matron of honor?"

"Oh, June!" she exclaimed in a rather weak breath. "Oh, June!"

"I hope that was a yes."

"Oh, June, yes!" And then she wept into the phone.

"Stop it!" June commanded. "This is supposed to be a happy occasion."

"You couldn't possibly honor me more," Nancy said.

"Isn't it odd," June said, "the way things come around?"

Jim was at the café at the agreed-upon time, but no June. They were going to get a marriage license, so he wore a tie but not a jacket. He had a cup of coffee, then a second. Sam wandered in, then Tom.

"That a tie?" Sam asked Jim.

Jim lifted one brow. "Been that long since you've seen one?" he returned.

"Going to a funeral?" Tom asked, smiling.

"Nope."

"Then he must be getting married," Sam reasoned.

"Not exactly," Jim said, not wishing to say more.

"You want a grilled cheese to go with that coffee?" George asked him.

But Jim hoped he would get something to eat with June after they got the license. "No, thanks." He glanced out the window toward the clinic and saw June coming toward the café, but most certainly not to meet him and drive to the courthouse. She wore her white lab coat, stethoscope around her neck, no jacket. "Excuse me," he said to the men, going out the door to meet her halfway.

"I'm so sorry," she said as she neared him. She reached him and put her hands on his cheeks to kiss his mouth. "John had to go to the hospital for an emergency and Dad and I are swamped over there. I think everyone held their Christmas colds until after the holiday."

He shrugged. "I guess you can't help that."

"You're wearing a tie."

"I haven't ever done this before. I don't know how you dress for a license purchase."

"You're very cute. I didn't know you had a tie."

"I have two," he said, smiling.

"Do you have a suit? For New Year's Eve?"

"Am I going to need it?" he teased.

"Can you hang a little loose until this

387

afternoon? I'm sure I'll finish up early enough to go today."

He had his doubts. He wanted out of the tie, at once. He put his hands on her stomach, leaned down and said to his son, "If she's too busy to have you, you're on your own." Then he kissed it.

Inside the café the men watched. "I don't believe I've ever seen anything like that before," George said.

"Then you haven't lived," Tom assured him.

A few hours later, when the last prescription had been written, June called Jim. "Is it too late?"

"We'll have to try again tomorrow, honey. They close in fifteen minutes."

"Oh, damn! Do you hate me?"

Hate her? Never had he felt such admiration! That she could do all she did, so unselfishly, while heavy with his child, filled him with a sort of reverence. On top of this, he found her deliciously sexy, swollen ankles and all. Keeping his hands off her while she was this far along was torture, and he couldn't wait until she was unburdened and his again. But his sister was standing a few feet away from him, so he said, "We'll try again tomorrow. Annie is making a pot roast for dinner. You'll love her pot roast."

"I owe you," she said.

"I can't wait to collect. For years to come."

In the middle of the night, the phone rang next to June's head. She had been having a heated argument with Birdie in her dream, and she'd been winning! They weren't arguing about June getting married, and she couldn't remember what it had been, but . . . She answered the phone sleepily, looking at the clock. One-thirty.

"June, I'm sorry to do this to you," John said. "I'm at the hospital in Rockport and I just got a page from Mary Lou Granger. Her little one is having an asthma attack that isn't subsiding with the use of the inhaler."

"Sure, John. What's got you at Rockport?"

"One of my OBs is dilated to nine. I thought of calling Elmer, but he looked a little worn out at the end of the day today."

"No, I'm glad you didn't call him. I'll be happy to go. I don't have that many more night calls in me."

"I told Mary Lou to go to the clinic."

"Perfect. I'll pull on some sweats and get over there."

"Thanks, June. I'll make it up to you."

Actually, she thought, she was going to be making up to him for a while. He was doing

389

everything in his power to make this pregnancy and birth as uncomplicated and restful as possible.

"What is it?" Jim asked.

"I'm going to run over to the clinic to meet an asthmatic patient. I should be back in bed, putting my cold feet on you in an hour or less."

He sat up. "I'll go with you," he muttered.

"Why?" she asked, dressing quickly.

"I don't know. It's dark. Maybe icy."

"The temperature was dropping this afternoon. El Niño is back, melting everything in sight."

"It's very wet," he said.

She laughed at him. "And you're very sweet. Are you going to accompany me at night for the rest of my career in medicine, or is this a one-time thing?"

He lay back down. "You're right," he said. "Wear your rubbers."

"If you'd been wearing yours . . ." she began, but she stopped herself because, of course, she wouldn't change a thing. Before she left the room she could hear the soft purr of his snore.

She bundled up extra warm, shivering against the night because, El Niño or no, it was chilly. The cloudy sky blackened the earth and there was nothing darker than a small country town under a winter sky after midnight. If there were any insomniacs in Grace Valley, she didn't know them.

It was smart of John to send the Grangers to the clinic; they were on the opposite side of the valley from June. If she had to travel all the way out to their farm, precious time would be lost. Plus, if oxygen was needed, the supply in the clinic was easier for a big fat pregnant woman to handle than the tank she carried in her truck with her other emergency supplies.

She came down Valley Drive and turned into the clinic parking lot, pulling around to the back door. The Grangers hadn't arrived yet; she had time to set up a treatment room for them. Their little girl, Katie, must be seven or eight by now, the oldest of three. She was the only one with asthma and allergies, and had been stablized with medication. All this was going through June's mind as she exited the truck and headed for the back door.

An unusual sound caused her to pause. Water? Someone had left the water running? She looked around each side of the clinic, which was surrounded by blacktop, and saw that there wasn't even a hose hooked up. But why would there be? The rain had been almost constant since mid-October. The ground everywhere was one big soggy mess.

From the illumination of the streetlights she could see the slick dampness on the street. The night-lights were on in the back of the café, but the church and parsonage were depressingly dark. However, the parking lot that separated the buildings was not just wet, it was *moving.*

With a deep, sinking feeling inside, June went back to her little truck, got in, started the ignition and pulled around to the side of the clinic, her headlights pointing toward the café and church. It looked like the ocean had come inland. The river, usually a narrow ribbon of water that ran from the mountains to the sea a good football field behind the café, was now a fat and raging beast that had almost reached the buildings. It was already up to café and parsonage, and very likely the church basement was flooded.

She left the truck lights on, shining on the flooded river, then dashed for the clinic, as much as a woman in her condition could dash. She went in through the back door, flipped the lights on in her office and dialed Tom's number first. But she heard a noise. Shuffling. She put the phone on the desk and went back to the clinic hallway to investigate.

She never saw it coming as Conrad Davis gave her a right hook to the jaw. Her head bounced against the doorjamb and everything went dark as she slid down the wall to the floor, unconscious.

Conrad looked down at her. Several things came to his addled, drug-craving mind at once. This was June, the beloved town doctor he had struck unconscious. She was hugely pregnant besides. And he'd been rummaging around in the clinic for quite a while, failing to find narcotics or money. Fresh out of jail, this was the only place that had come to mind for him to rob.

He'd better either kill her or run. He was a badass with no conscience, but he'd never killed anyone. He might for drugs, but she didn't have drugs.

He bolted outside, his pockets painfully empty, and noticed her small truck was running, the lights shining on the rising river across the street. He had parked his truck behind a garage two blocks away. It was suddenly settled in his mind. He was through with this town, with the people, with Erline and her brats. He decided to run the truck north as far as the gas in the tank would take him, then he'd sell it. Buy something a little smaller, cheaper, and have money left over for some pot, some meth, some ecstasy. He jumped into the truck and headed out of town. The way that water was rising, there wouldn't be a town much longer, anyway.

It never occurred to him to sound the alarm.

Jim woke to the ringing of the phone. "Hullo?" he said.

"Oh. Hi. Is this Jim?"

"Mmm-hmm," he said sleepily.

"This is Mary Lou Granger. Can I speak to June, please?"

"She's at the clinic. Meeting someone with asthma, she said. You can get her there."

"I'm the one with asthma. My daughter, that is. Katie. And no one answers at the clinic. We can't get there."

"Wha . . . ?" He was sitting up now. One thing came pounding through. *No one answers at the clinic.* Car trouble? Accident? He was standing, turning on the light, tossing clothes around in search of jeans.

"The river's up and there's flooding in some of the low areas. We live out in the country, you know, the opposite side of the valley from you. We have to go so far around to cross the river, we might as well go to Rockport. To the emergency room there.

But where's June?"

"I don't know," he said, pulling on his pants. "I'm going to drive into town, to the clinic, to make sure she hasn't had trouble along the way."

Since 911 had not yet come to the valley, Jim dialed the police department. He got the answering machine, which gave him a pager number and cell phone number. He opted for the latter, dialing while he pulled on boots.

"Yeah, June," Tom said, obviously responding to the number on his cell phone's caller ID.

"It's Jim. June went to the clinic to meet a patient but the patient just called here saying she can't get to the clinic. Something about a river? And there's no answer there. So I'm going. What about this river?"

"Holy shit," Tom said.

"That can't be good."

"The river behind the café. The Windle. We've been watching it since fall. It hasn't flooded in twenty years, but —"

"I'll meet you at the clinic."

"Don't cross any low areas covered with water. Flash flooding is a danger."

"Could June have been caught in a flash flood?" Jim asked fearfully.

"It's doubtful. She knows better. See you

in a few."

Jim woke his sister and brother-in-law and told them why he was leaving. Though they were worried as well, they couldn't really go with him. There were the kids, asleep upstairs, and even with his big truck, it was a tight squeeze. Plus, he wasn't about to wait for anyone to get dressed.

He was almost out the door when he did an unexpected thing. He went back to the bedroom, tossed off his jacket and pulled his guns and double shoulder holster from the bottom of the trunk at the foot of the bed. Just about everyone in Grace Valley had guns, but not guns like these. It crossed his mind to get out his bulletproof vest, but he didn't want to take the time. On second thought, he pulled the vest from the trunk and took it with him. This was not the kind of vest a street cop wore, but what a SWAT officer might wear, weighing in the neighborhood of forty pounds. This was a vest that could stop a rifle shot. He didn't know why he had this feeling, but he never argued with instinct.

Annie, in robe and slippers, saw him march from the bedroom to the door, wearing guns and carrying the vest. "Jim! What is it? What's happened?"

"I don't know, Annie. But I don't want to

be unprepared. I'll call you when I find June."

June didn't know how long she'd been out, but she suspected not long. She felt a throbbing in her chin and at the back of her head. Something had hit her, then her head had hit the wall. She looked at her watch — 2:00 a.m. She thought that was just a few minutes from when she'd arrived at the clinic, but wasn't sure. She stayed very still, very quite, listening.

Yes, she remembered. She had heard some rustling. Shuffling. She had known there was someone in the clinic and had gone into the hall when *bam!* That was that.

Now all was quiet. But there was no way she wanted to get slugged again. More important, she wanted to be sure the baby was okay. It appeared she hadn't fallen on her stomach, but rather had slid down the wall and landed on her butt. It was once a tiny, bony butt, but now there was sufficient padding. She ran her hands in circular fashion around her swollen tummy and smiled at the sensation of kicking and wriggling. There was really no reason to fear for the health and safety of the baby. She would call her dad and Jim, be checked for concussion, but it appeared all was normal.

With the exception of the Windle.

She listened again. When she was sure there was no one about, she crawled into her office and got carefully to her feet. The phone was making that angry off-the-hook sound. She put it back in the cradle and it instantly rang. She picked it up. "June Hudson."

"Where have you been?" Jim demanded. She could hear the sound of his truck in the background and knew he was driving.

"Here. Someone broke in and slugged me. Knocked me out."

"What?" he yelled into the phone.

"I'm okay. Are you coming? Because the river is flooding and I have to call Tom. And my dad. And —"

"Who slugged you?" he demanded hotly.

It was the first time she had heard anger in his voice since she'd met him. He was enraged. She hadn't thought before telling him. She should have realized, the way he felt about her, about the baby . . .

"Who? Who?"

"Oh, Jim, I don't know. Someone was in here. Broke in. I didn't realize it. I never saw him . . . I assume it was a 'him.' But I'm all right. And I'll call my dad and have him check me for a concussion, but I don't think I have one. Jim . . . the baby's moving. It's all right. Just come."

"I'm coming," he said, sounding calmer.

Then she made her calls, getting her dad out of bed, learning that Tom was already on his way, and sounding the alarm. The river is up, she told them. We're coming, they said.

She went to find an ice pack for her head, and when she turned on the lights she saw that the clinic had been ransacked. Someone looking for money or drugs or both, she reasoned. Holding an ice pack to the back of her head, she went to the lavatory in the reception area. The linen cupboard was still closed, still locked. She smiled to herself. That was where they hid the small amount of narcotics and cash they kept in the office. Every morning before patients arrived, they took the strong boxes out and left the toilet paper, facial tissues and tampons in the little closet. Every night they put the strong boxes back and locked it up. Who would look for drugs and cash in the patients' bathroom?

She heard the whoop-whoop of the police car outside. She was afraid to look, afraid to see how high the water was.

EIGHTEEN

Grace Valley was an amazingly beautiful place. It had rich soil, majestic mountains covered with tall, lush trees and miles of gorgeous ocean coastline. It was like heaven — as long as it didn't flood or burn. While the unseasonably warm temperature melted the mountain snow, the rains came. And came, and came, and came.

When June went to the front door of the clinic and stepped outside, she saw that the water was up to the back door of the café. Deputy Lee Stafford was parked right in front of the clinic with his spotlight shining on the water. It resembled a lake, but there was that rushing sound. Back where the actual river flowed, where Sam and others liked to drop an occasional line, it was surging like white-water rapids. The water on the lawn and parking lot was its overflow.

Lee would be calling all the agencies — police, fire, flood control, parks and rec, forestry, fish and game, California Highway Patrol, County Sheriff.

She went back inside and, still holding an ice pack on the back of her head, called George and Sam and Burt Crandall — all of whom had their businesses on Valley Drive. Then she called Judge, Bud Burnham, Robbie Gilmore, Daniel Culley and, after a slight hesitation, Chris and Nancy. "Nancy, the river's up. It looks like it's reached the café and church already. Your house is high up and should be all right, but please send Chris. We're going to need help here."

"June, where are you?"

"I'm at the clinic. Please send him. I should make more calls."

"Right away. And you be careful."

The hanging up of the phone and the opening of the back door seemed to come simultaneously. She knew from the heaviness of the footfalls that it was Jim, not Elmer. He seemed to fill the frame of the door to her office. She nearly gasped aloud as she noted the vest and guns. "What are you made up for?" she asked.

"I don't know. For whoever popped you. Let me see," he said, lifting her chin. "You're getting a little purple."

"Yeah, well, that's not what hurts. I hit

401

the back of my head on the wall. I have a goose egg," she said, pressing the ice against it again. His hand covered her stomach. "The baby seems fine," she said. She covered his hand with hers. "See? He moves all around. He's never still."

"Like Mo." He pulled her close and hugged her. "Stop scaring me, June."

In all her years of taking care of the town she knew that people cared about her. Cared deeply. And worried over her, too. And of course there was Elmer and Myrna, always checking to be sure she was all right. Tom and the boys looked out for her, too. But she had never had anything like this.

She put her arms around his neck, pressed herself into his hard vest. She rubbed her cheek against his rough one. There was no mistaking it — he loved her devotedly. With everything he had. As she loved him.

She pulled away a little. "Are you going to shoot many people tonight?" she asked.

"Do you have a cabinet or drawer that locks?"

"They should be safe in my lower desk drawer. And there will be lots of people around, trust me. Have you seen the river?"

"I didn't even look. Where's your truck?"

"Right outside," she said.

"Right outside where?"

"Right outside the back —"

He was shaking his head.

"Oh, man, he stole my truck. It has lots of stuff in it. First aid stuff, oxygen, blankets . . . Oh, brother!"

Elmer came in the back door and went straight to her office. The first thing that filled his eyes was Jim, armed. "Now, that looks the part of a fed."

"A what?" Jim asked.

"Oh, stop it. Everyone knows you're a fed. No one minds that you don't want to admit it, but give me a break. We know how you met June, sneaking around, getting her pregnant, right before that pot raid in the mountains."

Jim's eyebrows shot up. Then his mouth twisted in a cynical line and he glanced at June. She shrugged. "What can I say? Welcome to your town. And go ahead, try to have a private life."

Elmer looked June up and down while shrugging out of his jacket. "So. You fell, you say?"

"Not exactly, Dad. I came here to meet Katie Granger, who was having an asthma attack. I heard someone shuffling around in here and when I went into the hall, bam! I got slugged in the jaw. Here," she said, lifting her chin.

He touched the chin. "You lose consciousness?"

"Briefly. Minutes. Maybe seconds. I hit the back of my head on the wall. When I woke, I was sitting up, leaning against the wall. I didn't hit my stomach, I don't think. It feels fine and the baby is active."

His fingers went around to the back of her head. "Nice goose egg," he said.

"Is that a medical term?" Jim asked.

"Let's look at your eyes," he said, leading the way to an examining room. "You feel okay? Headache? Nausea? Dizziness?" Then, when he saw that cupboards had been emptied all over the floor, he said, "Damn hoodlums."

"My goose egg throbs. I've been keeping ice on it. Dad, did you see the river?"

"Yeah. We're in serious trouble, I think. Jump up here," he said, indicating an examining table.

"I left my truck running with the headlights facing the café and the lake behind it. Whoever hit me took it. Minus one more truck. I seem to be losing about two a year."

"Expensive trend. Squeeze my fingers. Push against my hand," he instructed as he proceeded to give her a simple neurological test. "You're good. And I'm sure the baby's fine, but I'll defer to John. He may want to do a routine ultrasound just because you lost consciousness."

"We need to reach John and tell him the river's up and the clinic may be in jeopardy. . . ."

Jim wandered out of the examination room, sensing both that they were nearly done and that he should divest himself of his guns and armor. He went back to June's office, where they would be locked up and from there he heard the sounds of vehicles. Large vehicles. He looked outside and saw headlights bouncing around the street and buildings.

He called Annie to tell her that June was fine, but that there was a problem with the river being too high and they would probably be at the clinic a lot longer. He didn't want to worry his sister; he wasn't sure he even knew what to worry about.

They came throughout the night, first the townsfolk and farmers. They brought whatever they had, from shovels to plows. Flatbed trucks were stacked with burlap bags and piled with sand. Standard Roberts brought all the sand and clay he could spare from his nursery. Then came the forestry and fish and game departments, their trucks stacked with emergency flood equipment. And, as dawn approached, the National

Guard came from Fort Bragg.

June refused to leave the town as long as she felt all right, though she couldn't do much to help. It didn't take Jim long to leave her side and join the others in sandbagging right in back of the café. Once there were flatbed trucks and floodlights, George and his sons took a few large panes of glass out of the front of the café and began moving heavy equipment out — stoves, coolers, grills, pans, dishes, glassware — everything they could get out before it was too late. It was all driven the short distance to Sam's garage and kept there.

From her place on the clinic's front steps June could see her friends and neighbors at work alongside flood control personnel. She knew just about every truck, van and car parked along Valley Drive. Upriver, in the foothills, there were more crews trying to stave off and divert the flooding. And downriver the highway department was busily putting up barricades on patches of road that were underwater.

She saw Ricky Rios bring Frank Craven and two of his younger brothers to town, followed shortly by Lincoln Toopeek with four young Toopeeks. Hal Wassich had mobilized his entire family, and Mike Dickson and his father-in-law arrived with a

Bobcat backhoe on a trailer.

The Highway Department brought truck after truck of sand, dumping it as close to the water as possible without risking that it could get swept up in the stream and washed away before being bagged.

The next thing June saw brought a hiccup of emotion to her breast. Coming toward her, with a hood over her head, was her new best friend. Smiling. Her eyes alive and mischievous. "Boy, what some people will do to get out of sandbagging," she teased.

"Nancy! How long have you been here?"

"As soon as I woke Chris I realized that, if we could just get the boys to Judge and Birdie's, I could help. Birdie's not going to be out here, but —" she looked over her shoulder "— Judge wouldn't be kept away."

June reached out for her. "Oh, God, I'm glad you're here! How far down is the river flooded?"

"They're saying all the way down to where 482 crosses Valley. The café and church are in some danger, but unfortunately they're evacuating a lot of houses along the riverside. And you know the houses as well as I do — not very substantial ones. They could be lost before morning."

"Where are they taking the people they evacuate?"

"To the high school. And look," Nancy said, indicating the church. "They're pulling out the pews . . . and everything that isn't nailed down. The basement is underwater already. Listen, I have to get back to work, but I told Jim to bring the big coffeepot from the café over here and get it cranked up. Okay?"

"Sure. Good idea."

Nancy gave her a quick hug. "You sure you feel okay?" she asked. "Should you be sitting?"

"I feel fine. The baby's finally quieted down for a while."

"Maybe you should go to the back and lie down, see if you can catch a snooze."

"With all this going on?" June asked. "Don't worry. I'm used to not sleeping. And I imagine I'll be getting even more used to it when the little one arrives."

Soon John and Susan appeared, carrying the sleeping Sydney to one of the recovery room beds. Because of their presence, June was forced to lie down for fifteen minutes out of every hour to give her swollen ankles some relief. John and Susan didn't dare shovel or bag sand — John couldn't afford to risk injury to his hands, and Susan, it seemed, had a touch of pregnancy and was forced into the rest position with June once in a while. But fortunately, for the sake of the passage of time, there was lots of cleaning up to do around the clinic, which was still a mess from its ransacking. In the early hours of the morning Jessie arrived to help put away supplies and files that had been scattered.

Dawn came and so did the people, from neighboring towns and rural areas surrounding Grace Valley. Army engineers supervised the sandbagging and dam building, but no matter how hard they worked, the river kept rising. The Red Cross came from Garberville with a couple of lunch wagons they parked at the end of the street. They gave coffee, water and sandwiches to anyone who wandered over. Then came the high school and even the junior high students, ready to work to keep the river from taking over the town.

Annie called and begged that June have someone come for them; they were four able bodies and couldn't stand being stuck at home, doing nothing. "Pack up some leftovers, make some sandwiches, empty out the fridge if you have to. The Red Cross has brought food, but if we can feed ourselves here in the clinic, it would help. Dress warmly and as waterproof as possible. My front hall closet has some rain gear. My bedroom closet is full of jeans and sweat-shirts I can't get into, and boots that might work for you and Tracy . . . and even Mo if his feet haven't gotten too big yet. And bring every plastic trash bag I have. I'll give you an hour to do all that, okay? Oh, and would you please feed Sadie so you can bring her, too? I don't want to leave her another whole day."

June took Jim's truck with the double cab. Annie had made an impressive run through June's kitchen and put together a picnic that would bring big healthy smiles to the faces of the clinic staff. Then June watched Jim's family walk across the street to the new bank of the river. Jim paused and leaned on his shovel, watching them come. From where she stood she could see the sentimen-tal look on his face. He opened his arms to hug them, each one, before passing them on to a job.

Throughout the day they worked while June watched helplessly from the clinic. If it weren't for the few minor injuries brought to her attention, she would have felt even more useless. At midafternoon Tom Toop-eek came to the clinic. "We found your truck, June. It was Conrad Davis who broke in here, I guess. Conrad who hit you."

"And?"

"And Conrad who tried to drive under a flooded overpass and got washed away. If he'd stayed with the truck, he might've been okay, but he tried to get across on foot. Highway Patrol found his body washed up against a tree."

"What a waste."

"They're not going to tow your truck until the water's down. There are too many more important matters for everyone right now."

"Of course. Will you tell Erline?"

"I'm going to take Sam with me to do that."

"Are those houses okay over there? They're pretty close to the river."

"You have a bigger problem in the clinic than they do. But there's no use pretending — this is as bad as anyone's ever seen it. Worse than the last flood twenty years ago."

It was midnight before it became clear — they had to leave. There was nothing more they could do. Everyone was loading up and pulling out. Jim, John, Elmer, Annie, Mike and the kids and Jessie put everything in the clinic on the highest possible surface. There wasn't time to get it out, but they did bag up things like files, test kits, office equipment, accounting ledgers and books. Copiers, fax machines, phones and the like all went up on the top shelf in exam rooms.

Jim put the computer and printer in the back of the truck.

Elmer was pulling on June's elbow. "Come on, honey. We have to go. The water's two feet deep in the street."

"But that's a long way from getting in here! We're up three feet at least!"

"June, we won't be able to drive out of here pretty soon. Let's go."

"Oh, Dad," she said, tears coming to her eyes. "Are we going to lose it all? The whole town?"

"No, June, but it's gonna get real wet around here. Now, let's go!"

As they all piled into two trucks — Elmer's and Jim's — they could see others taking their most valuable possessions out of their houses. They took a side trip at June's request and went by Judge and Birdie's. The scene was the same — Chris and Nancy were loading up the back of Judge's little truck with possessions while the boys were already buckled into their seats in the family van.

June rolled down the window. "Where are you going?" she called.

"Our house," Nancy answered. "We're on high ground. You going home now?"

"Yes. I'll call you on the cell later."

"June," Nancy yelled, tears in her voice.

"I'm sorry. I hoped we could save it."

"Just hurry and go," she said. "We saved the most important stuff."

At noon the next day the report was on CNN. The town of Grace Valley was literally underwater. National Guardsmen were rescuing residents from their homes and the Red Cross was putting people up in the local schools and churches. The Forrests, Toopeeks, Hudsons and Claypools were all in houses untouched by the flood, as were the Stones and Cravens. George's café was underwater, but the family home was undamaged. Burt and Syl lost home and bakery, as did Sam with his home and station. Judge and Birdie, the Mulls, the Burnhams and Barstows were out of luck, and so was Erline.

Of course Myrna took in the Barstows, and Ricky and Corsica made sure that Erline and the children were sheltered. The Mulls were put up by VA facilities and most of the others had grown children in neighboring towns who took them in.

It rained and it rained and it rained.

In the days that followed, while it was impossible to do any cleaning up in the town, one would think that everyone would sit idle and wait for the sun to come out.

Not so. With the clinic closed, June, John and Elmer made house calls or saw patients in the clinic facilities at Valley Hospital. Emergency shelters needed volunteers to collect food, clothing and bedding, and to help within the makeshift shelters set up in schools.

Of course, Grace Valley wasn't alone in being victimized by the warm weather and relentless rains. Other small towns had taken beatings as their lakes and rivers overflowed. The Russian River, which flooded much more often, put in a vicious showing by knocking out a dozen houses and stranding a bus full of schoolchildren in a flash flood that obliterated a highway. Then there were the landslides all up and down the rocky northern California coast from the soaking the ground had taken.

To see the way the town rallied was inspiring, but not at all surprising. Nancy and Chris settled the boys with Judge and Birdie and spent long days helping out in and around shelters, moving people, collecting donations, whatever was needed. Jurea and her teenagers, despite being homeless themselves, worked hard at helping others relocate. The Presbyterian Women, whatever their circumstances, were picking up donated groceries and putting together boxes for needy families. And, of course, Annie and her family weren't content to sit around while the town was working and helping one another.

They were all so tired, most especially June. Thankfully she worked with John, who guarded her health closely, making sure she was eating and resting whenever possible. But still the end of the days came thankfully and everyone who had a bed fell into it gratefully and slept deeply.

A few days after the town was evacuated, Nancy found June at the hospital and asked if she had time for lunch in the cafeteria, or at least a coffee break. "If you can wait a little," June said. But she cocked her head to one side to study Nancy's face. Something was different. "Is everything all right?"

"Sure. But I'm missing you. And I know we have things to talk about."

"Hah! The whole world has changed. Go get us a table and I'll be along as soon as I finish up two exams that are waiting."

The whole world had changed, indeed. Nancy, wearing jeans, boots, a dirty rain slicker and plaid flannel shirt, went to the hospital cafeteria. There were two types of people there, people dressed pretty much like her and people wearing scrubs. She almost laughed out loud. Had she been mourning her suits? Her pumps? Had she complained to Chris that she wanted a challenging job, one that made her feel smart and necessary? She had never in her life felt more challenged and necessary than this past week.

She took her tray through the line and got herself a hearty bowl of soup, a sandwich and a big slice of chocolate cake to top it off. She found a small table in the corner, where she could see everyone coming and going, and was halfway through her lunch when June finally arrived.

"How have you been?" June asked her.

"I'm great, but what about you? Are you working too hard?"

"I don't get a chance to. My mother, John, is on me every second."

"Has there been any talk of a wedding?"

"Yes," June said. "It went something like this — we could find a justice of the peace if either of us had a second to spare, but right now it seems not quite a priority." She rubbed her stomach. "Even my dad understands."

"So much for New Year's Eve," Nancy said.

"That's okay. Right now there's too much else going on. Have you been volunteering all week?"

"Yup. Me and Chris, can you beat that?"

"*That's* what's different," June said. "You've decided not to kill him."

Nancy's eyes sparkled and her face broke into a grin. "June, I don't know when I've felt more alive. I'm just sorry to say it took a natural disaster to make me see the light."

June was speechless. Finally she asked, "What light?"

"I'm never leaving this town. Well, I'm going back to San Diego to empty out the rest of the house, have a giant garage sale and put a For Sale sign up. And to resign from my old job. Then I'm coming back here to stay."

"What about all your money problems? Did you get that worked out?"

"Not really. But one thing is glaringly clear. Chris is not a businessman, and he never will be. I, however, am a pretty good businesswoman. I'm thinking of taking over his insurance business. He said it a couple of times before I heard him. 'Nancy, you should be selling insurance, you'd be great at it.' "

"You would. But I bet there are a lot of things you're good at. Like helping people."

"That was easy for me, I had nothing to lose. But what changed my life was watching George and the volunteer fire department hauling people out of town with their few meager possessions when his business was lost. Or watching Jurea Mull collecting donated clothing for children when she's homeless herself. Or how about you, making sure you see the patients wherever there's space, even though your clinic, which you built and loved, is underwater. I never knew what it took to be a real neighbor. A real community. It's the most important thing that's ever happened to me. In my life."

June felt her eyes well up with tears. She reached across the table and grasped her friend's hand. "I'm so glad you're going to stay here."

"So am I. And June, did you happen to notice Chris at all through this last week?"

"I've seen him here and there. Why?"

Nancy sat back in her chair. "He's incredible. He's unstoppable. He's been all over the valley, helping anywhere he's needed. Encouraging people. Promising them everything is going to be all right. June, it is so wonderful to be proud of my husband again. I'm not so sure anymore that Chris fell down on the job of being a good partner. It might be that I did."

"What has he said about this decision?"

"We've barely had time to talk, there's

been so much to do. I did catch him as we were trading places in the shower this morning and I said, I can't give up on this place now. I've put too much into it. I thought his smile was going to go on forever!"

Right then, while they sat in the crowded cafeteria, a strong beam of sunlight came through the windows and lit the place. Those present began to cheer.

New Year's Eve was quiet for almost everyone from Grace Valley, and New Year's Day was soggy. But it hadn't rained in a couple of days, and the effect on the town was amazing. Many buildings and houses had waterlines at about three feet from the ground, but were still standing. It could have been so much worse. There was very little snow left in the foothills, and if spring was simply normal, the snows at the very peak of the mountain ranges would melt off slowly through the spring and summer.

Annie, Mike and the kids said an emotional goodbye to June, Annie promising to come back in the spring to spend a little time with the baby.

Cleanup began immediately, though June was unable to do much to help. She continued to spend most of her time at the hospital, seeing patients there with Susan's help, while John, Elmer and Jim began work to put the clinic right. Every structure in Grace Valley was getting attention, and it looked as if there would be renovation work for Chris and others like him for months to come.

The café was going to get a major face-lift, with new appliances, counters, furniture and booths. The church had survived very well, and once the floors were refinished, the pews could be moved back in. The Flower Shoppe, bakery and gas station were a genuine mess. Sam decided to put a For Sale sign on the station — if anyone wanted to buy it to rebuild, he'd give them a bargain. But the shop he was going to fix up and restock, because he thought it was still a good idea to have Jurea and Erline, if she came back to Grace Valley, working there. Burt and Syl wanted to rebuild the bakery; they had too many accounts dependent on them to just walk away. "Besides," Burt said, "it'll probably be another twenty years before that river floods again."

The temperature dropped, and while most people who had a great deal to do, much of it outside, would resent that, these people were grateful it — as long as it didn't rain or snow for a while.

■ ■ ■ ■

In mid-January, still weeks before the businesses on Valley Drive would be ready to reopen, George Fuller went to Sam and Elmer and said a letter had come from Harry. It was addressed to George, but in the first paragraph George was invited to share its contents with whomever he wished.

Sam read the letter, then Elmer. Then they called a meeting of the members of the Presbyterian Church to be held in the elementary school closest to the valley. When the roster was called, the congregation was told that a letter had finally come from Reverend Shipton. The number of people who came to the school was amazing and gratifying. George began to read.

" 'Dear George,
The two most central gathering places in Grace Valley are the church and the café, so it seemed appropriate to send this to you, and let you share it with whomever you choose. I have amends to make to you, and to lots of people.' "

"That ain't exactly so," George put in editorially. "I don't feel like Harry has any amends to make with me. We all got our problems, make mistakes, and I ain't no exception. But —"

"Just read the letter, George!" Judge commanded.

"Yes, sir. All right."

" 'When it comes down to it, I lied to everyone. The fact is, I have an addiction and it is gambling. I have no control over this desire to gamble, and I have never limited myself to a card game or horse race. I played the stock market, bet on sports, threw dice and horseshoes, bet on roulette, blackjack and dogs. Truthfully, I could turn anything into a bet, and have at one time or another. I never won much, just enough to make me think the Big One was just around the corner.

Well, I was right about that. The Big One was just around the corner. It turned out to be my rock bottom. I borrowed money from everyone — good people and bad people. I rarely repaid anyone and it finally caught up with me. Some of the bad people beat me within an inch of my life and it was by the grace of God that I am alive to tell about it. From the hospital I went into an addiction treatment center where I have spent more than two months and am not finished. It's extra long for me because I am an extra-hard case. I will be recovering for many, many years to come. I still am bemused by the fact that I, a reverend, could put every mortal matter in the hands of God but this one — my insatiable desire to gamble. Now, helpless, I give it to God.

Although I've been very removed from the events of the world, I have heard of floods in northern California and I pray every day that Grace Valley and our people are okay. I'm going to be in this treatment facility for another couple of weeks and then I'll begin what is called after care. I can work during that time, but it's not necessary that I do. You should know, the church has been very supportive. They want me to get well. If you would like to have another minister come to Grace Valley Presbyterian, as common sense tells me you should, you have only to contact the church office. They'll take it from there.

I still have many people in Grace Valley to thank, many to whom I must apologize. When I leave this facility, I'm going to travel through Grace Valley. I'll stop for a bit, maybe speak to you and a few others. I don't expect to be made welcome. I know I've been too deceitful for that, so don't worry that you have to pretend any feelings. It's only for my recovery that I do this. I must face my mistakes, atone for them, and move forward with a clean slate.

Thank you, George, for being a messenger. Thank you for your kindness in this and so many things.' "

George stopped and dropped the hand holding the letter to his side. "I wasn't all that kind," he said.

"What's Harry mean, you don't have to pretend any feelings?" Birdie asked. "Does he think we're all mad at him?"

"Did you get the impression he'd rather not be preacher here?" Myrna asked.

"Maybe he's just embarrassed," Leah pointed out. "He doesn't want anyone to feel they have to accept him back."

"I don't know," Elmer said. "Sounds like he's still a little shaky to me. Maybe *Harry* doesn't know what he wants. He's been through a lot."

"Now, wait," June said. "Just because the tone of the letter is —" She stopped suddenly, her hands going to her stomach. "Oh, my," she said, looking down. "Oh, dear."

There was a long pause while all eyes went her way. Water began to trickle down to the floor, making an impressive puddle. There was not going to be any sneaking out of this gracefully. "I forgot what I was going to say," she said.

"What the devil is that?" Jim asked, leaning over.

"Her water broke," John said. "We're having a baby." He grinned as handsomely and excitedly as if it were his.

"Yahoo!" Nancy said, jumping to her feet.

June turned to John and asked, "Is it too early?"

"Naw. You'll be fine," he assured her. "Shall we?"

"I don't guess there's much choice," she answered, getting to her feet slowly. "What a mess."

"It's all worth it in the end," Susan promised.

It was a little like a parade. Jim held June's left elbow, John held her right. Behind her were Susan and Elmer. Next came the Forrests, all four of them. Other friends and neighbors just automatically got up and followed, the meeting abruptly over.

Myrna looped her hand through Morton's and said, "She's been hell on floors since this whole thing started."

NINETEEN

Valley Hospital was swollen with interested parties awaiting the birth of June's child. It wasn't just the people of Grace Valley, though they were there in force, but also hospital staff who couldn't be kept away.

June had to draw the line somewhere, so she decided to have only Jim and Nancy with her in the birthing room, the place where she would have both labor and delivery and her brief hospital stay. She promised her dad that Jim would fetch him immediately, the moment they'd finished counting the baby's fingers and toes.

And so the hours passed. And passed.

"His heart is strong. I'd like him a little bigger, but he's not too small. How are the contractions, June?" John asked.

"You're joking, right? How do you think they are? They're a laugh a minute!"

"Ah, pissy. That would indicate we're getting close to transition. Let's have a look."

"You just had a look! What the hell difference is looking going to make?"

"June," Jim pleaded, trying to grasp hold of her hand.

"Do you have to keep *touching* me?" she yelped.

"I'm thinking a good eight centimeters," Nancy whispered to John. "Probably nine."

"All right," June said, hoisting up on her elbows. "All comedians out! Out!"

"I hope we're not too late for the epidural. Let's have a look, June. Right now," John said, snapping on the gloves. And then to Nancy he said, "Wanna bet?"

"I don't know. Betting leaves kind of a sour taste in my mouth after what we just heard. But okay. Ten bucks says it's nine."

"I'm going all the way — I think she's there. Ten says it's ten."

"You have an unfair advantage! You've done this a lot! I want a handicap!"

"For *God's* sake!" June yelled. And then her body seemed to lift off the bed slightly, bearing down with a will of its own.

"Pant," John said. "Don't push yet. Not yet. Let me see, let me see . . . Whoa. My ten bucks. Okay, Dr. Hudson, you went a little fast for us. We're not going to get that epidural after all. But heck, you're at the easy part now. All you have to do is push him out."

The contraction passed. June was raised up slightly on her elbows and she glared over the huge mound that was her son, staring daggers at John. "Oh, that's swell, John. You're supposed to be *ready* for things like this. You're supposed to *know*. Now all I have to do is give birth? Without anesthesia? Swell, John. Swell."

John just laughed at her. If her position hadn't been so completely compromised, she would have hit him in the head.

"You may push on the next contraction. Where do you want Jim? Holding your shoulders while you bear down, or down here watching the action?"

"Frankly, I could care less!"

The last moments of labor and delivery always brought out the best in a woman, John thought.

Nancy took her place behind June and indicated to Jim that he should join John at the foot of the bed, ready to play catch. While June worked on pushing, Susan and the pediatric nurse came in, ready to clean up the baby when he was born.

As June became more tired from the pushing, she also became less testy and more sentimental. "We didn't get married," she whined. Then pushed. "I have no experience with this," she complained. Then pushed.

It only took about a half an hour of that, and there he was. "Aaaah," said everyone in the room.

Jim was again at her side as she cradled the baby and looked down at him. He was a tad on the smallish side, but enormously handsome. His eyes were open already and he looked all around. "Look how intelligent he is," she said breathlessly. "Isn't he brilliant? And his color is fabulous. Have you ever seen a more beautiful baby? Ever? Jim?"

Jim was crying. Here was a big strong undercover cop, tears running down his ruddy cheeks.

June was all done being cranky. It was amazing how fast that transition passed. John saw it all the time. Eight to ten centimeters could turn a woman into a wild beast, but birth could bring her back as fast. She put her hand up to Jim's cheek, touched his tears and said, "Thank you."

It was as June had hoped it would be. To see her father and Aunt Myrna holding little Jamie — short for James E., short for James Elmer Hudson Post — filled her with more joy than any moment in her life had up until now.

He weighed in at five pounds, ten ounces,

and was pronounced approximately a month early. He nursed like a barracuda and left the hospital with his mother forty-eight hours later. Friends and family brought meals and help so that June and Jim could take their time getting to know Jamie and parenthood without all the pressures of cooking, cleaning and working at their jobs.

They were often asked when the wedding was and June said, "When we get our church back. And our preacher."

Harry was mortified to learn of all that Grace Valley had been through. He hadn't been watching the news or reading the papers — he'd been involved in an intense twelve-step program and was very focused on recovering from his addiction. But when he left the treatment center and went first to the church headquarters he learned that Grace Valley had been nearly wiped out by flooding.

There was a piece in the *San Francisco Chronicle* about how the people of this town were pitching in together, rebuilding, renewing, and had never lost their optimism, their belief that their town would be whole again. "But we might build a higher levee behind the church and café," George Fuller was quoted. "Just to be on the safe side."

Harry hadn't heard from anyone in Grace Valley since sending his letter. He hadn't expected to, really. And now, knowing what he knew about what had happened to the town, he imagined they were even angrier than ever with him. Not only had he lied to them all, played them for fools, but then he'd run off and left them. He hadn't been there for them when they needed him most!

He was so afraid. He wished he hadn't promised to go to Grace Valley and see a few of his old friends. If he hadn't made the promise, he wouldn't be doing it now. He'd thought about asking Brianna to go with him for moral support, but, truth to tell, he didn't want to be even further humiliated in front of his ex-wife when the town turned its back on him.

Brianna had been a real pal through his treatment. He'd only had contact with a couple of people — his boss and his ex. Brianna had even gone so far as to attend family week with him, even though she was no longer family. Or was she? She had said in front of God and everyone that she loved Harry, would always love him, but was afraid to share a life with him as long as he had his problem. Well, his problem, he had so painfully learned, was for life.

As he got closer to Grace Valley, he grew

more and more nervous. He had said "a couple of weeks" in his letter, so they didn't know exactly when he was coming. He would just drive into town, into the heart of town where there would no doubt be people working on houses and businesses, park somewhere in the middle by the café or church, speak to whomever happened to be around and then beat a path out of there as fast as possible. And if they asked him about his gambling? "Tell the truth," his sponsor had said. "You can choose not to talk about it, but it's very dangerous to lie. We're only as sick as our secrets and lies."

There had been enough lying to last him a lifetime. Every time he thought about the way he'd borrowed money, pretending his paycheck was late, pretending he'd repay right away when what he really intended to do was put the money on a horse or find a floating crap game, it brought tears to his eyes. Maybe today was the day he'd say, "I'm really sorry I lied to you" to Sam. Or Elmer. Or George or June. And there were more. They'd treated him with such love and acceptance. How could he have lied to them?

He just hoped his heart wouldn't explode inside his chest before he actually got there. The closer he got, the worse it became. He passed Standard Roberts's flower field and saw that he had yellow ribbons on the mailbox, trees, the antennae of his car. Was there some holiday he didn't know about? He'd really lost touch.

But yes, there was some event, some community project, because every mailbox he passed wore a yellow ribbon. Had someone been kidnapped? Oh, that would be horrid if someone from this wonderful town was missing. All he could think was that yellow ribbons were used to signify the safe return of someone missing, someone in danger, someone lost.

As he got closer, the yellow ribbons only increased. They were placed around tree trunks and daringly high in the trees. They were painted on the glass of windows, made of brick mosaic on lawns, fluttering like flags from poles.

Now he really wanted to run. Here he was, coming back to his town to try to explain his disease and apologize, when they obviously had something urgent and desperate going on here. What arrogance he had! He should turn the car around before disrupting these people even more than he had.

But he was stuck, for he had passed the ribbon-laden police department. Valley

Drive was busier than he'd ever seen it, with trucks and construction workers everywhere. Virtually every building on the street was being worked on, and some of them looked as if they were nearly completed. He was so relieved to see that the café was standing! And there was a yellow ribbon painted on every single pane of glass in front of the café.

He pulled up to the café and parked. Of everyone in town he was probably closest to George; he had had almost every meal at the café. That's why he'd addressed his letter to George. This was a good place to start. There appeared to be lots of carpentry going on inside and he thought he spotted George. As he unfolded his lanky frame from the car, someone saw him, pointed, and people inside began to talk rapidly to one another.

Oh, how he wished he could turn and run.

Sam found him first, coming up from behind. "Harry? Reverend?"

He turned. "Sam! How great to see you!" he said, surprised by how true a statement that was. The welcoming look on Sam's face made him immediately wonder what he'd been so afraid of. Then came George, as excited as ever. A couple of locals stopped what they were doing to shake his hand.

Next, Tom and Lincoln Toopeek wandered over from the police department. Then Elmer came out of the clinic, followed by John, Susan, Jim and, finally, there was June, carrying a bundle. The baby had come? So soon?

People were coming out of buildings, stopping their cars in the middle of the road, emerging from every corner of the town.

He couldn't stop his stupid smiling, he was so relieved to see them all. Despite what had befallen them, they looked happy, healthy and strong. When June stood before him he embraced her gently but clumsily. "The baby is here so soon?" he asked, peeking at the little red face.

"A bit early, but healthy as a horse. It's so good to see you, Harry. We've missed you so much."

"Have you? Have you?"

"Oh, yes, Harry. Can you doubt it? We love you!"

"My God, how kind you all are. But what's happening here? Are the yellow ribbons for the rebuilding of the town?"

"What?" June asked, confused.

"The yellow ribbons. They're everywhere. What are they for?"

June couldn't help herself, she laughed at him. He'd always been such a putz. She covered her mouth with a hand and then pointed to a banner that was stretched across the street from the café to the clinic. It was high off the ground; Harry must have been so focused on the road he'd missed it.

It read, Welcome Home, Harry.

When the floor of the church was reinforced and resurfaced, when the pews were installed and new hymnals purchased, when the pulpit was standing and flowers fashioned by Sam and Jurea beautified the front of the church, Harry stood at the altar in his vestments. There was hardly room for another soul when the organ began to play. Jim and Chris entered from the side to stand before Harry. Nancy walked down the aisle, slowly, carrying her bouquet. Behind her were June and Elmer, June once again slim as a reed and wearing a lavender satin dress that made her look a bit like a girl.

Elmer handed his daughter off to her intended, then took his place in the front pew beside his sister. Myrna handed him his grandson.

Myrna and Morton had talked about this day, and it was their intention to renew their vows as June and Jim spoke theirs. And though no one had said anything, Nancy and Chris had decided to do the same thing. For many people in Grace Valley, seeing June wed Jim, the man they'd all come to love as one of their own, watching her do this with her old beau as the best man and her old rival as her matron of honor, brought everything full circle.

"Who gives this woman in marriage?" Harry asked.

Elmer stepped into the aisle with his grandson in his arms and said, "I believe we all do, Harry. I believe we all do."

ABOUT THE AUTHOR

Robyn Carr is a RITA® Award-winning author of over twenty-five novels, including the critically acclaimed *The House on Olive Street*. Robyn and her husband live in Las Vegas, Nevada. You can visit Robyn Carr's Web site at www.robyncarr.com.